ALL SOU1

Hugh Walpole was born in Auckland,
sent to England to be educated. Bullieα ....ιserable at school, young Walpole took refuge in the library, where he devoured the novels of Austen, Scott,
Trollope and others, and he knew from an early age that he wanted to become
a novelist. From 1903 to 1906, Walpole studied at Emmanuel College, Cambridge, and it was during this time that he first began to acknowledge his
homosexuality. His attention was fixated for a time on A. C. Benson, whom
he met as an undergraduate and who helped Walpole enter into a correspondence with Henry James, whom Walpole greatly admired and whose works
would influence Walpole's own.

Walpole's first novel was *The Wooden Horse* (1909), but his first success
was *Mr. Perrin and Mr. Traill* (1911), which received good reviews and sold
well; it also earned the admiration of Arnold Bennett, who would go on to
be a good friend. Walpole's career was further aided by a 1914 article by James
in the *Times Literary Supplement*, in which he ranked Walpole with D. H.
Lawrence and Compton Mackenzie as one of the important young British
writers of his generation.

During the First World War, Walpole was rejected for service because of
poor eyesight, so he went to Russia and assisted at hospitals, on one occasion
single-handedly saving a Russian officer and earning the Cross of St. George.
His experiences in Russia helped form the basis for his successful novels *The
Dark Forest* (1916) and *The Secret City* (1919) and also earned him a CBE in
1918.

After the war, Walpole continued to write prolifically, usually publishing
at least one very long novel each year. His output was diverse and included
the popular 'Herries' cycle of novels set in 18th-century England, as well as
boys' stories featuring the character Jeremy, and what he called his 'macabre'
novels, including *Portrait of a Man with Red Hair* (1925). In addition to his
writing, Walpole toured America extensively as a public speaker, winning
great popularity and earning huge sales for his books in the United States.

During the 1930s, Walpole spent time in Hollywood, writing scripts for
the films *David Copperfield* (1935) and *Little Lord Fauntleroy* (1936), and in
1937 he accepted a knighthood. At the start of the Second World War, Walpole remained in London and continued to write, working on his final macabre novel, *The Killer and the Slain* (1942), which was published posthumously.
Walpole had long suffered from diabetes and his poor health, combined with
the strain of his furious writing pace, probably contributed to his early death
at age 57 in 1941.

Walpole's reputation had already begun to decline by the 1930s as he was
increasingly seen as outdated by many critics, and it took a devastating hit
when he was parodied in Somerset Maugham's *Cakes and Ale* (1930). A *Times*
obituary that characterized Walpole as a 'workmanlike' writer, 'ambitious,'
and 'a sentimental egotist' who 'was not popular among his fellow-writers'
further damaged his reputation, which is only now seeing signs of a revival.

By Hugh Walpole

E

ALL SOULS' NIGHT

A Book of Stories

With a new introduction by
JOHN HOWARD

VALANCOURT BOOKS

Dedication: For Two Wise Women, Sylvia Lynd & Rose Macaulay

All Souls' Night by Hugh Walpole
First published London: Macmillan, 1933
First Valancourt Books edition, 2016

Published by Valancourt Books, Richmond, Virginia
http://www.valancourtbooks.com

ISBN 978-1-943910-35-9
Also available as an electronic book.

All Valancourt Books publications are printed on acid free paper that meets all ANSI standards for archival quality paper.

Cover by Henry Petrides
Set in Adobe Caslon

INTRODUCTION

When Sir Hugh Walpole died in June 1941 (he had been knighted in 1937, reflecting in his journal 'I must confess that since Scott I can't think of a good novelist who accepted a knighthood ... Besides I shall like being a knight ... ') his old friend and antagonist the critic and essayist James Agate devoted a long entry to him in the fifth volume of *Ego*, his diary-autobiography. 'Heart of gold, soul of loyalty, tried and trusty friend ... His tragedy was that his fine qualities have nothing to do with being a great novelist ... His steady blue eyes, his willing smile, his resonant voice, his high scorn, his skill in banter, his sense of fun – all these things had become part of the fabric of literary life in London.' Agate wished to express his affection for the man whose hospitality and company he had enjoyed (and whose money he had borrowed) even as they had frequently locked horns over the 'plaguey business of [Agate's] disliking his handling of words.'

Although Agate, in common with many critics, was far from convinced of Hugh Walpole's eventual place in English literature, no one could have disputed his popularity – and sales figures. At the time of his death at the age of 57, Walpole was probably best known as a prolific writer, having published over thirty full-length (and often substantial) novels in about the same number of years. Several works of criticism and *belles-lettres* must be added to this reckoning – as well as a sizeable number of short stories. During his lifetime Walpole wrote enough short stories for them to be gathered into five volumes, with a further collection appearing after his death. Walpole's biographer Rupert Hart-Davis stated that 'he was never greatly interested in his own short stories, even when he was writing them. They were useful means of filling up gaps between novels and of adding to his income, but little else.' While this may well have been true, that casual 'little else' is deserving of some closer scrutiny.

Walpole's novels were usually expansive and rich works,

full of colour and incident. In many cases they chronicled the lives of a large cast of characters whose stories were sometimes unfolded over periods of time. In contrast, the necessarily brief compass that generally typifies short fiction provided Walpole with opportunities to match. His short stories proved him to be as skilled within the limits of that form as he was with the novel. Walpole was consistently able to create encounters with the uncanny and unexpected; to crystallise impressions of people and places, providing mood studies and vignettes of characters or experiences – all within the space of a few thousand words.

The narrators of Walpole's stories are often apparently rather like the author himself. Sometimes portrayed as a writer, he is artistic, knowledgeable, and a collector. He is often rather gauche, insecure, anxious, and above all single – and seeking that one special (male) friendship. Settings recur, and are often places that Walpole knew and loved: especially Cornwall, and above all Cumberland. His protagonists are always very English, often innocents abroad. And whether they are at home or abroad they experience the unexpected breaking into their lives. Something or someone has a powerful impact on them and leaves them profoundly changed. Of course it is a grievous mistake to assume that a story (especially if narrated in the first person) contains a projection of the author or is otherwise autobiographical. Nevertheless, because Walpole did seem to put himself so transparently into his short stories, that temptation is not easy to dismiss. It is as if all his characters put together could result in Hugh Walpole – yet something would still not be there, would remain secret. There would still be a trace of mystery to the man.

Throughout his career as a novelist Walpole wrote what he termed 'macabres' – as he once stated, 'I have been unable to keep fantasy out of my books'. *The Killer and the Slain* (1942) – the last novel he lived to complete – was probably his darkest and most personal 'macabre'. So it was only natural for Walpole, a lover of fantastic and macabre fiction, also to write numerous short stories in this vein. These can be found scattered like shards of black glass in the collections *The Silver Thorn*, *All Souls' Night*, *Head in Green Bronze*, and *Mr Huffam*. And like broken glass, they can draw blood.

The stories in Walpole's first collection *The Golden Scarecrow* (1915) were not so sharp as to cause too much hurt, yet they proved to share characteristics with what he was to write in later years. A series of connected stories about a child called Hugh Seymour (Walpole's middle name was Seymour), they are perhaps rather too sentimental in places for all tastes. But Walpole was able to capture the breathless wonder – and terror – of a child's experience of life, when each day brings something new and numinous, and friends and foes alike wait around every corner. Events are recounted with a child's sense of proportion. It was as if the adult Walpole were still intimately familiar with the small realm of childhood, and the sense of that larger world just beyond immediate experience: the house beyond the nursery door, the leafy square and city streets on the other side of the front door, all immense and uncharted spaces but terrifying to a little boy. Walpole's evocation of his near-namesake's milieu is affecting and credible because he seems never to have forgotten what it was like to be a lonely child.

In many later stories, too, the presumably mature protagonist or narrator will still find himself in much the same position as Hugh Seymour: having to venture into unknown territory and meet other people who might not have his best interests at heart. But there is no way to tell, to find out, except through experience – alarming, yet alluring. Walpole went on to write three novels about another child, Jeremy Cole, and his dog Hamlet. The pair also turned up in 'The Ruby Glass', reprinted here. Years afterwards Walpole could still recover memories of his early years and articulate them with vividness and immediacy. Among his friends he was notorious for frequently acting with a child-like impetuosity and over-sensitivity: throughout his life he was quick to anger and as quick to abjectly regret it, seeking forgiveness and the resumption of a friendship which the other party had tolerantly probably never considered imperilled.

A second collection, *The Thirteen Travellers* (1920) also made use of a linking theme, which Hart-Davis summarised as 'the effect of the [First World War] on the leisured classes and the "new poor"'. With *The Silver Thorn* (1928) Walpole moved in a different direction. The stories become more personal and conversational, pieces in which, through his narrators and characters, he made greater use of his own experiences and concerns, and into which he became willing to invest more of his adult self, in its varied aspects: 'some of the bits about other people are amusing, but *all* the parts about myself are priggish and silly.'

All Souls' Night was first published in 1933. The sixteen stories it collected were subtitled, simply, 'A Book of Stories'. Despite a title laden with atmospheric associations taken from W.B. Yeats's poem of the same name, not all the stories involve ghosts or other manifestations of the supernatural, although they do come. The reader is given fair warning. At the beginning of the book Walpole reprints the first few lines of the poem, where they lie across the page – the reader's point of entry to the stories within – and sit like a manifesto. The last line reproduced is 'For it is a ghost's right ...' So we have to watch out and be on our guard. We will not be having everything our way from now on. Here, others – other *things* – the Other – also have their rights.[*]

Three of Walpole's best known and most anthologised macabre stories are here. 'Tarnhelm' is subtitled 'The Death of my Uncle Robert'. Looking back over forty years to the events leading up to that death, the narrator recalls how he was sent as a child to live in Cumberland with his two elderly uncles, who thoroughly loathe each other. Liking his Uncle Constance as much as he dislikes his Uncle Robert, the boy makes friends with Armstrong, one of the servants, who consoles him when he suffers from a vivid nightmare of a particularly evil and repulsive dog. Eventually it seems that the terrible dog is in fact a real creature and has some sort of connection with Uncle Robert. The child witnesses Uncle Constance shoot the creature. Following the trail of blood, they find the body of Robert.

'Mrs. Lunt' is set in Cornwall. The narrator, Runciman, travels there to stay for Christmas with Robert Lunt, a writer of good but obscure novels, who is a recent widower. Almost as soon as Runciman arrives he sees an old woman standing just

---

[*] The remainder of the Introduction reveals plot elements of some of the stories. Readers may wish to return to it after they have finished reading the collection.

inside his bedroom, by the door. Lunt flies into a rage when the woman is mentioned, insisting that there is no one else in the house. But he quickly breaks down and begs his visitor to forgive him and stay. While out for a walk, Runciman sees the woman again – and Lunt seems to see her as well, although he angrily denies it. Seeking to help, Runciman finds out from Lunt that he is depressed over the death of his wife, which happened exactly a year before. The couple had hated each other, and Lunt had showed no sorrow at her death. On the anniversary of her death, he is obsessed with the idea that she would return. That same night Lunt falls prey to hallucinations, and dies of a seizure. There were also some marks on his neck and chest that were hard to explain . . .

Winter in Cornwall is also the background for 'The Snow'. The story is set in Polchester, Walpole's fictional tribute to the city of Truro where his father had been on the staff of its first bishop, the headstrong Edward White Benson (himself father of three sons destined to embrace the supernatural and occult in their fiction). Walpole also set other stories and several novels in Polchester, including *The Old Ladies*, a brooding study of obsession and fear, and *The Cathedral* and *The Inquisitor* – two entries in his 'Scenes from Provincial Life' sequence in which he revisited the clerical intrigues of Anthony Trollope's Barchester, stirring them in with measures of modernised gothic melodrama and displaying his partiality for abnormal character psychology. Walpole's strong sense of place gives Polchester a vibrant life of its own. It is a picturesque city, yet one in which the grotesque and violent are never far beneath the apparently placid surface.

'The Snow' symbolises the intrusion of the past into the lives of a seemingly ordinary couple, the Ryders, and their slowly cooling marriage – Herbert Ryder's second. But although the 'second Mrs. Ryder was a young woman not easily frightened', as Christmas approaches she has started to glimpse a female figure, someone who brings her terror and a growing irritation with her husband that she seems unable to control. Her behaviour drives them further apart: their present is in irredeemable danger due to the breakdown of communication. As the temperature drops and the snow falls, the apparition of the woman retains the power to provoke and divide – and to remove the unwanted newcomer in the relationship.

The stories in *All Souls' Night* are transactions with the transitory, with something glimpsed, with the inward and spiritual in counterpoint with the outward and solidly physical. Walpole tries to comprehend the living as much as the dead and their revenants. While not innovative, his short stories gain power and impact from their sources deep in the author's memories and experiences, together with his narrative drive and skill at mood-building and description. His material is of the rawest: the powers of sexuality, love and the fear of love, betrayal and loss, the void concealed behind the façade of the ordinary. New experiences bring new confrontations – and the loss of innocence. There can be no going back. Nowhere is safe. So it is well always to remember that whether or not wine is served, *a ghost may come, for it is a ghost's right* ... And while remaining in Hugh Walpole's company, to ignore or forget this basic point can carry a terrible price.

John Howard
March 16, 2016

JOHN HOWARD was born in London. He is the author of *The Defeat of Grief*, *Numbered as Sand or the Stars*, and *The Lustre of Time*, as well as the short story collections *The Silver Voices*, *Written by Daylight*, and *Cities and Thrones and Powers*. He has published essays on various aspects of the science fiction and horror fields, and especially on the work of classic authors such as Fritz Leiber, Arthur Machen, August Derleth, M.R. James, and writers of the pulp era. Many of these have been collected in *Touchstones: Essays on the Fantastic*.

Midnight has come, and the great Christ Church Bell,
And many a lesser bell, sound through the room;
And it is All Souls' Night,
And two long glasses brimmed with muscatel
Bubble upon the table. A ghost may come;
For it is a ghost's right. . . .

W. B. YEATS

CONTENTS

THE WHISTLE

Mrs. Penwin gave one of her nervous little screams when she saw the dog.

'Oh, Charlie!' she cried. 'You surely haven't bought it!' and her little brow, that she tried so fiercely to keep smooth, puckered into its customary little gathering of wrinkles.

The dog, taking an instant dislike to her, sank his head between his shoulders. He was an Alsatian.

'Well . . .' said Charlie, smiling nervously. He knew that his impulsiveness had led him once more astray. 'Only the other evening you were saying that you'd like a dog.'

'Yes, but *not* an Alsatian! You *know* what Alsatians are. We read about them in the paper every day. They are simply not to be trusted. *I'm* sure he looks as vicious as anything. And what about Mopsa?'

'Oh, Mopsa . . .' Charlie hesitated. 'He'll be all right. You see, Sibyl, it was charity really. The Sillons are going to London, as you know. They simply can't take him. It wouldn't be fair. They've found it difficult enough in Edinburgh as it is.'

'I'm sure they are simply getting rid of him because he's vicious.'

'No, Maude Sillon assured me. He's like a lamb——'

'Oh, Maude! She'd say anything!'

'You know that you've been wanting a companion for Mopsa——'

'A companion for Mopsa! That's good!' Sibyl laughed her shrill little laugh that was always just out of tune.

'Well, we'll try him. We can easily get rid of him. And Blake shall look after him.'

'Blake!' She was scornful. She detested Blake, but he was too good a chauffeur to lose.

'And he's most awfully handsome. You can't deny it.'

She looked. Yes, he was most awfully handsome. He had lain down, his head on his paws, staring in front of him, quite

5

motionless. He seemed to be waiting ironically until he should be given his next command. The power in those muscles, moulded under the skin, must be terrific. His long wolf ears lay flat. His colour was lovely, here silver-grey, there faintly amber. Yes, he was a magnificent dog. A little like Blake in his strength, silence, sulkiness.

She turned again to the note that she was writing.

'We'll try him if you like. Anyway, there are no children about. It's Blake's responsibility—and the moment he's tiresome he goes.'

Charlie was relieved. It hadn't been so bad after all.

'Oh, Blake says he doesn't mind. In fact he seemed to take to the dog at once. I'll call him.'

He went to the double windows that opened into the garden and called: 'Blake! Blake!'

Blake came. He was still in his chauffeur's uniform, having just driven his master and the dog in from Keswick. He was a large man, very fair in colouring, plainly of great strength. His expression was absolutely English in its complete absence of curiosity, its certainty that it knew the best about everything, its suspicion, its determination not to be taken in by anybody, and its latent kindliness. He had very blue eyes and was clean-shaven; his cap was in his hand, and his hair, which was fair almost to whiteness, lay roughly across his forehead. He was not especially neat but of a quite shining cleanliness.

The dog got up and moved towards him. Both the Penwins were short and slight; they looked now rather absurdly small beside the man and the dog.

'Look here, Blake,' said Charlie Penwin, speaking with much authority, 'Mrs. Penwin is nervous about the dog. He's your responsibility, mind, and if there's the slightest bit of trouble, he goes. You understand that?'

'Yes, sir,' said Blake, looking at the dog. 'But there won't be no trouble.'

'That's a ridiculous thing to say,' remarked Mrs. Penwin sharply, looking up from her note. 'How can you be sure, Blake? You know how uncertain Alsatians are. I don't know what Mr. Penwin was thinking about.'

Blake said nothing. Once again and for the hundred thousandth time both the Penwins wished that they could pierce him with needles. It was quite terrible the way that Blake didn't speak when expected to, but then he was so wonderful a chauffeur, so good a driver, so excellent a mechanic, so honest—and Clara, his wife, was an admirable cook.

'You'd better take the dog with you now, Blake. What's his name?'

'Adam,' said Charlie.

'Adam! What a foolish name for a dog! Now don't disturb Clara with him, Blake. Clara hates to have her kitchen messed up.'

Blake, without a word, turned and went, the dog following closely at his heels.

Yes, Clara hated to have her kitchen messed up. She was standing now, her sleeves rolled up, her plump hands and wrists covered with dough. Mopsa, the Sealyham, sat at her side, his eyes, glistening with greed, raised to those doughy arms. But at sight of the Alsatian he turned instantly and flew at his throat. He was a dog who prided himself on fighting instantly every other dog. With human beings he was mild and indifferently amiable. Children could do what they would with him. He was exceedingly conceited and cared for no one but himself.

He was clever, however, and hid this indifference from many sentimental human beings.

Blake with difficulty separated the two dogs. The Alsatian behaved quite admirably, simply restraining the Sealyham and looking up at Blake, saying, 'I won't let myself go here although I should like to. I know that you would rather I didn't.' The Sealyham, breathing deeply, bore the Alsatian no grudge. He was simply determined that he should have no foothold here.

Torrents of words poured from Clara. She had always as much to say as her husband had little. She said the same thing many times over, as though she had an idiot to deal with. She knew that her husband was not an idiot—very far from it—but she had for many years been trying to make some impression on him. Defeated beyond hope, all she could now do was to resort to old and familiar tactics. What was this great savage dog? Where had he come from? Surely the mistress didn't approve, and she wouldn't have the kitchen messed up, not for anybody, and as Harry (Blake) very well knew, nothing upset her like a dog-fight, and if they were going to be perpetual, which knowing Mopsa's character they probably would be, she must just go to Mrs. Penwin and tell her that, sorry though she was after being with her all these years, she just couldn't stand it and would have to go, for if there was one thing more than another that really upset her it was a dog-fight, and as Harry knew, having her kitchen messed up was a thing that she couldn't stand. She paused and began vehemently to roll her dough. She was short and plump with fair hair and blue eyes like her husband's. When excited, little glistening beads of sweat appeared on her forehead. No one in this world knew whether Blake was fond of her or no. Clara Blake least of all. She wondered perpetually; this uncertainty and her cooking were her two principal interests in life. There were times when Blake seemed very fond of her indeed, others when he appeared not to be aware that she existed.

All he said now was: 'The dog won't be no trouble,' then went out, the dog at his heels. The Sealyham thought for a moment that he would follow him, then, with a little sniff of greed, settled himself down again at Clara Blake's feet.

The two went out into the thin misty autumn sunshine, down through the garden into the garage. The Alsatian walked very close beside Blake, as though some invisible cord held them together. All his life, now two years in length, it had been his instant principle to attach himself to somebody. For, in this curious world where he was, not his natural world at all, every breath, every movement, rustle of wind, sound of voices, patter of rain, ringing of bells, filled him with nervous alarm. He went always on guard, keeping his secret soul to himself, surrendering nothing, a captive in the country of the enemy. There might exist a human being to whom he would surrender himself. Although he had been attached to several he had not, in his two years, yet found one to whom he could give himself. Now as he trod softly over the amber and rosy leaves he was not sure that this man beside whom he walked might not be the one.

In the garage Blake took off his coat, put on his blue overalls, and began to work. The dog stretched himself out on the stone floor, his head on his paws, and waited. Once and again he started, his pointed ears pricked, at some unexpected sound. A breeze blew the brown leaves up and down in the sun, and the white road beyond the garage pierced like a shining bone the cloudless sky.

Blake's thoughts ran, as they always did, with slow assurance. This was a fine dog. He'd known the first moment that he set eyes on him that this was the dog for him. At that first glance something in his heart had been satisfied, something that had for years been unfulfilled. For they had had no children, he and Clara, and a motorcar was fine to drive and look after, but after all it couldn't give you everything, and he wasn't one to make friends (too damned cautious), and the people he worked for were all right but nothing extra, and he really didn't know whether he cared for Clara or no. It was so difficult after so many years married to tell. There were lots of times when he couldn't sort of see her at all.

He began to take out the sparking-plugs to clean them. That was the worst of these Heldsons, fine cars, as good as any going, but you had to be for ever cleaning the sparking-plugs. Yes, that dog was a beauty. He was going to take to that dog.

The dog looked at him, stared at him as though he were saying something. Blake looked at the dog. Then, with a deep sigh, as though some matter, for long uncertain, were at last completely settled, the dog rested again his head on his paws, staring in front of him, and so fell asleep. Blake, softly whistling, continued his work.

A very small factor, in itself quite unimportant, can bring into serious conflict urgent forces. So it was now when this dog Adam came into the life of the Penwins.

Mrs. Penwin, like so many English wives and unlike all American wives, had never known so much domestic power as she desired. Her husband was of course devoted to her, but he was for ever just escaping her, escaping her into that world of men that is so important in England, that is, even in these very modern days, still a world in the main apart from women.

Charlie Penwin had not very many opportunities to escape from his wife and he was glad that he had not, for when they came he took them. His ideal was the ideal of most English married men (and of very few American married men), namely that he should be a perfect companion to his wife. He fulfilled this ideal; they were excellent companions, the two of them, so excellent that it was all the more interesting and invigorating when he could go away for a time and be a companion to someone else, to Willie Shaftoe for instance, with whom he sometimes stayed in his place near Carlisle, or even for a day's golf with the Rev. Thomas Bird, rector of a church in Keswick.

Mrs. Penwin, in fact, had never quite, in spite of his profound devotion to her, never entirely captured the whole of her husband—a small fragment eternally escaped her, and this escape was a very real grievance to her. Like a wise woman she did not make scenes—no English husband can endure scenes—but she was always attempting to stop up this one little avenue of escape. But most provoking! So soon as one avenue was closed another would appear.

She realised very quickly (for she was not at all a fool) that this Alsatian was assisting her husband to escape from her because his presence in their household was bringing him into closer contact with Blake. Both the Penwins feared Blake and admired him; to friends and strangers they spoke of him with intense pride—'What we should do without Blake I can't think!' —'But aren't we lucky in *these* days to have a chauffeur whom we can completely trust?'

Nevertheless, behind these sentiments, there was this great difference, that Mrs. Penwin disliked Blake extremely (whenever he looked at her he made her feel a weak, helpless, and idiotic woman), while Charlie Penwin, although he was afraid of him, in his heart liked him very much indeed.

If Blake only were human, little Charlie Penwin, who was a sentimentalist, used to think—and now, suddenly, Blake *was* human. He had gone 'dotty' about this dog, and the dog followed him like a shadow. So close were they the one to the other that you could almost imagine that they held conversations together.

Then Blake came into his master's room one day to ask whether Adam could sleep in his room. He had a small room next to Mrs. Blake's, because he was often out late with the car at night and must rise very early in the morning. Clara Blake liked to have her sleep undisturbed.

'You see, sir,' he said, 'he won't sort of settle down in the out-house. He's restless: I know he is.'

'How do you know he is?' asked Charlie Penwin.

'I can sort of feel it, sir. He won't be no sort of trouble in my room, and he'll be a fine guard to the house at night.'

The two men looked at one another and were in that moment friends. They both smiled.

'Very well, Blake. I don't think there's anything against it.'

Of course there *were* things against it. Mrs. Penwin hated the idea of the dog sleeping in the house. She did not really hate it; what she hated was that Blake and her husband should settle this thing without a word to her. Nor, when she protested, would her husband falter. Blake wanted it. It would be a good protection for the house.

Blake discovered a very odd whistle with which he called the dog. Putting two fingers into his mouth he called forth this strange note that seemed to penetrate into endless distance and that had in it something mysterious, melancholy, and dangerous. It was musical and inhuman; friends of the Penwins, comfortably at tea, would hear this thin whistling cry coming, it seemed, from far away beyond the Fells, having in it some part of the Lake and the distant sea tumbling on Drigg sands, and of the lonely places in Eskdale and Ennerdale.

'What's that?' they would say, looking up.

'Oh, it's Blake calling his dog.'

'What a strange whistle!'

'Yes, it's the only one the dog hears.'

The dog did hear it, at any distance, in any place. When Blake went with the car the Alsatian would lie on the upper lawn whence he could see the road, and wait for his return.

He would both see and hear the car's return, but he would not stir until Blake, released from his official duties, could whistle to him—then with one bound he would be up, down the garden, and with his front paws up against Blake's chest would show him his joy.

To all the rest of the world he was indifferent. But he was not hostile. He showed indeed an immense patience, and especially with regard to the Sealyham.

The dog Mopsa attempted twice at least every day to kill the Alsatian. He succeeded in biting him severely, but so long as Blake was there Adam showed an infinite control, letting Blake part them although every instinct in him was stirred to battle.

But, after a time, Blake became clever at keeping the two dogs separate; moreover, the Sealyham became afraid of Blake. He was clever enough to realise that when he fought the Alsatian he fought Blake as well—and Blake was too much for him.

Very soon, however, Blake was at war not only with the Sealyham but with his wife and Mrs. Penwin too. You might think that the words 'at war' were too strong when nothing was to be seen on the surface. Mrs. Blake said nothing, Mrs. Penwin said nothing, Blake himself said nothing.

Save for the fights with the Sealyham there was no charge whatever to bring against the Alsatian. He was never in anyone's way, he brought no dirt in the house, whenever Charlie Penwin took him in the car he sat motionless on the back seat, his wolf ears pricked up, his large and beautiful eyes sternly regarding the outside world, but his consciousness fixed only upon Blake's back, broad and masterly above the wheel.

No charge could be brought against him except that the devotion between the man and the dog was, in this little house of ordered emotions, routine habits, quiet sterility, almost terrible. Mrs. Blake, as her husband left her one night to return to his own room, broke out:

'If you'd loved me as you love that dog I'd have had a different life.'

Blake patted her shoulder, moist beneath her nightdress.

'I love you all right, my girl,' he said.

And Mrs. Penwin found that here she could not move her husband.

Again and again she said:

'Charlie, that dog's got to go.'

'Why?'

'It's dangerous.'

'I don't see it.'

'Somebody will be bitten one day and then you *will* see it.'

'There's a terrible lot of nonsense talked about Alsatians....'

And then, when everyone was comfortable, Mrs. Blake reading her *Home Chat,* Mrs. Penwin her novel, Mrs. Fern, Mrs. Penwin's best friend, doing a 'crossword,' over the misty dank garden, carried, it seemed, by the muffled clouds that floated above the Fell, would sound that strange melancholy whistle, so distant and yet so near, Blake calling his dog.

For Blake himself life was suddenly, and for the first time, complete. He had not known, all this while, what it was that he missed, although he had known that he missed something.

Had Mrs. Blake given him a child he would have realised completion. Mrs. Blake alone had not been enough for his heart. In this dog he found fulfilment because here were all the things that he admired—loyalty, strength, courage, self-reliance, fidelity, comradeship, and, above all, sobriety of speech and behaviour. Beyond these there was something more—love. He did not, even to himself, admit the significance of this yet deeper contact. And he analysed nothing.

For the dog, life in this dangerous, menacing country of the enemy was at last secure and simple. He had only one thing to do, only one person to consider.

But of course life is not so simple as this for anybody. A battle was being waged, and it must have an issue. The Penwins were not in Cumberland during the winter. They went to their little place in Sussex, very close to London and to all their London friends. Mrs. Penwin would not take the Alsatian to Sussex. But why not? asked Charlie. She hated it, Mrs. Blake hated it. That, said Charlie, was not reason enough.

'Do you realise,' said Mrs. Penwin theatrically, 'that this dog is dividing us?'

'Nonsense,' said Charlie.

'It is not nonsense. I believe you care more for Blake than you do for me.' She cried. She cried very seldom. Charlie Penwin was uncomfortable, but some deep male obstinacy was roused in him. This had become an affair of the sexes. Men must stand together and protect themselves or they would be swept away in this feminine flood....

Blake knew, Mrs. Blake knew, Mrs. Penwin knew, that the dog would go with them to Sussex unless some definite catastrophe gave Mrs. Penwin the victory. As he lay on his bed at night, seeing the grey wolf-like shadow of the dog stretched on the floor, Blake's soul for the first time in its history trembled at the thought of the slight movement, incident, spoken word, sound, that might rouse the dog beyond his endurance and precipitate the catastrophe. The dog was behaving magnificently, but he was surrounded by his enemies. Did he know what hung upon his restraint?

Whether he knew or no, the catastrophe arrived, and arrived with the utmost, most violent publicity. On a sun-gleaming russet October afternoon, on the lawn, while Charlie was giving Blake instructions about the car, and Mrs. Penwin put in also her word, Mopsa attacked the Alsatian, Blake ran to separate them, and the Alsatian, sharply bitten, bewildered, humiliated, snapped and caught Blake's leg between his teeth. A moment later he and Blake knew, both of them, what he had done. Blake would have hidden it, but blood was flowing. In the Alsatian's heart remorse, terror, love, and a sense of disaster, a confirmation of all that, since his birth, knowing the traps that his enemies would lay for him, he had suspected, leapt to life together.

Disregarding all else he looked up at Blake.

'And that settles it!' cried Mrs. Penwin, triumphantly. 'He goes!'

Blake's leg was badly bitten in three places; they would be scars for life. And it was settled. Before the week was out the dog would be returned to his first owners, who did not want him, who would give him to someone else who also, in turn, through fear or shyness of neighbours, would not want him. . . .

Two days after this catastrophe Mrs. Blake went herself to Mrs. Penwin.

'My husband's that upset . . . I wouldn't care if the dog stays, Mum.'

'Why, Clara, you hate the dog.'

'Oh, well, Mum, Blake's a good husband to me. I don't like to see him . . .'

'Why, what has he said?'

'He hasn't said anything, Mum.'

But Mrs. Penwin shook her head. 'No, Clara, it's ridiculous. The dog's dangerous.'

And Blake went to Charlie Penwin. The two men faced one another and were closer together, fonder of one another, man caring for man, than they had ever been before.

'But, Blake, if the dog bites *you* whom he cares for ... I mean, don't you see, he really *is* dangerous....'

'He wasn't after biting me,' said Blake slowly. 'And if he *had* to bite somebody, being aggravated and nervous, he'd not find anyone better to bite than me who understands him and knows he don't mean nothing by it.'

Charlie Penwin felt in himself a terrible disloyalty to his wife. She could go to ... Why should not Blake have his dog? Was he for ever to be dominated by women? For a brief, rocking, threatening moment his whole stable ordered world trembled. He knew that if he said the dog was to remain the dog would remain and that something would have broken between his wife and himself that could never be mended.

He looked at Blake, who with his blue serious eyes stared steadily in front of him. He hesitated. He shook his head.

'No, Blake, it won't do. Mrs. Penwin will never be easy now while the dog is there.'

Later in the day Blake did an amazing thing. He went to Mrs. Penwin.

During all these years he had never voluntarily, himself, gone to Mrs. Penwin. He had never gone unless he were sent for. She looked at him and felt, as she always did, dislike, admiration, and herself a bit of a fool.

'Well, Blake?'

'If the dog stays I'll make myself responsible. He shan't bite nobody again.'

'But how can you tell? You said he wouldn't bite anyone before and he did.'

'He won't again.'

'No, Blake, he's got to go. I shan't have a moment's peace while he's here.'

'He's a wonderful dog. I'll have him trained so he won't hurt a fly. He's like a child with me.'

'I'm sure he is. Irresponsible like a child. That's why he bit you.'

'I don't make nothing of his biting me.'

'You may not, but next time it will be someone else. There's something in the paper about them every day.'

'He's like a child with me.'

'I'm very sorry, Blake. I can't give way about it. You'll see I'm right in the end. My husband ought never to have accepted the dog at all.'

After Blake had gone she did not know why, but she felt uneasy, as though she had robbed a blind man, or stolen another woman's lover. Ridiculous! There could be no question but that she was right.

Blake admitted that to himself. She was right. He did not criticise her, but he did not know what to do. He had never felt like this in all his life before, as though part of himself were being torn from him.

On the day before the dog was to go back to his original owners, Blake was sent into Keswick to make some purchases. It was a soft bloomy day, one of those North English autumn days when there is a scent of spices in the sharp air and a rosy light hangs in shadow about the trees. Blake had taken the dog with him, and driving back along the Lake, seeing how it lay a sheet of silver glass upon whose surface the islands were painted in flat colours of auburn and smoky grey, a sudden madness seized him. It was the stillness, the silence, the breathless pause. . . .

Instead of turning to the right over the Grange bridge he drove the car straight on into Borrowdale. It was yet early in the afternoon; all the lovely valley lay in gold leaf at the feet of the russet hills and no cloud moved in the sky. He took the car to Seatoller and climbed with the dog the steep path towards Honister.

And the dog thought that at last what he had longed for was to come to pass. He and Blake were at length free; they would go on and on, leaving all the stupid, nerve-jumping world behind them, never to return to it. With a wild, fierce happiness such as he had never yet shown, he bounded forward, drinking in the cold streams, feeling the strong turf beneath his feet, running back to Blake to assure him of his comradeship. At last he was free, and life was noble as it ought to be.

At the turn of the road Blake sat down and looked back. All round him were hills. Nothing moved; only the stream close to him slipped murmuring between the boulders. The hills ran ranging from horizon to horizon, and between grey clouds a silver strip of sky, lit by an invisible sun, ran like a river into mist. Blake called the dog to him and laid his hand upon his head. He knew that the dog thought that they two had escaped for ever now from the world. Well, why not? They could walk on, on to the foot of the hill on whose skyline the mining-hut stood like a listening ear, down the Pass to Buttermere, past the Lake, past Crummock Water to Cockermouth. Then there would be a train. It would not be difficult for him to get work. His knowledge of cars (he had a genius for them) would serve him anywhere. And Clara? She was almost invisible, a white tiny blob on the horizon. She would find someone else. His hand tightened about the dog's head....

For a long while he sat there, the dog never moving, the silver river spreading in the sky, the hills gathering closer about him.

Suddenly he shook his head. No, he could not. He would be running away, a poor kind of cowardice. He pulled Adam's sharp ears; he buried his face in Adam's fur. He stood up, and Adam also stood up, placed his paws on his chest, licked his cheeks. In his eyes there shone great happiness because they two were going away alone together.

But Blake turned back down the path, and the dog, realising that there was to be no freedom, walked close beside him, brushing with his body sometimes the stuff of Blake's trousers.

Next day Blake took the dog back to the place whence he had come.

Two days later, the dog, knowing that he was not wanted, sat watching a little girl who played some foolish game near him. She had plump bare legs; he watched them angrily. He was unhappy, lonely, nervous, once more in the land of the enemy, and now with no friend.

Through the air, mingling with the silly laughter of the child and other dangerous sounds, came, he thought, a whistle. His heart hammered. His ears were up. With all his strength he bounded towards the sound. But he was chained. To-morrow he was to be given to a Cumberland farmer.

Mrs. Penwin was entertaining two ladies at tea. This was the last day before the journey south. Across the dark lawns came that irritating, melancholy whistle, disturbing her, reproaching her—and for what?

Why, for her sudden suspicion that everything in life was just ajar—one little push and all would be in its place—but would she be married to Charlie, would Mrs. Planty there be jealous of her pretty daughter, would Miss Tennyson, nibbling now at her pink piece of icing, be nursing her aged and intemperate father . . . ? She looked up crossly—

'Really, Charlie . . . that must be Blake whistling. I can't think why now the dog's gone. To let us know what he thinks about it, I suppose . . .' She turned to her friends. 'Our chauffeur—a splendid man—we *are* so fortunate. Charlie, do tell him. It's such a hideous whistle anyway—and now the dog is gone . . .'

Lindingö, Sweden,
  August 14, 1929

THE SILVER MASK

Miss Sonia Herries, coming home from a dinner-party at the Westons', heard a voice at her elbow.

'If you please—only a moment——'

She had walked from the Westons' flat because it was only three streets away, and now she was only a few steps from her door, but it was late, there was no one about and the King's Road rattle was muffled and dim.

'I am afraid I can't——' she began. It was cold, and the wind nipped her cheeks.

'If you would only——' he went on.

She turned and saw one of the handsomest young men possible. He was the handsome young man of all romantic stories, tall, dark, pale, slim, distinguished—oh! everything!—and he was wearing a shabby blue suit and shivering with the cold just as he should have been.

'I'm afraid I can't——' she repeated, beginning to move on.

'Oh, I know,' he interrupted quickly. 'Everyone says the same, and quite naturally. I should if our positions were reversed. But I *must* go on with it. I *can't* go back to my wife and baby with simply nothing. We have no fire, no food, nothing except the ceiling we are under. It is my fault, all of it. I don't want your pity, but I *have* to attack your comfort.'

He trembled. He shivered as though he were going to fall. Involuntarily she put out her hand to steady him. She touched his arm and felt it quiver under the thin sleeve.

'It's all right ...' he murmured. 'I'm hungry ... I can't help it.'

She had had an excellent dinner. She had drunk perhaps just enough to lead to recklessness—in any case, before she realised it, she was ushering him in, through her dark-blue painted door. A crazy thing to do! Nor was it as though she were too young to know any better, for she was fifty if she was a day and, although sturdy of body and as strong as a horse (except for a little unsteadiness of the heart), intelligent enough to be thin, neurotic and abnormal; but she was none of these.

Although intelligent she suffered dreadfully from impulsive kindness. All her life she had done so. The mistakes that she had made—and there had been quite a few—had all arisen from the triumph of her heart over her brain. She knew it—how well she knew it!—and all her friends were for ever dinning it into her. When she reached her fiftieth birthday she said to herself, 'Well, now at last I'm too old to be foolish any more.' And here she was, helping an entirely unknown young man into her house at dead of night, and he in all probability the worst sort of criminal.

Very soon he was sitting on her rose-coloured sofa, eating sandwiches and drinking a whisky and soda. He seemed to be entirely overcome by the beauty of her possessions. 'If he's acting he's doing it very well,' she thought to herself. But he had taste and he had knowledge. He knew that the Utrillo was an early one, the only period of importance in that master's work, he knew that the two old men talking under a window belonged to Sickert's 'Middle Italian,' he recognised the Dobson head and the wonderful green bronze Elk of Carl Milles.

'You are an artist,' she said. 'You paint?'

'No, I am a pimp, a thief, a what you like—anything bad,' he answered fiercely. 'And now I must go,' he added, springing up from the sofa.

He seemed most certainly invigorated. She could scarcely believe that he was the same young man who only half an hour before had had to lean on her arm for support. And he was a gentleman. Of that there could be no sort of question. And he was astoundingly beautiful in the spirit of a hundred years ago, a young Byron, a young Shelley, not a young Ramón Novarro or a young Ronald Colman.

Well, it was better that he should go, and she did hope (for his own sake rather than hers) that he would not demand money and threaten a scene. After all, with her snow-white hair, firm broad chin, firm broad body, she did not look like someone who could be threatened. He had not apparently the slightest intention of threatening her. He moved towards the door.

'Oh!' he murmured with a little gasp of wonder. He had

stopped before one of the loveliest things that she had—a mask in silver of a clown's face, the clown smiling, gay, joyful, not hinting at perpetual sadness as all clowns are traditionally supposed to do. It was one of the most successful efforts of the famous Sorat, greatest living master of Masks.

'Yes. Isn't that lovely?' she said. 'It was one of Sorat's earliest things, and still, I think, one of his best.'

'Silver is the right material for that clown,' he said.

'Yes, I think so too,' she agreed. She realised that she had asked him nothing about his troubles, about his poor wife and baby, about his past history. It was better perhaps like this.

'You have saved my life,' he said to her in the hall. She had in her hand a pound note.

'Well,' she answered cheerfully, 'I was a fool to risk a strange man in my house at this time of night—or so my friends would tell me. But such an old woman like me—where's the risk?'

'I could have cut your throat,' he said quite seriously.

'So you could,' she admitted. 'But with horrid consequences to yourself.'

'Oh no,' he said. 'Not in these days. The police are never able to catch anybody.'

'Well, good-night. Do take this. It can get you some warmth at least.'

He took the pound. 'Thanks,' he said carelessly. Then at the door he remarked: 'That mask. The loveliest thing I ever saw.'

When the door had closed and she went back into the sitting-room she sighed:

'What a good-looking young man!' Then she saw that her most beautiful white jade cigarette-case was gone. It had been lying on the little table by the sofa. She had seen it just before she went into the pantry to cut the sandwiches. He had stolen it. She looked everywhere. No, undoubtedly he had stolen it.

'What a good-looking young man!' she thought as she went up to bed.

Sonia Herries was a woman of her time in that outwardly she was cynical and destructive while inwardly she was a creature longing for affection and appreciation. For though she had white hair and was fifty she was outwardly active, young, could do with little sleep and less food, could dance and drink cocktails and play bridge to the end of all time. Inwardly she cared for neither cocktails nor bridge. She was above all things maternal and she had a weak heart, not only a spiritual weak heart but also a physical one. When she suffered, must take her drops, lie down and rest, she allowed no one to see her. Like all the other women of her period and manner of life she had a courage worthy of a better cause.

She was a heroine for no reason at all.

But, beyond everything else, she was maternal. Twice at least she would have married had she loved enough, but the man she had really loved had not loved her (that was twenty-five years ago), so she had pretended to despise matrimony. Had she had a child her nature would have been fulfilled; as she had not had that good fortune she had been maternal (with outward cynical indifference) to numbers of people who had made use of her, sometimes laughed at her, never deeply cared for her. She was named 'a jolly good sort,' and was always 'just outside' the real life of her friends. Her Herries relations, Rockages and Cards and Newmarks, used her to take odd places at table, to fill up spare rooms at house-parties, to make purchases for them in London, to talk to when things went wrong with them or people abused them. She was a very lonely woman.

She saw her young thief for the second time a fortnight later. She saw him because he came to her house one evening when she was dressing for dinner.

'A young man at the door,' said her maid Rose.

'A young man? Who?' But she knew.

'I don't know, Miss Sonia. He won't give his name.'

She came down and found him in the hall, the cigarette-case in his hand. He was wearing a decent suit of clothes, but he still looked hungry, haggard, desperate and incredibly handsome. She took him into the room where they had been before. He gave her the cigarette-case. 'I pawned it,' he said, his eyes on the silver mask.

'What a disgraceful thing to do!' she said. 'And what are you going to steal next?'

'My wife made some money last week,' he said. 'That will see us through for a while.'

'Do you never do any work?' she asked him.

'I paint,' he answered. 'But no one will touch my pictures. They are not modern enough.'

'You must show me some of your pictures,' she said, and realised how weak she was. It was not his good looks that gave him his power over her, but something both helpless and defiant, like a wicked child who hates his mother but is always coming to her for help.

'I have some here,' he said, went into the hall, and returned with several canvases. He displayed them. They were very bad —sugary landscapes and sentimental figures.

'They are very bad,' she said.

'I know they are. You must understand that my aesthetic taste is very fine. I appreciate only the best things in art, like your cigarette-case, that mask there, the Utrillo. But I can paint nothing but these. It is very exasperating.' He smiled at her.

'Won't you buy one?' he asked her.

'Oh, but I don't want one,' she answered. 'I should have to hide it.' She was aware that in ten minutes her guests would be here.

'Oh, do buy one.'

'No, but of course not——'

'Yes, please.' He came nearer and looked up into her broad kindly face like a beseeching child.

'Well . . . how much are they?'

'This is twenty pounds. This twenty-five——'

'But how absurd! They are not worth anything at all.'

'They may be one day. You never know with modern pictures.'

'I am quite sure about these.'

'Please buy one. That one with the cows is not so bad.'

She sat down and wrote a cheque.

'I'm a perfect fool. Take this, and understand I never want to see you again. Never! You will never be admitted. It is no use speaking to me in the street. If you bother me I shall tell the police.'

He took the cheque with quiet satisfaction, held out his hand and pressed hers a little.

'Hang that in the right light and it will not be so bad——'

'You want new boots,' she said. 'Those are terrible.'

'I shall be able to get some now,' he said and went away.

All that evening while she listened to the hard and crackling ironies of her friends she thought of the young man. She did not know his name. The only thing that she knew about him was that by his own confession he was a scoundrel and had at his mercy a poor young wife and a starving child. The picture that she formed of these three haunted her. It had been, in a way, honest of him to return the cigarette-case. Ah, but he knew, of course, that did he not return it he could never have seen her again. He had discovered at once that she was a splendid source of supply, and now that she had bought one of his wretched pictures—— Nevertheless he could not be altogether bad. No one who cared so passionately for beautiful things could be quite worthless. The way that he had gone straight to the silver mask as soon as he entered the room and gazed at it as though with his very soul! And, sitting at her dinner-table, uttering the most cynical sentiments, she was all softness as she gazed across to the wall upon whose pale surface the silver mask was hanging. There was, she thought, a certain look of the young man in that jolly shining surface. But where? The clown's cheek was fat, his mouth broad, his lips thick—and yet, and yet——

For the next few days as she went about London she looked in spite of herself at the passers-by to see whether he might not be there. One thing she soon discovered, that he was very much more handsome than anyone else whom she saw. But it was not for his handsomeness that he haunted her. It was because he wanted her to be kind to him, and because she wanted—oh, so terribly—to be kind to someone!

The silver mask, she had the fancy, was gradually changing, the rotundity thinning, some new light coming into the empty eyes. It was most certainly a beautiful thing.

Then, as unexpectedly as on the other occasions, he appeared again. One night as she, back from a theatre smoking one last cigarette, was preparing to climb the stairs to bed, there was a knock on the door. Everyone of course rang the bell—no one attempted the old-fashioned knocker shaped like an owl that she had bought, one idle day, in an old curiosity shop. The knock made her sure that it was he. Rose had gone to bed, so she went herself to the door. There he was—and with him a young girl and a baby. They all came into the sitting-room and stood awkwardly by the fire. It was at that moment when she saw them in a group by the fire that she felt her first sharp pang of fear. She knew suddenly how weak she was—she seemed to be turned to water at sight of them, she, Sonia Herries, fifty years of age, independent and strong, save for that little flutter of the heart —yes, turned to water! She was afraid as though someone had whispered a warning in her ear.

The girl was striking, with red hair and a white face, a thin graceful little thing. The baby, wrapped in a shawl, was soaked in sleep. She gave them drinks and the remainder of the sandwiches that had been put there for herself. The young man looked at her with his charming smile.

'We haven't come to cadge anything this time,' he said. 'But I wanted you to see my wife and I wanted her to see some of your lovely things.'

'Well,' she said sharply, 'you can only stay a minute or two. It's late. I'm off to bed. Besides, I told you not to come here again.'

'Ada made me,' he said, nodding at the girl. 'She was so anxious to see you.'

The girl never said a word but only stared sulkily in front of her.

'All right. But you must go soon. By the way, you've never told me your name.'

'Henry Abbott, and that's Ada, and the baby's called Henry too.'

'All right. How have you been getting on since I saw you?'

'Oh, fine! Living on the fat of the land.' But he soon fell into silence and the girl never said a word. After an intolerable pause Sonia Herries suggested that they should go. They didn't move. Half an hour later she insisted. They got up. But, standing by the door, Henry Abbott jerked his head towards the writing-desk.

'Who writes your letters for you?'

'Nobody. I write them myself.'

'You ought to have somebody. Save a lot of trouble. I'll do them for you.'

'Oh no, thank you. That would never do. Well, good-night, good-night——'

'Of course I'll do them for you. And you needn't pay me anything either. Fill up my time.'

'Nonsense ... good-night, good-night.' She closed the door on them. She could not sleep. She lay there thinking of him. She was moved, partly by a maternal tenderness for them that warmed her body (the girl and the baby had looked so helpless sitting there), partly by a shiver of apprehension that chilled her veins. Well, she hoped that she would never see them again. Or did she? Would she not to-morrow, as she walked down Sloane Street, stare at everyone to see whether by chance that was he?

Three mornings later he arrived. It was a wet morning and she had decided to devote it to the settling of accounts. She was sitting there at her table when Rose showed him in.

'I've come to do your letters,' he said.

'I should think not,' she said sharply. 'Now, Henry Abbott, out you go. I've had enough——'

'Oh no, you haven't,' he said, and sat down at her desk.

She would be ashamed for ever, but half an hour later she was seated in the corner of the sofa telling him what to write. She hated to confess it to herself, but she liked to see him sitting there. He was company for her, and to whatever depths he might by now have sunk, he was most certainly a gentleman. He behaved very well that morning; he wrote an excellent hand. He seemed to know just what to say.

A week later she said, laughing, to Amy Weston: 'My dear, would you believe it? I've had to take on a secretary. A very good-looking young man—but you needn't look down your nose. You know that good-looking young men are nothing to *me*—and he does save me endless bother.'

For three weeks he behaved very well, arriving punctually, offering her no insults, doing as she suggested about everything. In the fourth week, about a quarter to one on a day, his wife arrived. On this occasion she looked astonishingly young, sixteen perhaps. She wore a simple grey cotton dress. Her red bobbed hair was strikingly vibrant about her pale face.

The young man already knew that Miss Herries was lunching alone. He had seen the table laid for one with its simple appurtenances. It seemed to be very difficult not to ask them to remain. She did, although she did not wish to. The meal was not a success. The two of them together were tiresome, for the man said little when his wife was there, and the woman said nothing at all. Also the pair of them were in a way sinister.

She sent them away after luncheon. They departed without protest. But as she walked, engaged on her shopping that afternoon, she decided that she must rid herself of them, once and for all. It was true that it had been rather agreeable having him there; his smile, his wicked humorous remarks, the suggestion that he was a kind of malevolent gamin who preyed on the world in general but spared her because he liked her—all this had attracted her—but what really alarmed her was that during all these weeks he had made no request for money, made indeed no request for anything. He must be piling up a fine account, must have some plan in his head with which one morning he would balefully startle her! For a moment there in the bright sunlight, with the purr of the traffic, the rustle of the trees about her, she saw herself in surprising colour. She was behaving with a weakness that was astonishing. Her stout, thick-set, resolute body, her cheery rosy face, her strong white hair—all these disappeared, and in their place, there almost clinging for support to the Park railings, was a timorous little old woman with frightened eyes and trembling knees. What was there to be afraid of? She had done nothing wrong. There were the police at hand. She had never been a coward before. She went home, however, with an odd impulse to leave her comfortable little house in Walpole Street and hide herself somewhere, somewhere that no one could discover.

That evening they appeared again, husband, wife and baby. She had settled herself down for a cosy evening with a book and an 'early to bed.' There came the knock on the door.

On this occasion she was most certainly firm with them. When they were gathered in a little group she got up and addressed them.

'Here is five pounds,' she said, 'and this is the end. If one of you shows his or her face inside this door again I call the police. Now go.'

The girl gave a little gasp and fell in a dead faint at her feet. It was a perfectly genuine faint. Rose was summoned. Everything possible was done.

'She has simply not had enough to eat,' said Henry Abbott. In the end (so determined and resolved was the faint) Ada Abbott was put to bed in the spare room and a doctor was summoned. After examining her he said that she needed rest and nourishment. This was perhaps the critical moment of the whole affair. Had Sonia Herries been at this crisis properly resolute and bundled the Abbott family, faint and all, into the cold unsympathising street, she might at this moment be a hale and hearty old woman enjoying bridge with her friends. It was, however, just here that her maternal temperament was too strong for her. The poor young thing lay exhausted, her eyes closed, her cheeks almost the colour of her pillow. The baby (surely the quietest baby ever known) lay in a cot beside the bed. Henry Abbott wrote letters to dictation downstairs. Once Sonia Herries, glancing up at the silver mask, was struck by the grin on the clown's face. It seemed to her now a thin sharp grin—almost derisive.

Three days after Ada Abbott's collapse there arrived her aunt and her uncle, Mr. and Mrs. Edwards. Mr. Edwards was a large red-faced man with a hearty manner and a bright waistcoat. He looked like a publican. Mrs. Edwards was a thin sharp-nosed woman with a bass voice. She was very, very thin, and wore a large old-fashioned brooch on her flat but emotional chest. They sat side by side on the sofa and explained that they had come to enquire after Ada, their favourite niece. Mrs. Edwards cried, Mr. Edwards was friendly and familiar. Unfortunately Mrs. Weston and a friend came and called just then. They did not stay very long. They were frankly amazed at the Edwards couple and deeply startled by Henry Abbott's familiarity. Sonia Herries could see that they drew the very worst conclusions.

A week later Ada Abbott was still in bed in the upstairs room. It seemed to be impossible to move her. The Edwardses were constant visitors. On one occasion they brought Mr. and Mrs. Harper and their girl Agnes. They were profusely apologetic, but Miss Herries would understand that 'with the interest they took in Ada it was impossible to stay passive.' They all crowded into the spare bedroom and gazed at the pale figure with the closed eyes sympathetically.

Then two things happened together. Rose gave notice and Mrs. Weston came and had a frank talk with her friend. She began with that most sinister opening: 'I think you ought to know, dear, what everyone is saying——' What everyone was saying was that Sonia Herries was living with a young ruffian from the streets, young enough to be her son.

'You must get rid of them all and at once,' said Mrs. Weston, 'or you won't have a friend left in London, darling.'

Left to herself, Sonia Herries did what she had not done for years, she burst into tears. What had happened to her? Not only had her will and determination gone but she felt most unwell. Her heart was bad again; she could not sleep; the house, too, was tumbling to pieces. There was dust over everything. How was she ever to replace Rose? She was living in some horrible night-mare. This dreadful handsome young man seemed to have some authority over her. Yet he did not threaten her. All he did was to smile. Nor was she in the very least in love with him. This must come to an end or she would be lost.

Two days later, at tea-time, her opportunity arrived. Mr. and Mrs. Edwards had called to see how Ada was; Ada was down-stairs at last, very weak and pale. Henry Abbott was there, also the baby. Sonia Herries, although she was feeling dreadfully unwell, addressed them all with vigour. She especially addressed the sharp-nosed Mrs. Edwards.

'You must understand,' she said. 'I don't want to be unkind, but I have my own life to consider. I am a very busy woman, and this has all been forced on me. I don't want to seem brutal. I'm glad to have been of some assistance to you, but I think Mrs. Abbott is well enough to go home now—and I wish you all good-night.'

'I am sure,' said Mrs. Edwards, looking up at her from the sofa, 'that you've been kindness itself, Miss Herries. Ada recognises it, I'm sure. But to move her now would be to kill her, that's all. Any movement and she'll drop at your feet.'

'We have nowhere to go,' said Henry Abbott.

'But, Mrs. Edwards——' began Miss Herries, her anger rising.

'We have only two rooms,' said Mrs. Edwards quietly. 'I'm sorry, but just now, what with my husband coughing all night—'

'Oh, but this is monstrous!' Miss Herries cried. 'I have had enough of this. I have been generous to a degree——'

'What about my pay,' said Henry, 'for all these weeks?'

'Pay! Why, of course——' Miss Herries began. Then she stopped. She realised several things. She realised that she was alone in the house, the cook having departed that afternoon. She realised that none of them had moved. She realised that her 'things'—the Sickert, the Utrillo, the sofa—were alive with apprehension. She was fearfully frightened of their silence, their immobility. She moved towards her desk, and her heart turned, squeezed itself dry, shot through her body the most dreadful agony.

'Please,' she gasped. 'In the drawer—the little green bottle—oh, quick! Please, please!'

The last thing of which she was aware was the quiet handsome features of Henry Abbott bending over her.

When, a week later, Mrs. Weston called, the girl, Ada Abbott, opened the door to her.

'I came to enquire for Miss Herries,' she said. 'I haven't seen her about. I have telephoned several times and received no answer.'

'Miss Herries is very ill.'

'Oh, I'm so sorry. Can I not see her?'

Ada Abbott's quiet gentle tones were reassuring her. 'The doctor does not wish her to see anyone at present. May I have your address? I will let you know as soon as she is well enough.'

Mrs. Weston went away. She recounted the event. 'Poor Sonia, she's pretty bad. They seem to be looking after her. As soon as she's better we'll go and see her.'

The London life moves swiftly. Sonia Herries had never been of very great importance to anyone. Herries relations enquired.

They received a very polite note assuring them that so soon as she was better——

Sonia Herries was in bed, but not in her own room. She was in the little attic bedroom but lately occupied by Rose the maid. She lay at first in a strange apathy. She was ill. She slept and woke and slept again. Ada Abbott, sometimes Mrs. Edwards, sometimes a woman she did not know, attended to her. They were all very kind. Did she need a doctor? No, of course she did not need a doctor, they assured her. They would see that she had everything that she wanted.

Then life began to flow back into her. Why was she in this room? Where were her friends? What was this horrible food that they were bringing her? What were they doing here, these women?

She had a terrible scene with Ada Abbott. She tried to get out of bed. The girl restrained her—and easily, for all the strength seemed to have gone from her bones. She protested, she was as furious as her weakness allowed her, then she cried. She cried most bitterly. Next day she was alone and she crawled out of bed; the door was locked; she beat on it. There was no sound but her beating. Her heart was beginning again that terrible strangled throb. She crept back into bed. She lay there, weakly, feebly crying. When Ada arrived with some bread, some soup, some water, she demanded that the door should be unlocked, that she should get up, have her bath, come downstairs to her own room.

'You are not well enough,' Ada said gently.

'Of course I am well enough. When I get out I will have you put in prison for this——'

'Please don't get excited. It is so bad for your heart.'

Mrs. Edwards and Ada washed her. She had not enough to eat. She was always hungry.

Summer had come. Mrs. Weston went to Etretat. Everyone was out of town.

'What's happened to Sonia Herries?' Mabel Newmark wrote to Agatha Benson. 'I haven't seen her for ages. . . .'

But no one had time to enquire. There were so many things to do. Sonia was a good sort, but she had been nobody's business. . . .

Once Henry Abbott paid her a visit. 'I am so sorry that you are not better,' he said smiling. 'We are doing everything we can for you. It is lucky we were around when you were so ill. You had better sign these papers. Someone must look after your affairs until you are better. You will be downstairs in a week or two.'

Looking at him with wide-open terrified eyes, Sonia Herries signed the papers.

The first rains of autumn lashed the streets. In the sitting-room the gramophone was turned on. Ada and young Mr. Jackson, Maggie Trent and stout Harry Bennett were dancing. All the furniture was flung against the walls. Mr. Edwards drank his beer; Mrs. Edwards was toasting her toes before the fire.

Henry Abbott came in. He had just sold the Utrillo. His arrival was greeted with cheers.

He took the silver mask from the wall and went upstairs. He climbed to the top of the house, entered, switched on the naked light.

'Oh! Who—what——?' A voice of terror came from the bed.

'It's all right,' he said soothingly. 'Ada will be bringing your tea in a minute.'

He had a hammer and nail and hung the silver mask on the speckled, mottled wall-paper where Miss Herries could see it.

'I know you're fond of it,' he said. 'I thought you'd like it to look at.'

She made no reply. She only stared.

'You'll want something to look at,' he went on. 'You're too ill, I'm afraid, ever to leave this room again. So it'll be nice for you. Something to look at.'

He went out, gently closing the door behind him.

Brackenburn,
  October 21, 1930

THE STAIRCASE

It doesn't matter in the least where this old house is. There were once many houses like it. Now there are very few.

It was born in 1540 (you can see the date of its birth over the lintel of the porch, cut into the stone). It is E-shaped with central porch and wings at each end. Its stone is now, in its present age, weathered to a beautiful colour of pearl-grey, purple-shadowed. This stone makes the house seem old, but it is not old; its heart and veins are strong and vigorous, only its clothes now are shabby.

It is a small house as Tudor manor-houses go, but its masonry is very solid, and it was created by a spirit who cared that it should have every grace of proportion and strength. The wings have angle buttresses, and the porch rises to twisted terminals; there are twisted terminals with cupola tops also upon the gables, and the chimneys too are twisted. The mullioned windows have arched heads, and the porch has a Tudor arch. The arch is an entrance to a little quadrangle, and there are rooms above and gables on either side. Here and there is rich carving very fancifully designed.

It is set upon a little hill, and the lawn runs down to a small formal garden with box-hedges mounted by animals fancifully cut, a sundial, a little stone temple. Fields spread on either side of it and are bordered completely by a green tangled wood. The trees climb skywards on every side, but they are not too close about the house. They are too friendly to it to hurt it in any way. Over the arched porch a very amiable gargoyle hangs his head. He has one eye closed and a protruding chin from which the rain drips on a wet day, and in the winter icicles hang from it.

All the country about the house is very English, and the villages have names like Croxton, Little Pudding, Big Pudding, Engleheart and Applewain. A stream runs at the end of the lower field, runs through the wood, under the road, by other fields, so far as Bonnet, where it becomes a river, and broadens under bridges at Peckwit, the county town.

The house is called Candil Place and is very proud of its name. Its history for the last hundred years has been very private and personal. No one save myself and the house knows the real crises of its history, just as no one knows the real crisis of your history save yourself. You have doubtless been often surprised that neighbours think that such and such events have been the dramatic changing moments in your life—as when you lost your wife or your money or had scarlet fever—when in reality it was the blowing of a window curtain, the buying of a ship in silver, or the cry of a child on the stair.

So it has been with this house which has had its heart wrung by the breaking of a bough in the wind, a spark flying from the chimney, or a mouse scratching in the wainscot. From its birth it has had its own pride, its own reserve, its own consequence. Everything that has happened in it, every person who has come to it or gone from it, every song that has been sung in it, every oath sworn in it, every shout, every cry, every prayer, every yawn has found a place in its history.

Its heart has been always kindly, hospitable, generous; it has had as many intentions as we have all had, towards noble ends and fine charities. But life is not so easy as that.

Its first days were full of light and colour. Of course it was always a small house; Sir Mortimer Candil, who helped to create it, loved it, and the house gave him its heart. The house knew that he did for it what he could with his means; the house suffered with him when his first wife died of the plague, rejoiced with him when he married again so beautiful a lady, suffered with him once more when the beautiful lady ran away to Spain with a rascal.

There is a little room, the Priest's Room, where Sir Mortimer shut himself in and cried, one long summer day, his heart away. When he came out of there he had no heart any more, and the house, the only witness of that scene, put its arms about him, loved him more dearly than it had ever done, and mourned him most bitterly when he died.

The house after that had a very especial tenderness for the

Priest's Room, which was first hung with green tapestry, and then had dark panelling, and then was whitewashed, and then had a Morris wallpaper, and then discovered its dark panelling again, changing its clothes but never forgetting anything.

But the house was never a sentimental weakling. It was rather ironic in spirit because of the human nature that it saw and the vanity of all human wishes.

As to this business of human wishes and desires, the house has never understood them, having a longer vision and a quieter, more tranquil heart. After the experience that it has had of these strange, pathetic, obstinate, impulsive, short-sighted beings it has decided, perhaps, that they are bent on self-ruin and seem to wish for that.

This has given the house an air of rather chuckling tenderness.

Considering such oddities, its chin in its hand and the wood gathering round to listen, whether there should be anything worth listening to (for the house when it likes is a good story-teller), the eye of its mind goes back to a number of puzzling incidents and, most puzzling of all, to the story of Edmund Candil and his lady Dorothy, the events of a close summer evening in 1815, the very day that the house and its inhabitants had the news of Waterloo.

Sir Edmund Candil was a very restless, travelling gentleman, and all the trouble began with that.

The house could never understand what pleasure he found in all these tiresome foreign tours that he prosecuted when there was the lovely English country for him to spend his days in. His wife Dorothy could not understand this either.

There was a kind of fated air about them from the moment of their marriage. The house noticed it on their very wedding-day, and the Priest's Room murmured to the Parlour: 'Here's an odd pair!' and the Staircase whispered to the little dark Hall with the family pictures: 'This doesn't look too well,' and the Powder-Closet repeated to the Yellow Bedroom: 'No, this doesn't look well at all.'

They had, of course, all known Edmund from his birth. He was a swarthy, broad-shouldered baby, unusually long in the leg, and from the very beginning he was known for his tender heart and his obstinate will. These two qualities made him very silent. His tender heart caused him to be afraid of giving himself away, his obstinate will made him close his mouth and jut out his chin so that nobody could possibly say that his resolve showed signs of weakening.

He had a sister Henrietta, who was the cause of all the later trouble. The house never from the beginning liked Henrietta. It considered that always she had been of a sly, mean, greedy disposition. There is nothing like a house for discovering whether people are mean or greedy. Chests of drawers, open fireplaces, chairs and tables, staircases and powder-closets, these are the wise recipients of impressions whose confidence and knowledge you can shake neither by lies nor arrogances.

The house was willing to grant that Henrietta loved her brother, but in a mean, grasping, greedy manner, and jealousy was her other name.

They were children of a late marriage and their parents died of the smallpox when Edmund was nineteen and Henrietta twenty-one. After that Henrietta ruled the house because Edmund was scarcely ever there, and the house disliked exceedingly her rule. This house was, as I have said, a loyal and faithful friend and servant of the Candil family. Some houses are always hostile to their owners, having a great unreasoning pride of their own and considering the persons who inhabit them altogether unworthy of their good fortune. But partly for the sake of Sir Mortimer, who had created and loved it, and partly because it was by nature kindly, and partly because it always hoped for the best, the house had always chosen only the finest traits in the Candil character and refused to look at any other.

But, if there is one thing that a house resents, it is to be shabbily and meanly treated. When a carpet is worn, a window rattling in the breeze, a pipe in rebellion, a chair on the wobble, the house does everything towards drawing the attention of its master. This house had been always wonderfully considerate of expense and the costliness of all repair. It knew that its masters were not men of great wealth and must go warily with their purposes, but, until Henrietta, the Candils had been generous within their powers. They had had a pride in the house which made them glad to be generous. Henrietta had no such pride. She persisted in what she called an 'adequate economy,' declaring that it was her duty to her brother who drove her, but as the house (who was never deceived about anything) very well knew, this so-called 'economy' became her god and to save money her sensual passion.

She grew into a long bony woman with a faint moustache on her upper lip and a strange, heavy, flat-footed way of walking. The Staircase, a little conceited perhaps because of its lovely banisters that were as delicate as lace, hated her tread and declared that she was so common that she could not be a Candil. Several times the Staircase tripped her up out of sheer maliciousness. The Store-room hated her more than did any other part of the house. Every morning she was there, skimping and cheese-paring, making this last and doing without that, wondering whether this were not too expensive and that too 'outrageous.' Of course her maidservants would not stay with her. She found it cheapest to engage little charity-girls, and when she had them she starved them. It is true that she also starved herself, but that was no virtue; the house would see the little charity-girls crying from sheer hunger in their beds, and its heart would ache for them.

This was of course to some degree different when Edmund came home from his travels, but not very different, because he was always considerably under his sister's influence. He was softhearted and she was hard, and, as the house very well knew, the hard ones always win.

Henrietta loved her brother, but she was also afraid of him. She was very proud of him but yet more proud of her domination over him. When he was thirty and she thirty-two she was convinced that he would never marry. It had been once her terror that he should, and she would lie awake thinking one moment of the household accounts and the next of wicked girls who might entrap her brother. But it seemed that he was never in love; he returned from every travel as virgin as before.

She said to him one morning, smiling her rather grim smile: 'Well, brother, you are a bachelor for life, I think.'

It was then that he told her that he was shortly to marry Miss Dorothy Preston of Cathwick Hall.

He spoke very quietly, but, as the armchair in the Adam Room noticed, he was not quite at his ease. They were speaking in the Adam Room at the time, and this armchair had only recently been purchased by Edmund Candil. The room was not known then as the Adam Room (it had that title later) but it was the room of Edmund's heart. The fireplace was in the Adam style and so were the ceiling, and the furniture, the chairs, the table, the sofa, the commode Edmund had had made for him in London.

Very lovely they were, of satin-wood and mahogany, with their general effect of straight line but modified by lovely curves, delicate and shining. In the centre of the commode was a painted vase of flowers, on the ceiling a heavenly tracing of shell-like circles. Everywhere grace and strength and the harmony of perfect workmanship.

This room was for Edmund the heart of England, and he would stand in it, his dark eyes glowing, fingering his stock, slapping his tight thigh with his riding-whip, a glory at his heart. Many things he had brought with him from foreign countries. There was the Chinese room, and the little dining-room was decorated with Italian pictures. In his own room that he called the Library there was an ink-horn that had been (they said) Mirabeau's, a letter of Marie Antoinette's, a yellow lock cut from the hair of a mermaid and some of the feathers from the headdress of an African chieftain. Many more treasures than these. But it was the Parlour with the fine furniture bought by him in London that was England, and it was of this room that he thought when he was tossing on the Bay of Biscay or studying pictures in Florence or watching the ablutions of natives in the Sacred River.

It was in this room that he told his sister that he intended marriage.

She made no protest. She knew well enough when her brother's mind was made up. But it was a sunny morning when he told her, and as the sun, having embraced merrily the box-hedge peacocks and griffins, looked in to wish good-morning to the sofa and the round shining satin-wood table that balanced itself so beautifully on its slim delicate legs, it could tell that the table and chairs were delighted about something.

'What is it?' said the sun, rubbing its chin on the window-sill.

'There's a new mistress coming,' said the table and chairs.

And, when she came, they all fell at once in love with her. Was there ever anyone so charming and delicate in her primrose-coloured gown, her pretty straw bonnet and the grey silk scarf about her shoulders? Was there ever anyone so charming?

Of course Henrietta did not think so. This is an old story, this one of the family relations greeting so suspiciously the new young bride, but it is always actual enough in its tragedy and heartbreak however often it may have happened before.

Is it sentimental to be sorry because the new Lady Candil was sad and lonely and cried softly for hours at night while her husband slept beside her? At that time at least the house did not think so. Possibly by now it has grown more cynical. It cannot, any more than the humans who inhabit it, altogether be unaware of the feeling and colour of its time.

In any case the house loved Dorothy Candil and was deeply grieved at her trouble. That trouble was, one must realise, partly of her own making.

Her husband loved her, nay, he adored her with all the tenderness and tenacity that were part of his character. He adored her and was bored by her: as everyone knows, this is a most aggravating state of feeling. He thought her beautiful, good, amiable and honest, but he had nothing at all to say to her. For many a man she would have been exactly fitting, for it was not so much that she was stupid as that she had no education and no experience. He gave her none of these things as he should have done. Nor did he realise that this life, in the depths of English country, removed from all the enterprise and movement of the town, removed also by the weather from any outside intercourse for weeks at a time, was for someone without any great resources in herself depressing and enervating.

And then she was frightened of him. How well the house understood this! It too was, at times, afraid of him, of his silences, his obstinacy and easy capacity of semi-liveliness, a sensitiveness that his reticence forbade him to express.

How often in the months that followed the marriage did the house long to advise her as to her treatment of him. The sofa in the parlour was especially wise in such cases. Long before it had been covered with its gay cherry-coloured silk it had been famous among friends and neighbours for its delicacy in human tactics.

There came a morning when Lady Candil sat on a corner of it, her lovely little hand (she was delicate, slim, fragile, her body had the consistency of egg-shell china) clenching the shining wood of its strong arm for support, and a word from her would have put everything right. The sofa could feel the throbbing of her heart, and looking across to the thick, stiff, obstinate body of her husband, longed to throw her into his arms. But she could not say the word, and the mischanced moment became history for both of them. Had they not loved so truly it might have been easier for them; as it was, shyness and obstinacy built the barrier.

And of course Henrietta assisted. How grimly was she pleased as she sat in her ugly old russet gown, pretending to read Lord Clarendon's History (for she made a great pretence of improving her mind), but in reality listening to the unhappy silences between them and watching for the occasion when a word from her to her brother would skilfully widen the breach. For she hated poor Dorothy. She must in any case have done so out of jealousy and disappointment, but Dorothy was also precisely the example in woman whom she most despised. A weak, feckless, helpless thing whose pretty looks were an insult!

Then Dorothy felt her peril and rose to meet it. The house may have whispered in her ear!

Yes, she rose to meet it, but, as life only too emphatically teaches us, it is no good crying for the moon—and it is no good, however urgent we may be, begging for qualities that we have not got. She had a terrible habit of being affectionate at the wrong time. A kind of fate pursued her in this. He would return from his afternoon's ride, pleasantly weary, eager for his wife and happy in the thought of a little romantic dalliance, and she, fancying that he would not be disturbed, would leave him to snore beside the fire. Or a neighbour squire would visit him and he be off with him for the afternoon and she feel neglected.

Or he would be absorbed in a newsletter with a lively account of French affairs and she choose that moment to sit on his knee and tug his hair.

Dorothy was in truth one of those unfortunate persons—and they are among the most unfortunate in the world—who are insensitive to the moods and atmospheres of others. These err not through egotism nor stupidity, but rather through a sort of colour-blindness, so that they see their friend red when he is yellow and green when he is blue. Neither Dorothy nor Edmund had any gift of words.

So, a year and a half after his marriage, Edmund, with an ache in his heart, although he would own this to nobody, went once again to foreign parts. The house implored him not to go: he almost heard its protests.

On one of his last evenings there—a windy spring evening—he came in from a dark twilight walk, splashed with the mud of the country paths, the sense of the pale hedgerow primroses yet in his eye, the chatter of birds in his ear, and standing in the hall heard the William and Mary clock with the moon and stars, the banisters of the staircase, the curtains of the long hall window whisper to him:

'Don't go! Don't go! Don't go!'

He stood there and thought: 'By Gemini, I'll not leave this!' Dorothy came down the stairs to greet him and, seeing him lost in thought, stole upstairs again. In any case he had taken his seat in the coach, and his place in the packet-boat was got for him by a friend in London.

'Don't go!' said the portrait of old Uncle Candil.

He strode upstairs and Dorothy was reading *Grandison* by the fire, and although her heart was beating with love for him, was too timid to say so.

So to foreign parts he went again and, loving her so dearly, wrote letters to her which he tore up without sending lest she should think him foolish—such being the British temperament.

How the house suffered then, that Dorothy should be left to the harsh economies of sister Henrietta. Henrietta was not a bad woman, but she was mean, selfish, proud and stupid. She was also jealous. Very quickly and with little show of rebellion Dorothy submitted to her ways. If true love is in question absence does indeed make the heart grow fonder, and Dorothy thought of her husband night, morning, and night again.

She was snubbed, starved, and given a thorough sense of her insufficiencies. It is surprising how completely one human being can convince another of incompetence, ignorance and silly vanity if they be often alone together and one of them a woman. Women are more whole-hearted than men in what they do, whether for good or ill, and Henrietta was very whole-hearted indeed in this affair.

She convinced Dorothy before her husband's return that she was quite unworthy of his love, that he found her dull and unresponsive, that he was deeply disappointed in the issue of his marriage, and that she had deceived him most basely. You may say that she was a poor-spirited little thing, but she was very lonely, half-starved, and her love made her defenceless.

The appetite grows with what it feeds on, and Henrietta found that 'educating Dorothy,' as she called it, was a very worthy and soul-satisfying occupation. Dorothy began to be frightened, not only of herself and of Henrietta but of everything around her, the house, the gardens, the surrounding country.

The house did its utmost to reassure her. When she lay awake in her bed at night the house would hush any noise that might disturb her, the furniture of her room, the hangings above her bed, the old chest of Cromwell's time, the Queen Anne ward-robe, the warming-pan, the fire-irons that had the heads of grin-ning dogs, the yellow rug from Turkey, the Italian lamp beside her bed, they all crowded about her to tell her that they loved her. After a while she was conscious of their affection. Her bedroom and the parlour were for her the happiest places in the house, the only places indeed where she was not afraid.

She did not know that they were saying anything to her—she had not that kind of perception—but she felt reassured by them, and she would lock herself into her bedroom and sit there for hours thinking of her husband and wondering where he might be.

She became so painfully aware of Henrietta that she saw her when she wasn't there. She saw her always just around a corner, behind a tree, on the other side of the rose-garden wall, peering over the sundial, hiding behind the curtain. She became a slave to her, doing all that she was told, going where she was bid. The house considered it a disgusting business.

One evening she broke into a flash of rebellion.

'Edmund loves me!' she cried, her little breasts panting, her small hands clenched. 'And you hate me! Why do you hate me? I have never done you any harm.'

Henrietta looked at her severely.

'Hate! Hate! I have other things to do—and if he loves you, why does he stay so long away?'

Ah! why indeed? The house echoed the question, the very floors trembling with agitation. The stupid fool! Could he not see the treasure that he had? Did he think that such glories were to be picked up anywhere, any day, for the asking? The fire spat a piece of coal on to the hearthrug in contempt of human blindness.

When the time arrived at last for Edmund's return, Dorothy was in a fitting condition of miserable humility. Edmund did not love her. He was bored with her too dreadfully. But indeed how could he love her? How could anybody love her, poor incompetent stupid thing that she was! And yet in her heart she knew that she was not so stupid. Did Edmund love her only a little she could jump all the barriers and be really rather brilliant—much more brilliant than Henrietta, who was certainly not brilliant at all. It was this terrible shyness that held her back, that and Henrietta's assurance that Edmund did not love her. And indeed he did not seem to. It was but too likely that Henrietta was right.

As the time approached for Edmund's return Henrietta was in a fine bustle and the house was in one too. The house smiled contemptuously at Henrietta's parsimonious attempts to freshen it up. As though the house could not do that a great deal better than Henrietta ever could! Bees-waxing the floors, rubbing the furniture, shining up the silver—what were these little superficialities compared with the inner spiritual shake that the house gave itself when it wanted to? A sort of glow stole over windows, stairs and hall; a silver shine, a richer colour crept into the amber curtains, the cherry-coloured sofa; the faces in the por-

traits smiled, the fire-irons glittered, the mahogany shone again.
Edmund had been away too long; the house would not let him
go so easily next time.

The night before his return Dorothy did not sleep, but lay
there, her eyes burning, her heart thickly beating, determin-
ing on the bold demonstrative person she would be. She would
show Henrietta whether he loved her or no. But at the thought
of Henrietta she shivered and drew the bedclothes closely about
her. She seemed to be standing beside the bed, illumined in the
darkness by her own malignant fires, her yellow skin drawn
tightly across the supercilious bones, her hands curving over
some fresh mean economy, her ridiculous head-dress wagging
like a mocking spirit above her small red-rimmed eyes. Yes, if
only Henrietta were not there . . .

And the old chest murmured softly: 'If only Henrietta were
not there . . .'

The post-chaise came up to the door darkly like a ghost,
for it had been snowing all day, and the house was wrapped in
silence. The animals on the box-tree hedge stood out fantasti-
cally against the silver-grey of the evening sky, and the snow fell
like the scattering feathers of a heavenly geese-flock.

Edmund stepped into the hall and had Dorothy in his arms.
At that moment they knew how truly they loved one another.
He wondered as he flung his mind back in an instant's retrospect
over a phantasmagoria of Indian Moguls, Chinese rivers and the
flaming sunsets of Arabia how it could be that he had not known
that his life was here, here with his beloved house above him,
his adored wife in his arms. His head up like a conqueror's, he
mounted the stairs, almost running into his wonderful parlour,
to see once again the vase of flowers on the commode, the slender beautiful legs of his chair, the charming circles of his delicate
ceiling. 'How could I have stayed away?' he thought. 'I will never
leave this again!'

And that night, clasped in one another's arms, they discovered one another again: shyness fled and heart was open to heart.

Nevertheless there remained Henrietta. Would you believe
that one yellow-faced old maid could direct and dominate two
normal healthy creatures? You know that she can, and is doing it

somewhere or other at this very moment. And all for their good. No one ever did anything mean to anyone else yet save for their good, and so it will be until the end of this frail planet.

She told Edmund that she had been 'educating Dorothy.' He would find her greatly improved; she feared that her worst fault was Hardness of Heart. Hardness of Heart! A sad defect!

During those snowy days Henrietta tried to show her brother that no one in the world truly loved him but herself. She had shown him this before and found the task easy; now it was more difficult. Dorothy's shyness had been melted by this renewed contact; he could not doubt the evidence of his eyes and the many little unconscious things that spoke for her when she had no idea that they were speaking. Now they rode and walked together and he explained to her how *he* was, how that at a time his thoughts would be far, far away in Cairo or Ispahan and that she must not think that he did not care for her because he was dreaming, and she told him that when he had frightened her she had been stupid, but that now that he frightened her no longer she would soon be brilliant. . . . So Henrietta's task was difficult.

And then in the spring, when the daffodils blew among the long grasses and the white violets were shining in the copse, a chance word of hers showed her the way. She hated Dorothy now because she suspected that Dorothy was planning to be rid of her. The fear that she would be turned out of the house never left her, and so, as fear always does, it drove her to baser things than belonged truly to her nature. She hinted that in Edmund's absence Dorothy had found a neighbouring squire 'good company.' And there had been perhaps another or two . . . MEN . . . At that word every frustrated instinct in Henrietta's body turned in rebellion. She had not spoken before she believed it true. She had this imaginative gift, common to lonely persons. She was herself amazed at the effect of her words on Edmund. If she had ever doubted Edmund's love for his wife (and she had not really doubted it) she was certain of the truth at last. Dorothy . . . Dorothy . . . His stout body trembled; his eyes were wounded; he turned from his sister as though he were ashamed both of her and of himself. After that there was no peace.

It was now that the house wondered most deeply at these

strange human beings. The little things that upset them, the odd things that, at a moment, they would believe! Here, for instance, was their Edmund, whom they so truly admired, loving his Dorothy and entirely trusting her. Now, at a moment's word from a sour-faced virgin, there is a fire of torment in his heart. He looks on every male with an eager restless suspicion. While attempting to appear natural he watches Dorothy at every corner and counters in his mind her lightest word.

'Why,' said the Italian lamp (which from its nationality knew everything about jealousy) to the Cromwellian chest, 'I have never known so foolish a suspicion,' to which the Cromwellian chest replied in its best Roundhead manner: 'Woman ... the devil's bait ... always has been ... always will be.'

He attacked his sister again and again. 'With whom has she been? Has she ever stayed from the house a night? What friends has she made?'

To which Henrietta would indignantly reply: 'Brother, brother. What are you about? This jealousy is most unbecoming. I have suggested no impropriety ... only a little foolishness born of idleness.'

But it did not need time for Dorothy to discover that something was once again terribly amiss.

This strange husband of hers, so unable to express himself —she had but just won him back to her and now he was away again! With the courage born of their new relationship she asked him what was the trouble. And he told her: 'Nothing. . . . Nothing! Nothing at all! Why should there be trouble? You are for ever imagining ...' And then looked at her so strangely that she blushed and turned away as though she were indeed guilty. Guilty of what? She had not the least idea. But what she did know was that it was dear sister Henrietta who was responsible, and now, as May came with a flourish of birds and blossom and star-lit nights, she began to hate Henrietta with an intensity quite new to her gentle nature.

So, with jealousy and hatred, alive and burning, the house grew very sad. It hated these evil passions and had said long ago that they ruined with their silly bitterness every good house in the world. The little Chinese cabinet with the purple dragons on its doors said that in China everything was much simpler—you did not drag a situation to infinity as these sluggish English do, but simply called Death in to make a settlement—a much simpler way. In any case the house began to watch and to listen with the certainty that the moment was approaching when it must interfere.

Jealousy always heightens love, and so, if Edmund had loved Dorothy at the first, that cool, placid anticipation was nothing to the fevered passion which he now felt. When he was away from her he longed to have her in his arms, covering her with kisses and assuring her that he had never doubted her, and when he was with her he suspected her every look, her every word. And she, miserable now and angry and ill, could not tell what possessed him, her virtue being so secure that she could not conceive that anyone should suspect it. Only she was well aware that Henrietta was to blame.

These were also days of national anxiety and unrest; the days when Napoleon jumping from Elba alighted in France and for a moment promised to stay there. Warm, stuffy, breathless days, when everyone was waiting, the house with the rest.

On the staircase one summer evening Dorothy told Henrietta something of her mind. 'If I had my way,' she ended in a shaking rage, 'you would not be here plotting against us!'

So that was it! At last Henrietta's suspicions were confirmed. In a short while Dorothy would have her out of the house; and then where would she go? The thought of her desolation, loneliness, loss of power, gripped her heart like a cat's claws. The two little charity-girls had a time of it during those weeks and cried themselves to sleep in their attic that smelt of mice and apples, dreaming afterwards of strong lovers who beat their mistress into a pulp.

'Give me proof!' said Edmund, so bitterly tormented. 'If it is true, give me proof!'

And Henrietta answered, sulkily: 'I have never said anything,' and a window-ledge fell on his fingers and bruised them just to teach him not to be so damnable a fool.

Nevertheless Henrietta had her proof. She had been cherishing it for a year at least. This was a letter written by a young naval lieutenant, cousin of a neighbouring squire, after he had danced with Dorothy at a Christmas ball. It was only a happy careless boy's letter, he in love with Dorothy's freshness, and because he was never more than a moment in any one place, careless of consequences. He said in his letter that she was the most beautiful of God's creatures, that he would dream of her at sea, and the rest. Dorothy kept it. Henrietta stole it. . . .

The day came when the coach brought the news of the Waterloo victory. On that summer evening rockets were breaking into the pale sky above the dark soft shelter of the wood; on Bendon Hill they were waiting for dark to light the bonfire. You could hear the shouting and singing from the high road. The happiness at the victory and the sense that England was delivered blew some of the cobwebs from Edmund's brain; he took Dorothy into the garden and there, behind the sundial, put his arms around her and kissed her.

Henrietta, watching the rockets strike the sky from her window, saw them, and fear, malice, loneliness, greed, hurt pride and jealousy all rose in her together. She turned over the letter in her drawer and vowed that her brother should not go to bed that night before he had heard of it.

'Look out! Look out!' cried her room to the rest of the house. 'She will make mischief with the letter. We must prevent her . . .'

'She has done mischief enough,' chattered the clock from the hall. 'She must be prevented . . .' whistled the chimneys. Something must be done and at once. But how? By whom?

She is coming. She stands outside her door, glancing about the dim sunset passage. The picture of Ranelagh above her head wonders—shall it fall on her? The chairs along the passage watch her anxiously as she passes them. But what can they do? Each must obey his own laws.

Stop her! Stop her! Stop her! Edmund and Dorothy are coming in from the garden. The sun is sinking, the shadows lengthening across the lawn. One touch on his arm: 'Brother, may I have a word?' and all the harm is done—misery and distress, unhappiness in the house, separation and loneliness. Stop her! Stop her!

All the house is quivering with agitation. The curtains are

blowing, the chimneys are twisting, the tables and chairs are creaking: Stop her! Stop her! Stop her!

The order has gone out. She is standing now at the head of the staircase leading to the hall. She waits, her head bent a little, listening. Something seems to warn her. Edmund and Dorothy are coming in from the garden. The fireworks are beginning beyond the wood, and their gold and crimson showers are rivalling the stars.

Henrietta, nodding her head as though in certainty, has taken her step, some roughness in the wood has caught her heel (was it there a moment ago?), she stumbles, she clutches at the balustrade, but it is slippery and refuses to aid her. She is falling; her feet are away in air, her head strikes the board; she screams, once and then again; a rush, a flash of huddled colour, and her head has struck the stone of the hall floor.

How odd a silence followed! Dorothy and Edmund were still a moment lingering by the door looking back to the shower of golden stars, hearing the happy voices singing in the road. Henrietta was dead and so made no sound.

But all through the house there was a strange humming as though everything from top to bottom were whispering.

Everything in the house is moving save the woman at the bottom of the stairs.

A CARNATION FOR AN OLD MAN

Richard Herries, his sister Margaret, and their friend Miss Felstead arrived in Seville one February evening soon after midnight.

Their Seville adventure began unfortunately. As Margaret Herries always declared afterwards: 'We might have known that it was fated to end disastrously. It had so dismal a beginning.'

It had indeed. At each visit they expected to step out of the train into a glorious tumultuous mixture of castanets, bullfighters, carnations, Carmen and Andalusian dancers. Instead of this they were received by a gentle drizzle and a Square quite silent and occupied only by some somnolent motorcars.

They needed encouragement. It had been a long and wearisome journey from Granada. Why, as Margaret said over and over again in the course of it, when Granada and Seville were so close to one another on the map they should be such an infinite distance by train only the Spanish railway authorities could explain, and they, so she was informed, never explained anything. They had been already unfortunate at Granada, where it had been cold and where Miss Felstead (who was very romantic) had been unable, in spite of bribes, to persuade the custodian to allow her to see from the Alhambra Tower the sunset light up the Sierras. It would be too bad were Seville to be unfavourable also.

But it really started badly. They had engaged rooms at the Hotel Royal in the Plaza de San Fernando. This had been done only after a most vigorous and almost acrimonious discussion. The point was that the Hotel Royal was a Spanish hotel run for the Spanish and therefore cheaper than those which accommodated especially the English and American. Cheaper, yes, but, Margaret was sure, much nastier. Wasn't Spanish sanitation notorious? What about the smells they had smelt in Barcelona? And didn't the Spaniards cook everything in rancid oil? Economically minded though Margaret always was, for once she was against economy. She changed places indeed with her brother, who was the most generous soul alive. But the bill at the English hotel in Granada had seemed to him quite beyond justice, and an English lady (a very clean and particular English lady) had told him that she always patronised the Royal when she went to Seville. An excellent hotel, she told him, clean, the servants polite and remarkably willing. A marvellously cheap *pension,* and the food good and plentiful. So Richard had for once insisted.

And now behold the miserable commencement! Miss Felstead (who had eyes like gimlets) perceived at once that in the Square there were two hotel omnibuses asleep like everything else, and that on the windows of one of these were inscribed the magical words 'Hotel Royal,' so she marshalled the two young dreamy porters and steered them with the luggage in the proper direction.

On the steps of the omnibus was a hotel porter fast asleep. He was awakened, the luggage piled on the roof of the omnibus, and the three travellers installed inside. Then occurred the disgraceful event! After waiting for some ten minutes and drinking in the miserable fact that Seville station at midnight in the rain was worse than Sheffield on a Sunday, it occurred to Margaret Herries that nothing at all was happening. The hotel porter, who was again dozing off, explained to Richard—who had a literary rather than practical knowledge of Spanish—that the driver of the omnibus had, some half-hour before, disappeared into the station for conversation with a friend.

'Well,' suggested Richard, 'fetch him.'

The porter, who had all the individuality, nobility and gravity of his race, walked with dignified austerity to the edge of the station, looked at it, shook his head, and returned wrapped in melancholy and thinking, apparently, of lottery tickets. After a while he pressed, very gently, the hooter of the omnibus, but with no result. Then, strongly urged, he went once more to the edge of the station but returned empty-handed.

So half an hour was passed. By this time Margaret and her friend were frantic with railway-nerves, bodily hunger (they had had only twenty minutes at Bobadilla to snatch some food three hours earlier), weariness and disappointment. Finally all the luggage was taken off the omnibus, after another half an hour a taxicab was found, and they set off for the hotel. The last view they had of the porter he was curled up inside the omnibus, happily reposing.

As Margaret always afterwards said, this was an Omen. She had herself never believed very much in Omens before. Miss Felstead was the one for Omens—but after the horrible week in Seville with its dreadful ending she never laughed at Omens again.

But for her everything was wrong with Seville from the beginning and, oddly, for Richard everything was right. He was an old man now—seventy-five years of age—and of course wanted his comforts. As a matter of fact the Herries always did want their comforts and saw that they got them. But once and again there would be a 'freak' Herries who never seemed to know quite what he did want, and Richard had been rather like that. It was because he had been like that that his many sisters had always looked after him so thoroughly. First Hettie, and then, when she married, Florence, and then, when she married, Rosalind, and then, when she died, the youngest of them, Margaret. On two occasions Richard had almost married, might have been married altogether had he not been looked after so completely.

He had not, be it understood, objected to being looked after; he had rather liked it. He had felt perhaps that only so could he preserve his own secret life. And then they were immensely kind, especially Margaret.

Margaret had always adored her brother. She was not at all a sentimental person. She was a definite type of Englishwoman —a little mannish, thick-set and square, given to white collars, Scotch tweeds and brogues, rosy of complexion with strong black hair flecked now with grey, a snub nose, an obstinate mouth and a clear calm forehead. No other country could possibly produce a woman so calm, so determined, so masculine and yet feminine, so kind and so obtuse and so certain that all the things that she didn't know were unworthy of any sensible person's attention, so unsexual and yet so obviously designed for maternity.

She poured all her maternity on to Richard and yet apparently without a shadow of emotion. They never under any conditions showed emotion the one for the other, but they were devoted, self-sacrificing, and very good companions.

For seventy-five years Richard Herries had submitted to his sisters because he was both lazy and dreamy. He was the Herries type that dreams dreams, and they have always either submitted and been wrapped away to nothing or rebelled and been cast out.

People described him as a 'dear little old man.' He was short and fat with snow-white hair and rosy cheeks, clean-shaven and of an immaculate shining neatness. He had a delightful chuckle, a fashion of jingling his change in his wide trousers pocket. He seemed to enjoy everything. No one would have guessed that for some while now he had been one of the loneliest souls in Christendom.

It had begun a year or two before at a concert of modern music in Berlin. Schnabel was playing, and he, Richard, had suddenly realised that he was miserably unhappy, that he had wasted the whole of his life, that he had done none of the things that he ought to have done. Margaret was with him, and he bought her a tie-pin. Nevertheless, for some days he still felt miserable. This feeling returned at certain intervals: once when he watched 'Punch and Judy' outside the Garrick Theatre, once when he read Madariaga's *Englishmen, Frenchmen, Spaniards,* once when he ate too much at a dinner-party, once when he saw his reflection in a looking-glass, once when he was staying in Cumberland and watched the birds fly over Derwentwater on a September evening.... And now again on this visit to Spain!

He connected these distresses at once, like all good Herries, with his stomach. He liked his food and his wine, but when he was unhappy he had only a biscuit for luncheon.

He rearranged his pictures in his London flat, hanging the Utrillo over the piano and the Segonzac over the bookcase, hoping that that would put things right. He had fancied at the time that it had, but here he was now in Spain with no pictures to rehang and his stomach in perfect order.

He was unhappy, rebellious and discontented, and especially he detested Miss Felstead. When a very courteous, aged English gentleman detests an amiable lady, what is he to do about it? Avoid her company? Yes, but you cannot do that if you are travelling with her in a foreign country. Say as little as possible? This he tried, but his unusual silence at once aroused suspicion. Was he ill? Was he uncomfortable? Was he (Margaret hinted) simply sulking? Whenever Margaret thought that anything was wrong she was extremely sensible and cheerful. She was as sensible as a chemist's shop and as cheerful as a fine day on the Scottish moors. She was breezy and jolly and accommodating. Miss Felstead, on the other hand, was tender and gentle and mysterious. In shape Miss Felstead was as slender as an umbrella handle, and in complexion rather blotchy, so that, quite frankly, when she was tender she was awful.

Richard had never liked her, but she was one of those English maiden ladies with no money and no relations upon whom others are always taking pity. It was rumoured, too, that she was extremely intelligent, that she would have been an authoress of note had she not possessed so critical a mind. When she was young she read Dante in Italian and belonged to a Browning Society; now that she was no longer young she raved about a Czecho-Slovakian pianist and read papers like 'Light' and 'Whence? Why? Whither?' But Richard had always suspected her intelligence, and his suspicions were confirmed when in the Prado, before Las Hilanderas, she had said: 'Very fine, of course, but does one *like* it?'

That evening, in order to annoy her, he had passionately defended the bullfight and had sent her at once into a rocking wailing recitative of 'Ah, but the horses! The poor, poor horses!'

He suspected that in her heart she detested him as truly as he detested her. She was jealous, in the curious tenacious way that such maiden ladies have, of Margaret's affection for him. The thought that she perhaps detested him gave him some comfort.

In any case, and for whatever the reason, he had from the moment that he set foot in Seville the worst attack of rebellion he had ever known.

He was exceedingly fond of Spain and of the Spanish. It was by his firm wish that they were there now. Margaret did not like Spain; it seemed to her a lazy, purposeless, priest-ridden country.

She could not understand what Richard saw in it, but loved him too dearly to refuse his wish.

He timidly suggested that he should come this time without her. He, seventy-five years of age and travel alone?

'But I'm perfectly fit. I've been there before. I know the language.'

Margaret smiled then, one of those smiles peculiarly the property of the Herries women, a smile self-confident, indulgent, maternal, kindly and patronising, a smile that had, on more than one earlier occasion, made murder a conceivable practice.

'Dear Richard ... at *your* age ... and Spain of all countries to be alone in!'

Yes. 'Spain of all countries!' That was Margaret's honest view of it. She thought that Spain was bad for everybody and especially for the Spaniards.

So, whether it were Margaret's anti-Spanish feeling or Miss Felstead's romanticism or simply the air or the disappointment over the omnibus at the station or the fact that they were at a Spanish hotel, whatever the reason, from the very first moment in Seville Richard and Margaret were at loggerheads.

'If I only had known!' Margaret said again and again afterwards. But of course she did not know. No one, thank heaven, ever does.

Richard had never been to Seville before. His first visit, some ten years earlier, had been along the southern coast, Malaga, Algeciras and Cadiz. The second time, five years ago, had taken him into the Basque country and as far south as Madrid and Toledo. At present his favourite town in Spain was Segovia, but he had stayed there only two days because Margaret was homesick for Cumberland. He looked back on it as a lovely city of silver-grey stone, flowers and green trees. He wouldn't mind settling there, he had told Margaret, for a year or two.

He was thinking of Segovia this first morning in Seville. He had slipped out of his hotel without letting the women know and had almost the air of a guilty schoolboy as, seeing the tower of the Cathedral beckoning to him across the blue above the Spanish Bank, he turned in that direction.

After that first step his story enters into another world. How many other worlds are there? Millions, says one; none at all, says another. 'Two are all I need,' says the poet. Richard Herries had all his life known only one and longed always, like ancestors of his, for another. Margaret's account of it afterwards was: 'On that very first morning in Seville he was unwell. Of course for one thing we were staying in a hotel for Spaniards—a most unwise thing to do, but Richard would have it. Then he went out all by himself that first morning, a most unusual thing for him to do. If I had only known that first day how ill he was!'

Luckily she did not.

But he didn't feel ill at all. He had never felt so well in his life before.

Although the sky was blue there was a sharp nip in the air. It was eleven o'clock and everyone was beginning to wake up. At one all the shops would shut until four, the hour when everyone would *really* be awake. This was a sort of false dawn, and very pleasant it was. In February Seville knows nothing of tourists save for an occasional meteoric flash of a boat-load from Cadiz or Malaga or Gibraltar. Richard might be said to be the guest of all the town.

His head was undoubtedly queer—not unpleasantly so, but as though he had taken a draught of some very potent sparkling wine. His limbs were light, made of gauze, and he seemed to have no age at all.

He was accustomed to the quiet and removed but friendly dignity of the Spaniard. That was one of the things that he liked best about Spain. They never pressed you to buy anything or go anywhere or do anything active, with the important exception, of course, of the boys who wanted to clean your boots for you. If you were a pretty young woman and alone, they might stare at you and even follow you, because pretty young women do not walk about alone in Spain, but that was the only active interest they took. And yet they were friendly, kind, and beautifully polite. Richard loved good manners.

So to-day as Richard passed under the lovely portal that leads into the garden where the orange trees nestle under the Cathedral walls the audacious thought came to him that he would stay in Seville for many weeks, perhaps until June even, see the Holy

Week with its processions, enjoy the Feria, bask in the suns of May, and, best of all, bury his nose in carnations. Now all his life long his favourite flower had been the carnation, and especially that purple one that is divinely streaked with mauve and crimson.

It had been his thought when he had first come to Spain that he would find a country buried in carnations, but it had been on every occasion too early in the year, and he had been bitterly disappointed when offered a miserable bunch of these flowers, already half dead, for the exorbitant sum of four or five pesetas. Why, they were cheaper in Piccadilly!

But now standing in that lovely garden with its uneven and crooked flags beneath his feet, the Giralda at his left stretching to the heavens, and the Patio de los Naranjos, its stone encrusted as though with jewels, the Madonna above the great door regarding him so benignly, the birds flying from buttress to buttress, he trembled with the excitement of his new experience —he would stay here. Margaret and Miss Felstead should return without him. He had in his heart the sweet burning awe of falling once again in love. . . .

He gave some money to the old twisted beggar who, with trembling hand, lifted the black leather flap for him to enter, and passed inside.

Luncheon at the Royal was served from half-past twelve until half-past two, and at half-past two Richard had not yet returned. Margaret was a resolute, contained, sensible woman, but her distress was nevertheless acute and it was not made easier by Elsie Felstead's little wails: 'I know something has happened to him! How could we let him go out alone! He might be ill and neither of us know it for days! What about the police?'

'Oh, be quiet, Elsie!' Margaret seldom snapped at her friend, but when she did her friend knew it. 'Of course he's all right. Richard's not a child, and he knows Spanish far better than we do.' All the same, she could have flung her arms around him and kissed him when he came in at last through the hotel door.

Instead of kissing him, being English, she scolded him.

Richard was very quiet. He said he was sorry, but he had been in the Cathedral. He had not noticed the time. It was a very beautiful cathedral.

Every sympathy must be felt for Margaret. Here she was in a strange country and her only brother, who was in her charge, whom she loved very dearly, was ill and refused to admit it.

That evening she attacked him about it.

'Richard, you are not well. Go to bed and I'll have some dinner sent up to you.'

'I'm perfectly well.' His voice was testy and his eyes absent-minded.

'Now I know you're not. You can't deceive me after all these years. You are sickening for something, or that's what you look like. Elsie agrees with me.'

'Damn Elsie,' said Richard.

Margaret was upset and with reason. This was altogether unlike Richard. 'Will you let me take your temperature?'

'No.'

Then followed Margaret's most irritating method of persuasion, her jolly, patronising, friendly method.

'Now, old boy,' putting her hand on his shoulder, 'this is childish. What harm is there in my taking your temperature? After all, if you are going to be ill you may just as well know it.'

'But I am *not* going to be ill,' he answered with much firmness. 'As a matter of fact I never felt better.' Then he went on, looking at her in an odd way, rather as though he were seeing her now for the first time in his life. 'The fact is, Margaret, I'm going about by myself a bit while we're here. You and Elsie might go to Malaga or Cadiz perhaps if you are bored by Seville—just for a day or two——'

He looked at her sternly as though he were giving her an order. He had never looked at her like that in all their lives together before. But she simply answered:

'Very well, Richard. Perhaps we will.' And she said nothing more about temperatures.

She was deeply alarmed. She lay for a long while awake thinking. What had happened to her brother? Something had occurred during those hours when he was alone in the town? Love? Absurd at his age ... and yet one read in the newspapers the oddest stories about old men. A Spanish siren? They were pretty, some of these Spanish women with their combs and black shawls. But no ... not Richard.... He was not like that. She resolved that she would not let him escape her in the morning. Where he went so would she.

And then in the morning an awful thing occurred. Richard lied to them both. He had never, in Margaret's belief, lied to her before. Dressed and ready, Margaret knocked at his door. He poked his head out.

'All right, my dear. Go down and wait for me. I'll be with you in a moment.'

They sat, the two of them, in the little hall of the Royal and waited. They waited for a long time, very uncomfortable because the men also seated in the hall, and having apparently all the day in front of them, stared at them so markedly. At last they sent someone up to enquire. He came back. The señor was not there. The *femme-de-chambre* had seen him, half an hour before, with his hat and cane. Was there another exit to the hotel? Yes, there was another exit ... Margaret and Miss Felstead stared at one another in mutual horror.

Richard was not only unwell; he was also insane. But Richard was not insane; he was merely conscious of happiness as he had never been conscious of it before.

On making his escape he went straight to the Cathedral, passed through the Court of the Orange Trees, gave half a peseta to the blind beggar who lifted the black flap for him, and stepped into his true life.

That was how he now expressed it to himself, that was how he saw it. He was seventy-five years of age, had had on the whole a full, interesting and happy existence, and yet—had never been alive until yesterday! Had been asleep, mummified, blind, deaf, dumb and had not known it.

It was not, as he very well knew, that this church was of such marvellous beauty. He had seen cathedrals possibly of greater beauty, Chartres, St. Mark's in its own kind, even Ely on its slender scale. It was not that he was converted suddenly to any religious belief. Like most men he did not believe in very much but rather snatched at moments of love and beauty for confirmation of his unuttered hopes. It was not that he felt better or kinder or wiser since yesterday; it was simply that he was alive, alive to his finger-tips. It was like falling in love, but there was no one to fall in love with.

If it was not the most beautiful cathedral that he had ever seen, it was nevertheless the most alive. It gave him an impression of vastness as no other cathedral had done. But it was a vastness perfectly lighted. Although far from the darkness of a cathedral like Barcelona, it was quite without the shrill brightness that takes away mystery. The light came from many sources, now in long paths of softening colour, now in splashes of blue and purple that seemed almost to spring like fountains from the ground, now in dim misty gold from behind the shadowy pillars. In all this clarity there was no especial neatness or spruceness. What especially pleased him was that the building seemed always to continue its own natural life, crumbling here, breaking away a little there, stiffening in one place, failing in another. The magnificent colour of the highly placed windows was enrapturing. Never in his life had he seen such true deeps of rose and opal and onyx and crimson. High in air the windows sailed like magical clouds on the points of the vast pillars and the great gates, thin like black silver or a wall of gold, like the gate before the altar, or a mist of cloud, were everywhere.

On this second day he realised that the church was like a town: here women were kneeling, there children playing, priests passed swiftly on some business, on a seat near to him a woman was suckling a child, before a neighbouring chapel two dogs were playing, two old men were sweeping with brooms, some men in a group near by were discussing their affairs. Life, heightened by the beauty and majesty of the place, was going on everywhere around him, and to himself too something especial was about to happen.

He looked up, a smile on his lips, as though he knew what was coming, and encountered the grave, happy eyes of Santa Emilia.

Santa Emilia has been waiting (for how many years I shouldn't like to say) very patiently in the right corner of a picture that hangs in a chapel that shall be nameless, nameless because it would be a piece of the worst impertinence if, in the course of this little history, I were to reveal her exact position. I will not even assert definitely that her name is Emilia.

On one of the walls of one of these chapels, then, there is a large painting (by Murillo, perhaps, as so many of the paintings in this city are by that artist), and it is flanked on either side by some six other paintings in the shape of panels. These panels are of a lovely gentle colouring—soft rose and silver, the palest of greens and of dove grey. It was in the largest of these panels that Emilia had for so many years been so sweetly and patiently sitting. In her picture the heavens open and someone, God the Father Himself, perhaps, is delivering judgment, and several Saints seated on the grass listen in a mild surprise.

It is impossible to suppose that Santa Emilia herself was watching for any casual comer. For one thing her chapel was dark, well defended by its high iron gates, and it was but seldom that visitors penetrated that obscurity. Then she had other things to do. Her face, young, eager, ardent, was raised to the sky in an attitude of worship, her hands with their lovely slender fingers folded on her lap, a green scarf falling lightly over the white meshes of her robe. Why, after all these years, should she notice Richard Herries? The answer to that is that obviously it must have been astonishing to her that anyone should notice her at all, choose her from among so many others. She was carrying in one hand a red flower that might have been a carnation (Richard was certain that it was), and it was the agitation of this flower against her fingers that warned her that something exceptional was occurring. So she turned and looked towards the gates and at once in that first glance exchanged they loved one another.

She had been waiting always for just such an experience as this. She had never known anything of earthly love. From her babyhood her life had been dedicated to Christ and she had wanted nothing else. When the Pestilence had struck her convent in Seville she had been only twenty-three years of age, but was even then distinguished among the others for the purity and goodness of her life.

The Pestilence was raging throughout Seville and she had gone into the town and wrought so many services there in caring for the sick and comforting the bereaved that, at her death from that same disease, she had been canonised.

She was only a very minor Saint; she had not lived long

enough nor caused enough public attention (for with Saint-hood as with everything else, advertisement is a great help) to be remembered very dearly by anyone. And then her position was obscure, seated there in one of the most obscure paintings in one of the darkest of the chapels. She was nevertheless most happy, for to worship God continually when you are certain of His existence is the happiest of all possible lives.

Nevertheless she was, and always had been, a completely human being as well as a Saint, and now, looking down into the rosy, earnest face of that old man who was so very like the child that she might have had, had life been different, she loved him as she would, had it been so ordered, have loved her son.

Richard stayed there a long time. He told her many things that he had never told anyone in his life before. Then he went away....

His life was at once, from that moment, so immensely heightened, intensified and ennobled that anyone, encountering him, must perceive the change. All true love must of course ennoble the possessor of it, but here was a miracle—not because Santa Emilia had turned her head and smiled at him—Saints are continually engaged in these acts of mercy—but because this experience had come to him so very late in his life when everything might have been supposed to be over for him.

Back in his hotel he wanted very badly to give some sort of explanation to the two ladies. But what could he say? He was not so rapt in his own miracle but that he could realise perfectly well that to say to Margaret: 'You must excuse me if I seem a little absent-minded. The fact is that I have fallen in love with a Saint in the Cathedral,' would be simply to invite her instantly to summon a doctor.

So he said nothing at all. But he was in fact so charming, so gentle and so happy that Margaret asked him no questions. One thing that pleased her greatly was to see that he had quite altered his attitude to Miss Felstead. He was not irritated any longer by her remarks, did not snap at her romanticism, was patient with her sentiment. He was patient with everyone and everything and his eyes shone with a happy light.

'We were quite wrong,' his sister said to her friend, 'to think him ill. Seville seems to be doing him a world of good. We may as well stay on for a while, although I can't say that I like either the hotel or the town.'

He had now, it was plain, a passion for the Cathedral, and in that, too, they allowed him to have his way. After all, it did no one any harm.

In many places of worship it would soon have attracted attention that a little elderly gentleman should stay for so long, day after day in the same position, his face close to the iron gates, staring in front of him. But in this cathedral nothing human was either odd or vulgar.

He told her everything, he who had never told anyone anything before. Few people realise the tomb-like silence in which most Englishmen spend their lives. Their education trains them to silence, their marriage system encourages it, their belief in physical exercise makes intellectual silence easy.

No one, standing near at hand, would have heard anything: Richard's lips indeed did not move, but Santa Emilia heard everything. So many things that she could not have believed possible! How far from her cloistered Spanish life of four hundred years before was this strange English one; a family life, made up of gardens shadowed by old trees and guarded by rose-red walls, of sports desperately important, of sisters and sisters and sisters, of many months of rain and mist and fog, of a religion that was no religion, and, finally, what drew her heart just as four hundred years ago it would have been drawn, a sense of babyhood, a perpetual nursery with rocking cradles and the good God coming laden with gifts for good children down through the chimney—as though this little old man with the white hair were the child for whom, although she did not know it, she had always longed.

Yes, he told her everything—even that he had thought that Spain would be filled with carnations, but that, alas, he had found only some faded ones. Was that a carnation that she held in her hand? Yes, she told him that it was. It had not been one until that moment. As she spoke it became one.

She spoke, but no one watching beside Richard would have seen her lips move. He alone saw and heard.

In another place and at another time he would have known that he was very unwell. His heart had been for many years weak and all the symptoms that he so greatly dreaded were now present. But he did not realise them. He was not aware of his body. He was happy as one is happy in a dream when one suddenly, after æons of disappointment, has perfect satisfaction. Santa Emilia went with him everywhere. Margaret and Miss Felstead of course did not know this. Margaret was worried a little about his appearance. Like many good women she was especially proud of detecting the approach of illness in anyone. She was certain that Richard 'was sickening for something.' But he denied any ailment. He had never, he told her, felt so well in his life before, and that indeed was true.

Taking Santa Emilia everywhere, he found Seville most enchanting. Even the Museo, with its too saccharine Murillo, its pathetic air of desertion, its courtyard that echoed so sadly the weary feet of the tourists, seemed to him beautiful because of Santa Emilia's pride in it. Seville, in spite of its energy and jollity and measure of full, healthy life, is especially the city of children and old men. Nowhere in Spain—and I suspect nowhere else in the world—are there such marvellous old men with such marvellous faces, and nowhere else are the children so gay. No matter where—in the crowded Sierpes, along the banks of the brown Guadalquivir, in the quiet fountain-singing gardens of Murillo —it is the old men and the children who are everywhere.

When at last Santa Emilia knew how deeply she loved her friend, she asked Santa Isabela what she must do. Santa Isabela had always stood, a tall and gracious figure, at her side, looking up towards God coming in Judgment.

'I have been here,' Santa Emilia said, 'such a very long time. There are so many parts of Heaven that I have not visited. We should be so very happy together.'

'Perhaps,' said Santa Isabela, 'he does not want to leave the world yet. I have noticed how strongly men cling to the world.'

'I will ask him,' said Santa Emilia.

She asked him.

He said that he would go wherever she would take him. She promised that he should see gardens and gardens of carnations.

He told her that he wanted only the one that she carried in her hand.

It was afternoon when she told him this, and Vespers were just over. Two choir-boys were showing some tourists the carving in the Choir and one of them swung on the foot of the great bronze lectern to show the tourists what a Spanish choir-boy dared to do. Many women were kneeling in the vast church, and their prayers rose up to the Madonna above the High Altar; she bent upon them glances of the utmost tenderness and protection.

'Yes,' said Santa Isabela. 'You are permitted to go. Santa Rosa will take your place here.'

So they went together into Heaven.

A little crowd gathered. The Englishman had fallen suddenly in a faint. No, alas, he was dead. Of heart failure, said one of the canons who had been passing and knew something of medicine.

Behind Margaret's deep distress there were two consolations: she had known for days that he was not well although he said otherwise, and on his face there was a look of radiant happiness.

It was not until many weeks later that the Dean of the Cathedral, who was an authority on the pictures, taking some friends into the little chapel, was puzzled.

'I always had thought,' he explained, 'that Santa Emilia held a flower. I was wrong. I must have been deceived by the light.'

'And who was Santa Emilia?' asked a friend.

'A minor Saint. Nothing much is known about her. She died young, very young, in this city of the Plague.'

TARNHELM

I was, I suppose, at that time a peculiar child, peculiar a little by nature, but also because I had spent so much of my young life in the company of people very much older than myself.

After the events that I am now going to relate, some quite indelible mark was set on me. I became then, and have always been since, one of those persons, otherwise insignificant, who have decided, without possibility of change, about certain questions.

Some things, doubted by most of the world, are for these people true and beyond argument; this certainty of theirs gives them a kind of stamp, as though they lived so much in their imagination as to have very little assurance as to what is fact and what fiction. This 'oddness' of theirs puts them apart. If now, at the age of fifty, I am a man with very few friends, very much alone, it is because, if you like, my Uncle Robert died in a strange manner forty years ago and I was a witness of his death.

I have never until now given any account of the strange proceedings that occurred at Faildyke Hall on the evening of Christmas Eve in the year 1890. The incidents of that evening are still remembered very clearly by one or two people, and a kind of legend of my Uncle Robert's death has been carried on into the younger generation. But no one still alive was a witness of them as I was, and I feel it is time that I set them down upon paper.

I write them down without comment. I extenuate nothing; I disguise nothing. I am not, I hope, in any way a vindictive man, but my brief meeting with my Uncle Robert and the circumstances of his death gave my life, even at that early age, a twist difficult for me very readily to forgive.

As to the so-called supernatural element in my story, everyone must judge for himself about that. We deride or we accept, according to our natures. If we are built of a certain solid practical material the probability is that no evidence, however definite, however first-hand, will convince us. If dreams are our daily portion, one dream more or less will scarcely shake our sense of reality.

However, to my story.

My father and mother were in India from my eighth to my thirteenth year. I did not see them, except on two occasions when they visited England. I was an only child, loved dearly by both my parents, who, however, loved one another yet more. They were an exceedingly sentimental couple of the old-fashioned kind. My father was in the Indian Civil Service and wrote poetry. He even had his epic, *Tantalus: A Poem in Four Cantos,* published at his own expense.

This, added to the fact that my mother had been considered an invalid before he married her, made my parents feel that they bore a very close resemblance to the Brownings, and my father even had a pet name for my mother that sounded curiously like the famous and hideous 'Ba.'

I was a delicate child, was sent to Mr. Ferguson's Private Academy at the tender age of eight, and spent my holidays as the rather unwanted guest of various relations.

'Unwanted' because I was, I imagine, a difficult child to understand. I had an old grandmother who lived at Folkestone, two aunts who shared a little house in Kensington, an aunt, uncle and a brood of cousins inhabiting Cheltenham, and two uncles who lived in Cumberland. All these relations, except the two uncles, had their proper share of me, and for none of them had I any great affection.

Children were not studied in those days as they are now. I was thin, pale and bespectacled, aching for affection but not knowing at all how to obtain it; outwardly undemonstrative but inwardly emotional and sensitive, playing games because of my poor sight very badly, reading a great deal more than was good for me, and telling myself stories all day and part of every night.

All of my relations tired of me, I fancy, in turn, and at last it was decided that my uncles in Cumberland must do their share. These two were my father's brothers, the eldest of a long family of which he was the youngest. My Uncle Robert, I understood, was nearly seventy, my Uncle Constance some five years younger. I remember always thinking that Constance was a funny name for a man.

My Uncle Robert was the owner of Faildyke Hall, a country house between the lake of Wastwater and the little town of Seascale on the sea coast. Uncle Constance had lived with Uncle Robert for many years. It was decided, after some family correspondence, that the Christmas of this year, 1890, should be spent by me at Faildyke Hall.

I was at this time just eleven years old, thin and skinny, with a bulging forehead, large spectacles and a nervous, shy manner. I always set out, I remember, on any new adventures with mingled emotions of terror and anticipation. Maybe *this* time the miracle would occur: I should discover a friend or a fortune, should cover myself with glory in some unexpected way; be at last what I always longed to be, a hero.

I was glad that I was not going to any of my other relations for Christmas, and especially not to my cousins at Cheltenham, who teased and persecuted me and were never free of earsplitting noises. What I wanted most in life was to be allowed to read in peace. I understood that at Faildyke there was a glorious library.

My aunt saw me into the train. I had been presented by my uncle with one of the most gory of Harrison Ainsworth's romances, *The Lancashire Witches,* and I had five bars of chocolate cream, so that that journey was as blissfully happy as any experience could be to me at that time. I was permitted to read in peace, and I had just then little more to ask of life.

Nevertheless, as the train puffed its way north, this new country began to force itself on my attention. I had never before been in the North of England, and I was not prepared for the sudden sense of space and freshness that I received.

The naked, unsystematic hills, the freshness of the wind on which the birds seemed to be carried with especial glee, the stone walls that ran like grey ribbons about the moors, and, above all, the vast expanse of sky upon whose surface clouds swam, raced, eddied and extended as I had never anywhere witnessed. . . .

I sat, lost and absorbed, at my carriage window, and when at last, long after dark had fallen, I heard 'Seascale' called by the porter, I was still staring in a sort of romantic dream. When I stepped out on to the little narrow platform and was greeted by the salt tang of the sea wind my first real introduction to the North Country may be said to have been completed. I am writing now in another part of that same Cumberland country, and beyond my window the line of the fell runs strong and bare against the sky while below it the Lake lies, a fragment of silver glass at the feet of Skiddaw.

It may be that my sense of the deep mystery of this country had its origin in this same strange story that I am now relating. But again perhaps not, for I believe that that first evening arrival at Seascale worked some change in me, so that since then none of the world's beauties—from the crimson waters of Kashmir to the rough glories of our own Cornish coast—can rival for me the sharp, peaty winds and strong, resilient turf of the Cumberland hills.

That was a magical drive in the pony-trap to Faildyke that evening. It was bitterly cold, but I did not seem to mind it. Everything was magical to me.

From the first I could see the great slow hump of Black Combe jet against the frothy clouds of the winter night, and I could hear the sea breaking and the soft rustle of the bare twigs in the hedgerows.

I made, too, the friend of my life that night, for it was Bob Armstrong who was driving the trap. He has often told me since (for although he is a slow man of few words he likes to repeat the things that seem to him worth while) that I struck him as 'pitifully lost' that evening on the Seascale platform. I looked, I don't doubt, pinched and cold enough. In any case it was a lucky appearance for me, for I won Armstrong's heart there and then, and he, once he gave it, could never bear to take it back again.

He, on his side, seemed to me gigantic that night. He had, I believe, one of the broadest chests in the world: it was a curse to him, he said, because no ready-made shirts would ever suit him.

I sat in close to him because of the cold; he was very warm, and I could feel his heart beating like a steady clock inside his rough coat. It beat for me that night, and it has beaten for me, I'm glad to say, ever since.

In truth, as things turned out, I needed a friend. I was nearly asleep and stiff all over my little body when I was handed down from the trap and at once led into what seemed to me an immense hall crowded with the staring heads of slaughtered animals and smelling of straw.

I was so sadly weary that my uncles, when I met them in a vast billiard-room in which a great fire roared in a stone fireplace like a demon, seemed to me to be double.

In any case, what an odd pair they were! My Uncle Robert was a little man with grey untidy hair and little sharp eyes hooded by two of the bushiest eyebrows known to humanity. He wore (I remember as though it were yesterday) shabby country clothes of a faded green colour, and he had on one finger a ring with a thick red stone.

Another thing that I noticed at once when he kissed me (I detested to be kissed by anybody) was a faint scent that he had, connected at once in my mind with the caraway-seeds that there are in seed-cake. I noticed, too, that his teeth were discoloured and yellow.

My Uncle Constance I liked at once. He was fat, round, friendly and clean. Rather a dandy was Uncle Constance. He wore a flower in his buttonhole and his linen was snowy white in contrast with his brother's.

I noticed one thing, though, at that very first meeting, and that was that before he spoke to me and put his fat arm around my shoulder he seemed to look towards his brother as though for permission. You may say that it was unusual for a boy of my age to notice so much, but in fact I noticed everything at that time. Years and laziness, alas! have slackened my observation.

II

I had a horrible dream that night; it woke me screaming, and brought Bob Armstrong in to quiet me.

My room was large, like all the other rooms that I had seen, and empty, with a great expanse of floor and a stone fireplace like the one in the billiard-room. It was, I afterwards found, next to the servants' quarters. Armstrong's room was next to mine, and Mrs. Spender's, the housekeeper's, beyond his.

Armstrong was then, and is yet, a bachelor. He used to tell me that he loved so many women that he never could bring his mind to choose any one of them. And now he has been too long my personal bodyguard and is too lazily used to my ways to change his condition. He is, moreover, seventy years of age.

Well, what I saw in my dream was this: They had lit a fire for me (and it was necessary; the room was of an icy coldness), and I dreamt that I awoke to see the flames rise to a last vigour before they died away. In the brilliance of that illumination I was conscious that something was moving in the room. I heard the movement for some little while before I saw anything.

I sat up, my heart hammering, and then to my horror discerned, slinking against the farther wall, the evilest-looking yellow mongrel of a dog that you can fancy.

I find it difficult, I have always found it difficult, to describe exactly the horror of that yellow dog. It lay partly in its colour, which was vile, partly in its mean and bony body, but for the most part in its evil head—flat, with sharp little eyes and jagged yellow teeth.

As I looked at it, it bared those teeth at me and then began to creep, with an indescribably loathsome action, in the direction of my bed. I was at first stiffened with terror. Then, as it neared the bed, its little eyes fixed upon me and its teeth bared, I screamed again and again.

The next I knew was that Armstrong was sitting on my bed, his strong arm about my trembling little body. All I could say over and over was, 'The Dog! the Dog! the Dog!'

He soothed me as though he had been my mother.

'See, there's no dog there! There's no one but me! There's no one but me!'

I continued to tremble, so he got into bed with me, held me close to him, and it was in his comforting arms that I fell asleep.

III

In the morning I woke to a fresh breeze and a shining sun and the chrysanthemums, orange, crimson and dun, blowing against the grey stone wall beyond the sloping lawns. So I forgot about my dream. I only knew that I loved Bob Armstrong better than anyone else on earth.

Everyone during the next days was very kind to me. I was so deeply excited by this country, so new to me, that at first I could think of nothing else. Bob Armstrong was Cumbrian from the top of his flaxen head to the thick nails under his boots, and, in grunts and monosyllables, as was his way, he gave me the colour of the ground.

There was romance everywhere: smugglers stealing in and out of Drigg and Seascale, the ancient Cross in Gosforth church-yard, Ravenglass, with all its seabirds, once a port of splendour.

Muncaster Castle and Broughton and black Wastwater with the grim Screes, Black Combe, upon whose broad back the shadows were always dancing—even the little station at Sea-scale, naked to the sea-winds, at whose bookstalls I bought a publication entitled the *Weekly Telegraph* that contained, week by week, instalments of the most thrilling story in the world.

Everywhere romance—the cows moving along the sandy lanes, the sea thundering along the Drigg beach, Gable and Scafell pulling their cloud-caps about their heads, the slow voices of the Cumbrian farmers calling their animals, the little tinkling bell of the Gosforth church—everywhere romance and beauty.

Soon, though, as I became better accustomed to the coun-try, the people immediately around me began to occupy my attention, stimulate my restless curiosity, and especially my two uncles. They were, in fact, queer enough.

Faildyke Hall itself was not queer, only very ugly. It had been built about 1830, I should imagine, a square white building, like a thick-set, rather conceited woman with a very plain face. The rooms were large, the passages innumerable, and everything covered with a very hideous whitewash. Against this whitewash hung old photographs yellowed with age, and faded, bad water-colours. The furniture was strong and ugly.

One romantic feature, though, there was—and that was the little Grey Tower where my Uncle Robert lived. This Tower was at the end of the garden and looked out over a sloping field to the Scafell group beyond Wastwater. It had been built hundreds of years ago as a defence against the Scots. Robert had had his study and bedroom there for many years and it was his domain; no one was allowed to enter it save his old servant Hucking, a bent, wizened, grubby little man who spoke to no one and, so they said in the kitchen, managed to go through life without sleeping. He looked after my Uncle Robert, cleaned his rooms, and was supposed to clean his clothes.

I, being both an inquisitive and romantic-minded boy, was soon as eagerly excited about this Tower as was Bluebeard's wife about the forbidden room. Bob told me that whatever I did I was never to set foot inside.

And then I discovered another thing—that Bob Armstrong hated, feared and was proud of my Uncle Robert. He was proud of him because he was head of the family, and because, so he said, he was the cleverest old man in the world.

'Nothing he can't seemingly do,' said Bob, 'but he don't like you to watch him at it.'

All this only increased my longing to see the inside of the Tower, although I couldn't be said to be fond of my Uncle Robert, either.

It would be hard to say that I disliked him during those first days. He was quite kindly to me when he met me, and at meal-times, when I sat with my two uncles at the long table in the big, bare, whitewashed dining-room, he was always anxious to see that I had plenty to eat. But I never liked him; it was perhaps because he wasn't clean. Children are sensitive to those things. Perhaps I didn't like the fusty, seed-caky smell that he carried about with him.

Then there came the day when he invited me into the Grey Tower and told me about Tarnhelm.

Pale slanting shadows of sunlight fell across the chrysanthemums and the grey stone walls, the long fields and the dusky hills. I was playing by myself by the little stream that ran beyond the rose garden, when Uncle Robert came up behind me in the soundless way he had, and, tweaking me by the ear, asked me whether I would like to come with him inside his Tower. I was, of course, eager enough; but I was frightened, too, especially when I saw Hucking's moth-eaten old countenance peering at us from one of the narrow slits that pretended to be windows.

However, in we went, my hand in Uncle Robert's hot dry one. There wasn't, in reality, so very much to see when you were inside—all untidy and musty with cobwebs over the doorways, and old pieces of rusty iron and empty boxes in the corners, and the long table in Uncle Robert's study covered with a thousand things—books with the covers hanging on them, sticky green bottles, a looking-glass, a pair of scales, a globe, a cage with mice in it, a statue of a naked woman, an hour-glass—everything old and stained and dusty.

However, Uncle Robert made me sit down close to him, and told me many interesting stories. Among others the story about Tarnhelm.

Tarnhelm was something that you put over your head, and its magic turned you into any animal that you wished to be. Uncle Robert told me the story of a god called Wotan, and how he teased the dwarf who possessed Tarnhelm by saying that he couldn't turn himself into a mouse or some such animal; and the dwarf, his pride wounded, turned himself into a mouse, which the god easily captured and so stole Tarnhelm.

On the table, among all the litter, was a grey skullcap.

'That's my Tarnhelm,' said Uncle Robert, laughing. 'Like to see me put it on?'

But I was suddenly frightened, terribly frightened. The sight of Uncle Robert made me feel quite ill. The room began to run round and round. The white mice in the cage twittered. It was stuffy in that room, enough to turn any boy sick.

IV

That was the moment, I think, when Uncle Robert stretched

out his hand towards his grey skull-cap—after that I was never happy again in Faildyke Hall. That action of his, simple and apparently friendly though it was, seemed to open my eyes to a number of things.

We were now within ten days of Christmas. The thought of Christmas had then—and, to tell the truth, still has—a most happy effect on me. There is the beautiful story, the geniality and kindliness, still, in spite of modern pessimists, much happiness and goodwill. Even now I yet enjoy giving presents and receiving them—then it was an ecstasy to me, the look of the parcel, the paper, the string, the exquisite surprise.

Therefore I had been anticipating Christmas eagerly. I had been promised a trip into Whitehaven for present-buying, and there was to be a tree and a dance for the Gosforth villagers. Then after my visit to Uncle Robert's Tower, all my happiness of anticipation vanished. As the days went on and my observation of one thing and another developed, I would, I think, have run away back to my aunts in Kensington, had it not been for Bob Armstrong.

It was, in fact, Armstrong who started me on that voyage of observation that ended so horribly, for when he had heard that Uncle Robert had taken me inside his Tower his anger was fearful. I had never before seen him angry; now his great body shook, and he caught me and held me until I cried out.

He wanted me to promise that I would never go inside there again. What? Not even with Uncle Robert? No, most especially not with Uncle Robert; and then, dropping his voice and looking around him to be sure that there was no one listening, he began to curse Uncle Robert. This amazed me, because loyalty to his masters was one of Bob's great laws. I can see us now, standing on the stable cobbles in the falling white dusk while the horses stamped in their stalls, and the little sharp stars appeared one after another glittering between the driving clouds.

'I'll not stay,' I heard him say to himself. 'I'll be like the rest. I'll not be staying. To bring a child into it . . .'

From that moment he seemed to have me very specially in his charge. Even when I could not see him I felt that his kindly eye was upon me, and this sense of the necessity that I should be guarded made me yet more uneasy and distressed.

The next thing that I observed was that the servants were all fresh, had been there not more than a month or two. Then, only a week before Christmas, the housekeeper departed. Uncle Constance seemed greatly upset at these occurrences; Uncle Robert did not seem in the least affected by them.

I come now to my Uncle Constance. At this distance of time it is strange with what clarity I still can see him—his stoutness, his shining cleanliness, his dandyism, the flower in his button-hole, his little brilliantly shod feet, his thin, rather feminine voice. He would have been kind to me, I think, had he dared, but something kept him back. And what that something was I soon discovered: it was fear of my Uncle Robert.

It did not take me a day to discover that he was utterly subject to his brother. He said nothing without looking to see how Uncle Robert took it; suggested no plan until he first had assurance from his brother; was terrified beyond anything that I had before witnessed in a human being at any sign of irritation in my uncle.

I discovered after this that Uncle Robert enjoyed greatly to play on his brother's fears. I did not understand enough of their life to realise what were the weapons that Robert used, but that they were sharp and piercing I was neither too young nor too ignorant to perceive.

Such was our situation, then, a week before Christmas. The weather had become very wild with a great wind. All nature seemed in an uproar. I could fancy when I lay in my bed at night and heard the shouting in my chimney that I could catch the crash of the waves upon the beach, see the black waters of Wast-water cream and curdle under the Screes. I would lie awake and long for Bob Armstrong—the strength of his arm and the warmth of his breast—but I considered myself too grown a boy to make any appeal.

I remember that now almost minute by minute my fears increased. What gave them force and power who can say? I was much alone, I had now a great terror of my uncle, the weather was wild, the rooms of the house large and desolate, the servants mysterious, the walls of the passages lit always with an unnatu-

ral glimmer because of their white colour, and although Armstrong had watch over me he was busy in his affairs and could
not always be with me.

I grew to fear and dislike my Uncle Robert more and more.
Hatred and fear of him seemed to be everywhere, and yet he was
always soft-voiced and kindly. Then, a few days before Christmas, occurred the event that was to turn my terror into panic.

I had been reading in the library Mrs. Radcliffe's *Romance
of the Forest,* an old book long forgotten, worthy of revival. The
library was a fine room run to seed, bookcases from floor to ceiling, the windows small and dark, holes in the old faded carpet.
A lamp burnt at a distant table. One stood on a little shelf at my
side.

Something, I know not what, made me look up. What I saw
then can even now stamp my heart in its recollection. By the
library door, not moving, staring across the room's length at me,
was a yellow dog.

I will not attempt to describe all the pitiful fear and mad
freezing terror that caught and held me. My main thought, I
fancy, was that that other vision on my first night in the place had
not been a dream. I was not asleep now; the book in which I had
been reading had fallen to the floor, the lamps shed their glow, I
could hear the ivy tapping on the pane. No, this was reality.

The dog lifted a long, horrible leg and scratched itself. Then
very slowly and silently across the carpet it came towards me.

I could not scream; I could not move; I waited. The animal
was even more evil than it had seemed before with its flat head,
its narrow eyes, its yellow fangs. It came steadily in my direction,
stopped once to scratch itself again, then was almost at my chair.

It looked at me, bared its fangs, but now as though it grinned
at me, then passed on. After it was gone there was a thick foetid
scent in the air—the scent of caraway-seed.

V

I think now on looking back that it was remarkable enough
that I, a pale nervous child who trembled at every sound, should

have met the situation as I did. I said nothing about the dog to any living soul, not even to Bob Armstrong. I hid my fears—and fears of a beastly and sickening kind they were, too—within my breast. I had the intelligence to perceive—and *how* I caught in the air the awareness of this I can't, at this distance, understand —that I was playing my little part in the climax to something that had been piling up, for many a month, like the clouds over Gable.

Understand that I offer from first to last in this no kind of explanation. There is possibly—and to this day I cannot quite be sure—nothing to explain. My Uncle Robert died simply—but you shall hear.

What was beyond any doubt or question was that it was after my seeing the dog in the library that Uncle Robert changed so strangely in his behaviour to me. That may have been the merest coincidence. I only know that as one grows older one calls things coincidence more and more seldom.

In any case, that same night at dinner Uncle Robert seemed twenty years older. He was bent, shrivelled, would not eat, snarled at anyone who spoke to him and especially avoided even looking at me. It was a painful meal, and it was after it, when Uncle Constance and I were sitting alone in the old yellow-papered drawing-room—a room with two ticking clocks for ever racing one another—that the most extraordinary thing occurred. Uncle Constance and I were playing draughts. The only sounds were the roaring of the wind down the chimney, the hiss and splutter of the fire, the silly ticking of the clocks. Suddenly Uncle Constance put down the piece that he was about to move and began to cry.

To a child it is always a terrible thing to see a grown-up person cry, and even to this day to hear a man cry is very distressing to me. I was moved desperately by poor Uncle Constance, who sat there, his head in his white plump hands, all his stout body shaking. I ran over to him, and he clutched me and held me as though he would never let me go. He sobbed incoherent words about protecting me, caring for me . . . seeing that that monster. . . .

At the word I remember that I too began to tremble. I asked my uncle what monster, but he could only continue to murmur incoherently about hate and not having the pluck, and if only he had the courage. . . .

Then, recovering a little, he began to ask me questions. Where had I been? Had I been into his brother's Tower? Had I seen anything that frightened me? If I did, would I at once tell him? And then he muttered that he would never have allowed me to come had he known that it would go as far as this, that it would be better if I went away that night, and that if he were not afraid. . . . Then he began to tremble again and to look at the door, and I trembled too. He held me in his arms; then we thought that there was a sound and we listened, our heads up, our two hearts hammering. But it was only the clocks ticking and the wind shrieking as though it would tear the house to pieces.

That night, however, when Bob Armstrong came up to bed he found me sheltering there. I whispered to him that I was frightened; I put my arms around his neck and begged him not to send me away; he promised me that I should not leave him and I slept all night in the protection of his strength.

How, though, can I give any true picture of the fear that pursued me now? For I knew from what both Armstrong and Uncle Constance had said that there was real danger, that it was no hysterical fancy of mine or ill-digested dream. It made it worse that Uncle Robert was now no more seen. He was sick; he kept within his Tower, cared for by his old wizened manservant. And so, being nowhere, he was everywhere. I stayed with Armstrong when I could, but a kind of pride prevented me from clinging like a girl to his coat.

A deathly silence seemed to fall about the place. No one laughed or sang, no dog barked, no bird sang. Two days before Christmas an iron frost came to grip the land. The fields were rigid, the sky itself seemed to be frozen grey, and under the olive cloud Scafell and Gable were black.

Christmas Eve came.

On that morning, I remember, I was trying to draw—some childish picture of one of Mrs. Radcliffe's scenes—when the double doors unfolded and Uncle Robert stood there. He stood there, bent, shrivelled, his long, grey locks falling over his collar, his bushy eyebrows thrust forward. He wore his old green suit and on his finger gleamed his heavy red ring. I was frightened, of course, but also I was touched with pity. He looked so old, so frail, so small in this large empty house.

I sprang up. 'Uncle Robert,' I asked timidly, 'are you better?'

He bent still lower until he was almost on his hands and feet; then he looked up at me, and his yellow teeth were bared, almost as an animal snarls. Then the doors closed again.

The slow, stealthy, grey afternoon came at last. I walked with Armstrong to Gosforth village on some business that he had. We said no word of any matter at the Hall. I told him, he has reminded me, of how fond I was of him and that I wanted to be with him always, and he answered that perhaps it might be so, little knowing how true that prophecy was to stand. Like all children I had a great capacity for forgetting the atmosphere that I was not at that moment in, and I walked beside Bob along the frozen roads, with some of my fears surrendered.

But not for long. It was dark when I came into the long, yellow drawing-room. I could hear the bells of Gosforth church pealing as I passed from the ante-room.

A moment later there came a shrill, terrified cry: 'Who's that? Who is it?'

It was Uncle Constance, who was standing in front of the yellow silk window curtains, staring at the dusk. I went over to him and he held me close to him.

'Listen!' he whispered. 'What can you hear?'

The double doors through which I had come were half open. At first I could hear nothing but the clocks, the very faint rumble of a cart on the frozen road. There was no wind.

My uncle's fingers gripped my shoulder. 'Listen!' he said again. And now I heard. On the stone passage beyond the drawing-room was the patter of an animal's feet. Uncle Constance and I looked at one another. In that exchanged glance we confessed that our secret was the same. We knew what we should see.

A moment later it was there, standing in the double doorway, crouching a little and staring at us with a hatred that was mad and sick—the hatred of a sick animal crazy with unhappiness, but loathing us more than its own misery.

Slowly it came towards us, and to my reeling fancy all the room seemed to stink of caraway-seed.

'Keep back! Keep away!' my uncle screamed.

I became oddly in my turn the protector.

'It shan't touch you! It shan't touch you, uncle!' I called.

But the animal came on.

It stayed for a moment near a little round table that contained a composition of dead waxen fruit under a glass dome. It stayed here, its nose down, smelling the ground. Then, looking up at us, it came on again.

Oh God!—even now as I write after all these years it is with me again, the flat skull, the cringing body in its evil colour, and that loathsome smell. It slobbered a little at its jaw. It bared its fangs.

Then I screamed, hid my face in my uncle's breast and saw that he held, in his trembling hand, a thick, heavy, old-fashioned revolver.

Then he cried out:

'Go back, Robert. . . . Go back!'

The animal came on. He fired. The detonation shook the room. The dog turned and, blood dripping from its throat, crawled across the floor.

By the door it halted, turned and looked at us. Then it disappeared into the other room.

My uncle had flung down his revolver; he was crying, sniffling; he kept stroking my forehead, murmuring words.

At last, clinging to one another, we followed the splotches of blood, across the carpet, beside the door, through the doorway.

Huddled against a chair in the outer sitting-room, one leg twisted under him, was my Uncle Robert, shot through the throat.

On the floor, by his side, was a grey skull-cap.

MR. ODDY

This may seem to many people an old-fashioned story; it is perhaps for that reason that I tell it. I can recover here, it may be, for myself something of the world that is already romantic, already beyond one's reach, already precious for the things that one might have got out of it and didn't.

London of but a few years before the war! What a commonplace to point out its difference from the London of to-day and to emphasise the tiny period of time that made that difference!

We were all young and hopeful then; we could all live on a shilling a year and think ourselves well off; we could all sit in front of the lumbering horse buses and chat confidentially with the omniscient driver; we could all see Dan Leno in Pantomime and watch Farren dance at the Empire; we could all rummage among those cobwebby streets at the back of the Strand where Aldwych now flaunts her shining bosom and imagine Pendennis and Warrington, Copperfield and Traddles cheek by jowl with ourselves; we could all wait in the shilling queue for hours to see Ellen Terry in *Captain Brassbound* and Forbes-Robertson in *Hamlet*; we could all cross the street without fear of imminent death, and above all we could all sink ourselves into that untidy, higgledy-piggledy, smoky and beery and gas-lampy London gone utterly and for ever.

But I have no wish to be sentimental about it; there is a new London which is just as interesting to its new citizens as the old London was to myself. It is my age that is the matter; before the war one was so *very* young.

I like, though, to try and recapture that time, and so, as a simple way to do it, I seize upon a young man; Tommy Brown we will call him. I don't know where Tommy Brown may be now; that Tommy Brown who lived as I did in two very small rooms in Glebe Place, Chelsea, who enjoyed hugely the sparse but economical meals provided so elegantly by two charming ladies at The Good Intent down by the river, that charming hostelry

whence looking through the bow windows you could see the
tubby barges go floating down the river, and the thin outline of
Whistler's Battersea Bridge, and in the small room itself were
surrounded by who knows what geniuses in the lump, geniuses
of Art and Letters, of the Stage and of the Law.

For Tommy Brown in those days life was Paradisal.

He had come boldly from Cambridge to throw himself upon
London's friendly bosom; despite all warnings to the contrary he
was certain that it would be friendly; how could it be otherwise
to so charming, so brilliant, so unusually attractive a young man?
For Tommy was conceited beyond all that his youth warranted,
conceited indeed without any reason at all.

He had, it is true, secured the post of reviewer to one of the
London daily papers; this seemed to him when he looked back
in later years a kind of miracle, but at the time no miracle at all,
simply a just appreciation of his extraordinary talents. There was
also reposing in one of the publishers' offices at that moment the
manuscript of a novel, a novel that appeared to him of astonishing brilliance, written in the purest English, sparkling with wit,
tense with drama.

These things were fine and reassuring enough, but there was
more than that; he felt in himself the power to rise to the greatest
heights; he could not see how anything could stop him, it was his
destiny.

This pride of his might have suffered some severe shocks
were it not that he spent all of his time with other young gentlemen quite as conceited as himself. I have heard talk of the
present young generation and its agreeable consciousness of its
own merits, but I doubt if it is anything in comparison with that
little group of twenty-five years ago. After all, the war has inter-
vened—however young we may be and however greatly we may
pretend, this is an unstable world and for the moment heroics
have departed from it. But for Tommy Brown and his friends
the future was theirs and nobody could prevent it. Something
pathetic in that as one looks back.

Tommy was not really so unpleasant a youth as I have
described him—to his elders he must have appeared a baby, and
his vitality at least they could envy. After all, why check his con-

fidence? Life would do that heavily enough in its own good time.

Tommy, although he had no money and no prospects, was already engaged to a young woman, Miss Alice Smith. Alice Smith was an artist sharing with a girl friend a Chelsea studio, and she was as certain of her future as Tommy was of his.

They had met at a little Chelsea dance, and two days after the meeting they were engaged. She had no parents who mattered, and no money to speak of, so that the engagement was the easiest thing in the world.

Tommy, who had been in love before many times, was certain, as he told his friend Jack Robinson so often as to bore that gentleman severely, that this time at last he knew what love was. Alice ordered him about—with her at any rate his conceit fell away—she had read his novel and pronounced it old-fashioned, the severest criticism she could possibly have made, and she thought his reviews amateur. He suffered then a good deal in her company. When he was away from her he told himself and everybody else that her critical judgment was marvellous, her comprehension of all the Arts quite astounding, but he left her sometimes with a miserable suspicion that perhaps after all he was not going to do anything very wonderful and that he would have to work very hard indeed to rise to her astonishing standards.

It was in such a mood of wholesome depression that he came one beautiful April day from the A.B.C. shop where he had been giving his Alice luncheon, and found his way to an old bookshop on the riverside round the corner from Oakley Street. This shop was kept by a gentleman called Mr. Burdett Coutts, and the grand associations of his name gave him from the very first a sort of splendour.

It was one of those old shops of which there are, thank God, still many examples surviving in London, in which the room was so small and the books so many that to move a step was to imperil your safety. Books ran in thick, tight rows from floor to ceiling everywhere, were piled in stacks upon the ground and hung in perilous heaps over chairs and window ledges.

Mr. Burdett Coutts himself, a stout and grizzled old man enveloped always in a grey shawl, crouched behind his spectacles in a far corner and took apparently no interest in anything save that he would snap the price at you if you brought him a volume and timorously enquired. He was not one of those old booksellers dear to the heart of Anatole France and other great men who would love to discourse to you of the beauties of *The Golden Ass,* the possibility of Homer being a lady, or the virtues of the second *Hyperion* over the first. Not at all; he ate biscuits which stuck in his grizzly beard, and wrote perpetually in a large worm-eaten ledger which was supposed by his customers to contain all the secrets of the universe.

It was just because Mr. Coutts never interfered with you that Tommy Brown loved his shop so dearly. If he had a true genuine passion that went far deeper than all his little superficial vanities and egotisms, it was his passion for books—books of any kind.

He had at this time no fine taste—all was fish that came to his net. The bundles of Thackeray and Dickens, parts tied up carelessly in coarse string, the old broken-backed volumes of Radcliffe and Barham and Galt, the red and gold Colburn's Novelists, all these were exciting to him, just as exciting as though they had been a first Gray's *Elegy* or an original *Robinson Crusoe.*

He had, too, a touching weakness for the piles of fresh and neglected modern novels that lay in their discarded heaps on the dusty floor; young though he was, he was old enough to realise the pathos of these so short a time ago fresh from the bursting presses, so eagerly cherished through months of anxious watching by their fond authors, so swiftly forgotten, dead almost before they were born.

So he browsed, moving like a panting puppy with inquisitive nose from stack to stack with a gesture of excitement, tumbling a whole racket of books about his head, looking then anxiously to see whether the old man would be angry with him, and realising for the thousandth time that the old man never was.

It was on this day, then, rather sore from the arrogancies of his Alice, that he tried to restore his confidence among these friendly volumes. With a little thrill of excited pleasure he had just discovered a number of the volumes born of those romantic and tragedy-haunted 'Nineties.' Here in little thin volumes were the stories of Crackanthorpe, the poems of Dowson, the *Key-*

notes of George Egerton, *The Bishop's Dilemma* of Ella d'Arcy, *The Happy Hypocrite* of Max Beerbohm.

Had he only been wise enough to give there and then for that last whatever the old man had asked him for it he would have been fortunate indeed, but the pennies in his pocket were few— he was not yet a book collector, but rather that less expensive but more precious thing, a book adorer. He had the tiny volume in his hand, when he was aware that someone had entered the shop and was standing looking over his shoulder.

He turned slowly and saw someone who at first sight seemed vaguely familiar, so familiar that he was plunged into confusion at once by the sense that he ought to say 'How do you do?' but could not accurately place him. The gentleman also seemed to know him very well, for he said in a most friendly way, 'Ah yes, the "'Nineties," a very fruitful period.'

Tommy stammered something, put down the Max Beerbohm, moved a little, and pulled about him a sudden shower of volumes. The room was filled with the racket of their tumbling, and a cloud of dust thickened about them, creeping into eyes and mouth and nose.

'I'm terribly sorry,' Tommy stammered, and then, looking up, was sorry the more when he saw how extremely neat and tidy the gentleman was and how terribly the little accident must distress him.

Tommy's friend must have been between sixty and seventy years of age, nearer seventy perhaps than sixty, but his black hair was thick and strong and stood up *en brosse* from a magnificent broad forehead. Indeed, so fine were the forehead and the turn of the head that the face itself was a little disappointing, being so round and chubby and amiable as to be almost babyish. It was not a weak face, however, the eyes being large and fine and the chin strong and determined.

The figure of this gentleman was short and thick-set and inclined to stoutness; he had the body of a prize-fighter now resting on his laurels. He was very beautifully clothed in a black coat and waistcoat, pepper-and-salt trousers, and he stood leaning a little on a thick ebony cane, his legs planted apart, his whole attitude that of one who was accustomed to authority. He had the look of a magistrate, or even of a judge, and had his face been less kindly Tommy would have said good-day, nodded to Mr. Burdett Coutts, and departed, but that was a smile difficult to resist.

'Dear me,' the gentleman said, 'this is a very dusty shop. I have never been here before, but I gather by the way that you knock the books about that it's an old friend of yours.'

Tommy giggled in a silly fashion, shifted from foot to foot, and then, desiring to seem very wise and learned, proved himself only very young and foolish.

'The "'Nineties" are becoming quite romantic,' he said in his most authoritative voice, 'now that we're getting a good distance from them.'

'Ah, you think so!' said the gentleman courteously; 'that's interesting. I'm getting to an age now, I'm afraid, when nothing seems romantic but one's own youth and, ah, dear me! that was a very long time ago.'

This was exactly the way that kindly old gentlemen were supposed to talk, and Tommy listened with becoming attention.

'In my young day,' his friend continued, 'George Eliot seemed to everybody a magnificent writer: a little heavy in hand for these days, I'm afraid. Now who is the god of your generation, if it isn't impertinent to enquire?'

Tommy shifted again from foot to foot. Who was the god of his generation? If the truth must be told, in Tommy's set there were no gods, only young men who might be gods if they lived long enough.

'Well,' said Tommy awkwardly, 'Hardy, of course—er—it's difficult to say, isn't it?'

'Very difficult,' said the gentleman.

There was a pause then, which Tommy concluded by hinting that he was afraid that he must move forward to a very important engagement.

'May I walk with you a little way?' asked the gentleman very courteously. 'Such a very beautiful afternoon.'

Once outside in the beautiful afternoon air everything was much easier; Tommy regained his self-confidence, and soon was talking with his accustomed ease and freedom. There was nothing very alarming in his friend after all; he seemed so very eager to hear everything that Tommy had to say. He was strangely ignorant too; he seemed to be interested in the Arts, but to know very little about them; certain names that were to Tommy household words were to this gentleman quite unknown. Tommy began to be a little patronising. They parted at the top of Oakley Street.

'I wonder if you'd mind,' the gentleman said, 'our meeting again? The fact is, that I have very little opportunity of making friends with your generation. There are so many things that you could tell me. I am afraid it may be tiresome for you to spend an hour or two with so ancient a duffer as myself, but it would be very kind of you.'

Tommy was nothing if not generous; he said that he would enjoy another meeting very much. Of course he was very busy and his spare hours were not many, but a walk another afternoon could surely be managed. They made an appointment, they exchanged names; the gentleman's name was Mr. Alfred Oddy.

That evening, in the middle of a hilarious Chelsea party, Tommy suddenly discovered to his surprise that it would please him very much to see Mr. Oddy walk in through the door.

Although it was a hilarious party Tommy was not very happy; for one thing, Spencer Russell, the novelist, was there and showed quite clearly that he didn't think Tommy very interesting. Tommy had been led up and introduced to him, had said one or two things that seemed to himself very striking, but Spencer Russell had turned his back almost at once and entered into eager conversation with somebody else.

This wasn't very pleasant, and then his own beloved Alice was behaving strangely; she seemed to have no eyes nor ears for anyone in the room save Spencer Russell, and this was the stranger in that only a week or so before she had in public condemned Spencer Russell's novels, utterly and completely, stating that he was written out, had nothing to say, and was as good as dead. To-night, however, he was not dead at all, and Tommy had the agony of observing her edge her way into the group surrounding him and then listen to him not only as though he were the fount of all wisdom, but an Adonis as well, which last was absurd seeing that he was fat and unwieldy and bald on the top of his head.

After a while Tommy came up to her and suggested that they should go, and received then the shock of his life when she told him that he could go if he liked, but that he was not to bother her. And she told him this in a voice so loud that everybody heard and many people tittered.

He left in a fury and spent then a night that he imagined to be sleepless, although in truth he slept during most of it.

It was with an eagerness that surprised himself that he met Mr. Oddy on the second occasion. He had not seen Alice for two days. He did not intend to be the one to apologise first; besides, he had nothing to apologise for; and yet during these two days there was scarcely a moment that he had not to restrain himself from running round to her studio and making it up.

When he met Mr. Oddy at the corner of Oakley Street he was a very miserable young man. He was so miserable that in five minutes he was pouring out all his woes.

He told Mr. Oddy everything, of his youth, his wonderful promise, and the extraordinary lack of appreciation shown to him by his relatives, of the historical novels that he had written at the age of anything from ten to sixteen and found only the cook for an audience, of his going to Cambridge, and his development there so that he became Editor of *The Lion*, that remarkable but very short-lived literary journal, and the President of 'The Bats,' the most extraordinary Essay Club that Cambridge had ever known; of how, alas, he took only a third in History owing to the perverseness of examiners; and so on and so on, until he arrived in full flood at the whole history of his love for Alice, of her remarkable talents and beauty, but of her strange temper and arrogance and general feminine queerness.

Mr. Oddy listened to it all in the kindest way. There's no knowing where they walked that afternoon; they crossed the bridge and adventured into Battersea Park, and finally had tea in a small shop smelling of stale buns and liquorice drops. It was only as they turned homewards that it occurred to Tommy that he had been talking during the whole afternoon. He had the grace to see that an apology was necessary.

'I beg your pardon, sir,' he said, flushing a little, 'I'm afraid I have bored you dreadfully. The fact is that this last quarrel with Alice has upset me very badly. What would you do if you were in my position?'

Mr. Oddy sighed. 'The trouble is,' he said, 'that I realise only too clearly that I shall never be in your position again. My time for romance is over, or at least I get my romance now in other ways. It wasn't always so; there was a lady once beneath whose windows I stood night after night merely for the pleasure of seeing her candle outlined behind the blind.'

'And did she love you,' Tommy asked, 'as much as you loved her?'

'Nobody, my dear boy,' Mr. Oddy replied, 'loves you as much as you love them; either they love you more or they love you less. The first of these is often boring, the second always tragic. In the present case I should go and make it up; after all, happiness is always worth having, even at the sacrifice of one's pride. She seems to me a very charming young lady.'

'Oh, she is,' Tommy answered eagerly. 'I'll take your advice, I'll go this very evening; in fact, if you don't mind, I think it would be rather a good time to find her in now.'

Mr. Oddy smiled and agreed; they parted to meet another day.

On the third occasion of their meeting, which was only two days after the second, Tommy cared for his companion enough to wish to find out something about him.

His scene of reconciliation with his beautiful Alice had not been as satisfactory as he had hoped; she had forgiven him indeed, but given him quite clearly to understand that she would stand none of his nonsense either now or hereafter. The satisfactory thing would have been for Tommy there and then to have left her, never to see her again; he would thus have preserved both his pride and his independence; but, alas, he was in love, terribly in love, and her indignation made her appear only the more magnificent.

And so, on this third meeting with his friend, he was quite humble and longing for affection.

And then his curiosity was stirred. Who was this handsome

old gentleman with his touching desire for Tommy's companionship? There was an air about him that seemed to suggest that he was someone of importance in his own world; beyond this there was an odd sense that Tommy knew him in some way, had seen him somewhere; so on this third occasion Tommy came out with his questions.

Who was he? Was he married? What was his profession, or was he perhaps retired now? And another question that Tommy would have liked to ask, and had not the impertinence, was as to why this so late interest in the Arts and combined with this interest this so complete ignorance?

Mr. Oddy seemed to know a great deal about everything else, but in this one direction his questions were childish. He seemed never to have heard of the great Spencer Russell at all (which secretly gave Tommy immense satisfaction), and as for geniuses like Mumpus and Peter Arrogance and Samuel Bird, even when Tommy explained how truly great these men were, Mr. Oddy appeared but little impressed.

'Well, at least,' Tommy burst out indignantly, 'I suppose you've read something by Henry Galleon? Of course he's a back number now, at least he is not modern, if you know what I mean, but then he's been writing for centuries. Why, his first book came out when Trollope and George Eliot were still alive. Of course, between ourselves I think *The Roads*, for instance, a pretty fine book, but you should hear Spencer Russell go for it.'

No, Mr. Oddy had never heard of Henry Galleon.

But there followed a most enchanting description by Mr. Oddy of his life when he was a young man and how he once heard Dickens give a reading of *A Christmas Carol,* of how he saw an old lady in a sedan chair at Brighton (she was cracked, of course, and even then a hundred years after her time, but still he had seen it), of how London in his young day was as dark and dirty at night as it had been in Pepys' time, of how crinolines when he was young were so large that it was one of the sights to see a lady getting into a cab, of how in the music-halls there was a chairman who used to sit on the stage with a table in front of him, ring a bell and drink out of a mug of beer, of how he heard Jean de Reszke in *Siegfried* and Ternina in *Tristan,* and of how he had been at the first night when Ellen Terry and Irving had delighted the world with *The Vicar of Wakefield.*

Yes, not only had Mr. Oddy seen and done all these things, but he related the events in so enchanting a way, drew such odd little pictures of such unexpected things and made that old London live so vividly, that at last Tommy burst out in a volley of genuine enthusiasm: 'Why, you ought to be a writer yourself! Why don't you write your reminiscences?'

But Mr. Oddy shook his head gently: there were too many reminiscences, everyone was always reminiscing; who wanted to hear these old men talk?

At last, when they parted, Mr. Oddy had a request—one thing above all things that he would like would be to attend one of these evening gatherings with his young friend to hear these young men and women talk. He promised to sit very quietly in a corner—he wouldn't be in anybody's way.

Of course Tommy consented to take him; there would be one next week, a really good one; but in his heart of hearts he was a little shy. He was shy not only for himself but also for his friend.

During these weeks a strange and most unexpected affection had grown up in his heart for this old man; he really did like him immensely, he was so kind and gentle and considerate.

But he would be rather out of place with Spencer Russell and the others; he would probably say something foolish, and then the others would laugh. They were on the whole a rather ruthless set and were no respecters of persons.

However, the meeting was arranged; the evening came and with it Mr. Oddy, looking just as he always did, quiet and gentle but rather impressive in some way or another. Tommy introduced him to his hostess, Miss Thelma Bennet, that well-known futuristic artist, and then carefully settled him down in a corner with Miss Bennet's aunt, an old lady who appeared occasionally on her niece's horizon but gave no trouble because she was stone deaf and cared only for knitting.

It was a lively evening; several of the brighter spirits were there, and there was a great deal of excellent talk about literature. Every writer over thirty was completely condemned save for those few remaining who had passed eighty years of age and ceased to produce.

Spencer Russell especially was at his best; reputations went down before his vigorous fist like ninepins. He was so scornful that his brilliance was, as Alice Smith everywhere proclaimed, 'simply withering.' Everyone came in for his lash, and especially Henry Galleon. There had been some article in some ancient monthly written by some ancient idiot suggesting that there was still something to be said for Galleon and that he had rendered some service to English literature. How Russell pulled that article to pieces! He even found a volume of Galleon's among Miss Bennet's books, took it down from the shelf and read extracts aloud to the laughing derision of the assembled company.

Then an odd thing occurred. Tommy, who loved to be in the intellectual swim, nevertheless stood up and defended Galleon. He defended him rather feebly, it is true, speaking of him as though he were an old man ready for the almshouse who nevertheless deserved a little consideration and pity. He flushed as he spoke, and the scorn with which they greeted his defence altogether silenced him. It silenced him the more because Alice Smith was the most scornful of them all; she told him that he knew nothing and never would know anything, and she imitated his piping excited treble, and then everyone joined in.

How he hated this to happen before Mr. Oddy! How humiliating after all the things that he had told his friend, the implication that he was generally considered to be one of England's most interesting young men, the implication above all that although she might be a little rough to him at times Alice really adored him, and was his warmest admirer. She did not apparently adore him to-night, and when he went out at last with Mr. Oddy into the wintry, rain-driven street it was all he could do to keep back tears of rage and indignation.

Mr. Oddy had, however, apparently enjoyed himself. He put his hand for a minute on the boy's shoulder.

'Good-night, my dear boy,' he said. 'I thought it very gallant of you to stand up for that older writer as you did: that needed courage. I wonder,' he went on, 'whether you would allow me to come and take tea with you one day—just our two selves. It would be a great pleasure for me.'

And then, having received Tommy's invitation, he vanished into the darkness.

On the day appointed, Mr. Oddy appeared punctually at Tommy's rooms. That was not a very grand house in Glebe Place where Tommy lived, and a very soiled and battered landlady let Mr. Oddy in. He stumbled up the dark staircase that smelt of all the cabbage and all the beef and all the mutton ever consumed by lodgers between these walls, up again two flights of stairs, until at last there was the weather-beaten door with Tommy's visiting-card nailed upon it. Inside was Tommy, a plate with little cakes, raspberry jam, and some very black-looking toast.

Mr. Oddy, however, was appreciative of everything; especially he looked at the books. 'Why,' he said, 'you've got quite a number of the novels of that man you defended the other evening. I wonder you're not ashamed to have them if they're so out of date.'

'To tell you the truth,' said Tommy, speaking freely now that he was in his own castle, 'I like Henry Galleon awfully. I'm afraid I pose a good deal when I'm with those other men; perhaps you've noticed it yourself. Of course Galleon is the greatest novelist we've got, with Hardy and Meredith, only he's getting old, and everything that's old is out of favour with our set.'

'Naturally,' said Mr. Oddy, quite approving, 'of course it is.'

'I have got a photograph of Galleon,' said Tommy. 'I cut it out of a publisher's advertisement, but it was taken years ago.'

He went to his table, searched for a little and produced a small photograph of a very fierce-looking gentleman with a black beard.

'Dear me,' said Mr. Oddy, 'he does look alarming!'

'Oh, that's ever so old,' said Tommy. 'I expect he's mild and soft now, but he's a great man all the same; I'd like to see Spencer Russell write anything as fine as *The Roads* or *The Pattern in the Carpet.*'

They sat down to tea very happy and greatly pleased with one another.

'I do wish,' said Tommy, 'that you'd tell me something about yourself; we're such friends now, and I don't know anything about you at all.'

'I'd rather you didn't,' said Mr. Oddy. 'You'd find it so uninteresting if you did; mystery's a great thing.'

'Yes,' said Tommy, 'I don't want to seem impertinent, and of course if you don't want to tell me anything you needn't, but —I know it sounds silly, but, you see, I like you most awfully. I haven't liked anybody so much for ever so long, except Alice, of course. I don't feel as though you were of another generation or anything; it's just as though we were the same age!'

Mr. Oddy was enchanted. He put his hand on the boy's for a moment and was going to say something, when they were interrupted by a knock on the door, and the terrible-looking landlady appeared in the room. She apologised, but the afternoon post had come and she thought the young gentleman would like to see his letters. He took them, was about to put them down without opening them, when suddenly he blushed. 'Oh, from Alice,' he said. 'Will you forgive me a moment?'

'Of course,' said Mr. Oddy.

The boy opened the letter and read it. It fell from his hand on to the table. He got up gropingly as though he could not see his way, and went to the window and stood there with his back to the room. There was a long silence.

'Not bad news, I hope,' said Mr. Oddy at last.

Tommy turned round. His face was grey and he was biting his lips. 'Yes,' he answered, 'she's—gone off.'

'Gone off?' said Mr. Oddy, rising from the table.

'Yes,' said Tommy, 'with Russell. They were married at a register office this morning.'

He half turned round to the window, put out his hands as though he would shield himself from some blow, then crumpled up into a chair, his head falling between his arms on the table.

Mr. Oddy waited. At last he said: 'Oh, I'm sorry: that's dreadful for you!'

The boy struggled, trying to raise his head and speak, but the words would not come. Mr. Oddy went behind him and put his hands on his shoulders.

'You know,' he said, 'you mustn't mind me. Of course, I'll go if you like, but if you could think of me for a moment as your oldest friend, old enough to be your father, you know.'

Tommy clutched his sleeve, then, abandoning the struggle altogether, buried his head in Mr. Oddy's beautiful black waistcoat.

Later he poured his heart out. Alice was all that he had; he knew that he wasn't any good as a writer, he was a failure altogether; what he'd done he'd done for Alice, and now that she'd gone——

'Well, there's myself,' said Mr. Oddy. 'What I mean is that you're not without a friend; and as for writing, if you only write to please somebody else, that's no use; you've got to write because you can't help it. There are too many writers in the world already for you to dare to add to their number unless you're simply compelled to. But there—I'm preaching. If it's any comfort to you to know, I went through just this same experience myself once—the lady whose candle I watched behind the blind. If you cared to, would you come and have dinner with me to-night at my home? Only the two of us, you know; but don't if you'd rather be alone.'

Tommy, clutching Mr. Oddy's hand, said he would come.

About half-past seven that evening he had beaten up his pride. Even in the depth of his misery he saw that they would never have got on together, he and Alice. He was quickly working himself into a fine state of hatred of the whole female race, and this helped him—he would be a bachelor all his days, a woman-hater; he would preserve a glorious independence. How much better this freedom than a houseful of children and a bagful of debts.

Only, as he walked to the address that Mr. Oddy had given him he held sharply away from him the memory of those hours that he had spent with Alice, those hours of their early friendship when the world had been so wonderful a place that it had seemed to be made entirely of golden sunlight. He felt that he was an old man indeed as he mounted the steps of Mr. Oddy's house.

It was a big house in Eaton Square. Mr. Oddy must be rich. He rang the bell, and a door was opened by a footman. He asked for Mr. Oddy.

The footman hesitated a little, and then, smiling, said: 'Oh yes, sir, will you come in?'

He left his coat in the hall, mounted a broad staircase, and then was shown into the finest library that he had ever seen. Books! Shelf upon shelf of books, and glorious books, editions de luxe and, as he could see with half an eye, rare first editions and those lovely bindings in white parchment and vellum that he so longed one day himself to possess. On the broad writing-table there was a large photograph of Meredith; it was signed in sprawling letters, 'George Meredith, 1887.' What could this mean? Mr. Oddy, who knew nothing about literature, had been given a photograph by George Meredith and had this wonderful library! He stared bewilderedly about him.

A door at the far end of the library opened and an elegant young man appeared. 'Mr. Galleon,' he said, 'will be with you in a moment. Won't you sit down?'

SEASHORE MACABRE

A MOMENT'S EXPERIENCE

We had gone to our usual summer residence, a farm perched on the steep hill above Gosforth—Gosforth in Cumberland, where the Druid Cross is in the graveyard, so that foreigners come from the far ends of the earth to see it. For the rest the farm was hay and chickens' eggs, and wallflowers in hot dusty clusters under the narrow garden-wall, and the ducks walking into the kitchen, and Mrs. A——, the friendly, soft-hearted and deeply pessimistic farmer's wife, making cakes, hot and spicy, in the cavernous black oven.

But this incident, so clearly and sharply remembered, so symbolic, Mr. Freud perhaps would tell me, of all my older life, has nothing to do with the farm, except that it starts from there. It starts from there because on fine days we bicycled three miles into Seascape.

Seascale was the nearest seaside resort. It looked then as though one day it might become a true resort. It had long, lazy sands, a new golf course, a fine hotel, and there were little roads and lanes in and about that looked as though, with the slightest encouragement, they might become quite busy shop-haunted streets. Nevertheless, little roads and lanes now after thirty years they still are. Seascale has never taken that step upward into commercial prosperity that once perhaps was hoped for it. I myself am glad that it has not. It is the one place of my childhood that is not altered. The flat, passive sands are damp and windblown as they always were, the little station—sticky in the warm weather with a sort of sandy grit, damp in the wet weather like a soaked matchbox—stands just as it always did, as though with a rather stupid finger to its lip it were wondering whether it should go or stay.

No, not on the face of it a romantic place, Seascale—and yet to myself one of the romantic places of the world!

We bicycled—my father, my sister and I—while my mother and small brother were driven the three miles in a pony-trap. Then, if the weather permitted us, we spent the day on Seascale sands. We bathed in water that had always a chill in it quite special to itself, we ate ham sandwiches, hard-boiled eggs and gingerbreads under the shelter of the one small rock that the beach possessed (if that rock were not already occupied), and we read—my mother and father *The Egoist;* I—if priggish—*Le Rouge et le Noir,* if unpriggish, *Saracinesca.*

Now it happened that one day in the week was specially glorious to me; this was the day of my weekly pocket-money, threepence the amount, if not already owed for reasons of discipline, sin or back-answering. Now it also occurred that on the same day that I received my pocket-money was published the new number of a paper, yet I believe (and hope) in a flourishing condition—*The Weekly Telegraph.*

The Weekly Telegraph was my love and my dear. It cost, I think, only a penny. Its dry and rather yellow-tinted sheets (smelling of straw, liquorice and gunpowder, I fancy in reminiscence) held an extraordinary amount of matter, and especially they held the romantic short stories of Robert Murray Gilchrist, the serial narratives of young Mr. Phillips Oppenheim, and even, best of all as I remember it, *The Worldlings,* by Mr. Leonard Merrick. There were also 'Country Notes,' tinged deeply with Cumberland sights and sounds, jests, quips and oddities, ways of cleaning knives and forks, making pillowslips and curing a child of the croup.

What I suppose I am trying to emphasise is the contrast of these happy simplicities with—well, reader (as Charlotte Brontë always said), be patient and you shall hear!

You can see me, small, spindle-shanked and wind-blown, while my family sat huddled beneath the one Seascale rock, struggling through the spidery sand to the little station, my threepenny piece damply clutched. It was, as I remember it, a day of bright, glittering sun and a high wind. I am at least certain of a general glitter in the heavens and fragments of burning sand about my eyes.

I fought my way up the slope, sand in my shoes, sand in my

eyes, sand in my throat. I stood on the higher ground, rubbed the sand from my eyes and looked back to the distant plum-coloured hills where the Screes run down sheer to Wastwater and Gable rolls his shoulder. Then into the little station that burnt in the sun so that its paint sizzled. I asked for *The Weekly Telegraph*. I cannot remember what he was like who gave it to me, but I do know that I did not take two steps before I had opened the paper to see whether there were a Gilchrist 'Peakland' story, all about My Lady Swarthmore and tinkling spinets and a room darkly hung with tapestries, and some fair child working a picture in delicate silks. Yes, there it was! The horn was blowing through Elfland, the long slow sands below me were lit with mother-of-pearl, and there were mermaids near the shore. Mr. Oppenheim was also there—*A Prince of Swindlers*, Chap. XVII. 'As he walked down the steps of the Hotel Splendide, wondering whether he should try his luck at the Tables or no, Prince Serge ...' I drew a deep breath of satisfaction, took a step out of the station and almost collided with the wickedest human being it has ever been my luck to behold. Now, wicked human beings are rare! I have, I think, never beheld another. The majority of us are fools with or without a little knavery. This old man was, although, as you will see, I never exchanged a word with him, really wicked—capable, I am sure, of real, fine, motiveless villainy like Iago.

He was a little man, bent in the back, wearing a rather floppy black hat and carrying an umbrella. He had, I remember, a sallow complexion, a hooked nose, and a wart on his chin. I say I remember, but indeed he is as vivid to me as though he were standing by my side at this moment—which in fact he may be for all I know to the contrary.

And now, how strange what followed! As I have said, I almost stumbled on him. He stood aside and looked at me, and *I* looked at him! His look as I recall it was cold, sneering and mean-faced. Then he turned on his heel and, waving his bulging umbrella in the air, walked down the road.

Why, of all things in the world, did I follow him? I cannot imagine. I was on the whole a timid child, a good deal of a coward. Moreover, I had in my hand my adored *Weekly Telegraph* and was longing to read in it. Nevertheless, I followed him.

Looking back across all those years it seems to me that a cloud passed over the sun as we walked along, that the walls of the houses shone with a less brilliant reflection, that a chill creeping little wind began to wander. That is doubtless imagination. What is true is that the little man walked without making any sound upon the road. He was wearing, I suppose, shoes soled in felt or something of the kind. What is also true is that I was drawn after him as though I were led by a string.

Now I have said that I knew him to be wicked. How did I know? Was it only the idlest fancy? At that time I had but a child's knowledge of the world, and wickedness was far from my experience. The nearest to wickedness that I had then reached perhaps was the sight of a schoolfellow who had pulled the wings from a fly, or the lustful anger in the eyes of a schoolmaster beating one of my companions. Well, this little old man with the umbrella had something of that about him. Cruelty and meanness? Are there any other sorts of wickedness? I am sure that this little man could be both cruel and mean.

Did he know that I was following him? He must have heard my step. He gave no sign. With his head forward, his back bent, waving his umbrella, so under the windy sun he pursued his way.

Beyond the little town we reached paths soft in sand and with stiff sea-grasses sprouting there. We approached the sea and I fancy that the wind increased in volume, began to blow a hurricane. My heart was beating with terror, a sort of sickly pleasure, an odd mixture of daring and foreboding.

The little man came to a cottage knee-deep in sand, on the very edge, in fact, of a dune that ran down to a sea where waves were flinging in a succession of fiery silver wheels. Although the sun shone so brilliantly, the cottage looked dark and chill. There was, as I remember it, no warmth here, and the wind tugged at my trouser-legs. The little man vanished into the cottage. Clutching my *Weekly Telegraph,* I followed. And then—how did I have the courage? What spell was laid upon me so that I did something utterly against my nature? Or was it that my true nature was for once permitted the light?

In any case I paused, my heart hammering, the little cottage as still as a picture. Then—I turned the handle of the door and looked in.

What I saw was a decent-sized kitchen with a yawning black oven, dressers—but on them no plates; windows—but uncurtained. In a rocking-chair beside the fire sat an old man, the very spit of the old gentleman I had followed. The room was dark, for the windows were small; it was lit by candles and the candles were placed, two at one end of a trestle, two at another. And on the trestle lay a corpse.

I had never until that moment seen a dead person. This figure lay wrapped in white clothes; a white bandage was round his chin; his cheeks were waxen and yellow. So he lay. There was a silence, as there should be, of the grave itself. The corpse, as, with horror clutching my throat, I more persistently gazed, was that of an old man, the image again of the old boy with the umbrella, of the old boy in the chair. Nothing stirred. I could hear the solemn tick of a clock.

But, in my agitation, unknowing, I held the door open. A sudden gust of wind rushed past me and instantly—most horrible of all my life's recollections!—everything sprang to life. The little man whom I had followed appeared at the head of the kitchen-stairs and, in the most dreadful way, he pointed his umbrella as though condemning me to instant death. The little man in the chair sprang out of his sleep, and I shudder now when I remember his loose eye with its pendulous lid and an awful toneless grin as he stepped towards me. But worst of all was the way in which the thin silver hair of the corpse began to blow and his grave-clothes to flutter.

The room was filled with the wind. Sand came blowing in. Everything was on the move; it seemed to me that the yellow-faced corpse raised his hand ...

Screaming, I ran for my life. Stumbling, falling, bruising my knees, tearing my hands against the spiky grass, I frantically escaped.

A moment's experience—yes, but Mr. Freud might say—a lifetime's consequence.

LILAC

Frederick Anstey moved the Rodin Balzac a little so that the light of the spring evening should catch the strong curve of the nose and the high broad lines of the forehead.

'Marvellous!' he murmured, as though he had never seen it before. 'And he put a lot of extra work into this one. In fact there's not two of them alike. The one Mr. Bernard Shaw has . . .'

'Yes,' said Mr. Litehouse cautiously. 'If only it weren't so like Lloyd George. I should never be able to get it out of my head. "Why, it's the image of Lloyd George," was the very first thing my wife said when she came in to see it yesterday. And you can't deny. . . . Two hundred guineas, did you say?' he asked with sudden suspicion, as though Frederick Anstey might have forgotten what he *had* said.

'Two hundred,' said Frederick, smiling his round rubicund smile that was, he knew, bad for business but he never could check it. Bad for business because when a customer saw it he concluded instantly that Frederick was a creature of no stamina and could be easily beaten down.

'All right, I'll take it,' said Mr. Litehouse suddenly. (Five minutes before he had declared quite firmly that nothing would induce him to buy it.) 'That is if I can take it away now in my car—at once. I want to show it to somebody.' (You could always tell a true collector by his insistence on taking things with him, as though the object would disappear the moment his back was turned.)

'Of course you can,' said Frederick, his whole body smiling now. Then he was grave and sincere. It wouldn't do (for the hundredth time he told himself) to look as though selling the Balzac had pleased him. His gesture must be that if Mr. Litehouse didn't buy it, someone else would in half a minute!

Mr. Litehouse wouldn't allow it to be wrapped up. He ordered it to be carried at once into his car, and there, on the back seat, Balzac sat with Mr. Litehouse's bony and beautifully dressed person beside him, looking out on to the busy London streets as though he didn't care a damn.

'Sold the Balzac,' Frederick said carelessly to Pecking, whose attitude always was that no one save himself could sell anything.

'Litehouse?' asked Pecking.

Frederick nodded.

'Too good for him. . . . Still, he's got some fine things. It's only snobbery of course. Doesn't know one thing from another.'

'Lucky for us,' said Frederick, laughing.

'You look cheerful,' said Pecking resentfully. 'Come into a fortune?'

'No,' said Frederick. 'Expect it's the spring weather.'

He knew that it was not, or at least only a little. It had been a wonderful day and now the evening was lovely, but he regarded the selling of the Balzac as an omen. And he needed good omens, for in a quarter of an hour's time he was going to ask Lily Brocket to marry him. Everything helped. The Balzac helped. The spring evening helped. And if she refused him, nothing would be of any use at all!

He went into the farther room where the Zzierzcky pictures hung. This was the first Zzierzcky show in London and it had been a wonderful success. Nearly every picture had sold. A success of snobbery of course. The people who liked the pictures hadn't been able to afford to buy them: the people who had bought them had most certainly not liked them. Zzierzcky was very modern indeed. His landscapes were entitled 'Pond in Snow,' 'The Mountain Pass,' 'Winter Sunlight' and so on, but unless you were the kind of person who was ready for anything in pictures you would never guess what the pictures were about. Nevertheless, they had grown on Frederick during the month of their exhibition. He had, in the last three years, explained so many modern pictures to so many stupid and reluctant people that he had come to have modern tastes himself.

When he had come first to the Gallery he had actually thought Dawson a good painter! Now Dawson made him sick. Or would have done had he not a kindly feeling for Dawson. That was his trouble, that he had a kindly feeling for almost everyone. He was a very modest, kindly-hearted little man and had he ever considered what he was (which he never did) he would have wished fervently that he was anything else in the world.

But that was his trouble, that no one ever took him seriously. It had not been a real trouble (because formerly he had not taken himself seriously) until he had fallen in love with Lily Brocket. He wanted her to take him seriously. If she did not he might as well go and drown himself. And then at the thought of that he couldn't help but smile. The picture of his going to drown himself was so very absurd.

While he was washing his hands in the little cupboard off the passage and peering at himself in the glass, he hated, for the hundred-thousandth time, his round rosy face. It was the face of an infant, a good-natured infant who had just enjoyed a good feed from its bottle! Anything less distinguished! And his body too, round and short, thick in the leg, short in the arm. Who could take seriously such a body? The only thing he could do with it was to keep it clean and neat....

He shrugged his shoulders, wiped his hands with a kind of careful ceremony on the towel, and then forgot about himself. He never could think about himself for long. Something would keep breaking in: a joke or a meal, a pretty girl, or selling a picture, a game of golf (which he enjoyed and played very badly), or meeting a friend. He was an ordinary dull kind of fellow like thousands of others. That was what he thought of himself. He *could* not imagine what Lily saw in him.

But perhaps she saw nothing at all. This thought came to him as he put on his overcoat; so awful was it that for a moment his heart stopped beating. When it came to it you could not tell with a girl, could you? You could never tell what a girl was thinking. Were she really fond of him would she not have married him a year ago? There was, of course, her old father, that ridiculous old man of skin and bone with his greed and rheumatism and voice like a mouse in the wainscot.

She said that she couldn't leave him, but couldn't she? Ah, that was the question. Wouldn't she leave him if she really loved Frederick? How was Frederick to tell?

No, all he knew about it was that he adored her, could not live without her. That was the old hackneyed phrase, but in his case it was real and authentic. In spite of his chubby face and passion for seeing the cheerful side of everything, if Lily married someone else—that ridiculous tobacconist, for instance—he, Frederick, would decline and die—and no one in the whole world would care a halfpenny!

Lord! what melancholy thoughts for so lovely an evening! He was walking up Duke Street, and every shop was a little magic of fire and splendour, and overhead the sky swam in a mist of blue and silver light. People did not look at the sky enough in London. They walked with their noses straight in front of them or hurried like nervous rabbits or talked to their friends.

Perhaps he himself would not now have looked at the sky had it not been for his love of Lily. But spring was in the air and pushing up through the very pavement. You could almost, were your fancy poetic enough, detect violets in the corners of the grey stone and primroses clustered in the doorways.

Five minutes later he was thinking of nothing but Lily. She was waiting for him at the corner of the Green Park, the entrance near the Ritz corner, and they moved away down the Park in the direction of Buckingham Palace, at first not speaking.

'What a lovely evening!' she said softly. She was herself lovely in her little grey hat and silver-grey coat, with her rosy cheeks, black, black eyes and her way of moving as though she loved the world and couldn't have enough of it.

Someone had given her a bunch of primroses. She had pinned them into her coat. He was instantly jealous.

'Who gave you those primroses?' he asked huskily.

'Never *you* mind,' she answered him, laughing. And then, lest she should have hurt him, she added hastily: 'It was old Mr. Deering. He's always doing something kind.'

'Oh, is he?' said Frederick scornfully. 'Old man of his age. He ought to be thinking of the next world.'

'Now look here,' she said, putting her hand on his arm; his body trembled at her touch. 'Don't let's waste time talking of old nothings like Mr. Deering. We haven't got a minute. I oughtn't to have come really, but I knew you'd be so disappointed. Aunt Clara's turned up unexpectedly from Brighton. There's no one in the house but father, and he's got one of his toothaches. I've simply got to go straight back.'

There was rage in Frederick's heart, passionate hatred of Aunt Clara, bitter disappointment, a sense that life had once again dealt him a knock-down blow, a physical pain about his heart, an impulse to rage at Lily like a maniac, tear her hat from her head and trample on her bunch of primroses—and a surprising, incredible desire to break down and cry like a child.

She felt at once his bitter, desperate disappointment, pressed her hand into his arm, and, in a voice more loving than any that she had ever used to him before, said:

'Fred, dear ... you're not more disappointed than I am. It's a rotten shame. I never dreamt of Aunt Clara coming. It's just like her. It's our luck. I'm wretched about it.'

And she was! He knew at once that she meant what she said; he knew that she cared for him and in that knowledge the filmy silver sky, the dazzling friendly lights, the dark, obscure trees danced and turned and danced again, and his eyes were dim.

'See here, Lily,' he said, turning her towards him so that she looked into his eyes. 'I love you. You know I do. I've loved you for two years and now I love you so that it eats me up. It does truly. You've got to marry me. I've asked you before. Three times I've asked you, but never like to-night. It's so serious that I can't live ... I can't live ... if you don't....'

Her face was tender, maternal, gravely anxious as she looked at him. 'Yes, Fred ... I know ... but there's father.'

'Damn your father,' he answered (and she saw that to-night there was something new in his face, something really desperate). 'Isn't he seventy-six? Are our lives to be ruined for an old man like that? Isn't it a wicked thing for an old man to stop two people's lives ...?'

'But you don't understand——'

'I do understand, perfectly. You've told me again and again. And I tell you that if you're going to let your father interfere any longer, I'll never see you again after to-night. This is the last time. I can't stand it.... It isn't fair.'

'No; it isn't fair,' she answered him frankly. 'I've been thinking that for a long time. It isn't fair to you and it isn't fair to me, really.'

He felt an impulse of intense irritation and exasperation.

'Well, then, if it isn't fair, it's got to be ended ... Are you going to marry me?'

'But there's father——'

'Father can come and live with us. I've told you so over and over again.' He looked at her, tears in his eyes. He saw everything —sky and trees and coloured lights—in a trembling mist. 'If you loved me,' he said, his voice shaking, 'you wouldn't have hesitated. I might have known. It's because you don't love me that you can talk about your father.'

She shook her head, looking at him with great tenderness. 'It isn't as easy as that, Fred. It isn't indeed.... But it isn't fair either.... You're right there. I tell you what I'll do.'

He looked at her with new hope. His eyes cleared. The Park seemed suddenly to have a scent of flowers.

'I've got to go, but I'll write a line, telling you what I feel, and I'll send it along by Alfred to Garland Square. Before ten anyway. That's the best I can do, really it is, Fred.'

'A note?' he said, bewildered.

'Yes; saying how I feel. I'll settle it to-night. There are things I can say better in a letter. I'll send it by Alfred before ten.... Good-bye. I've got to run.' And she was gone, without a pressure of the hand, without another word, swallowed up by the Park as though she had never been.

He stayed there, staring in front of him; then, after a minute or two, started on his way home. He didn't know what to think. No, but he was hopeful, more hopeful than he had ever been before. And, whatever way it might go, to-night would settle it. Whatever way it might go!

At the thought that it might go the wrong way his body shrank within its clothes as though a giant hand were compressing it. Supposing she should say no! Oh, suppose ... He was nearly killed by a car, a voice shouted at him, lights flashed and danced, he was on the farther pavement. A lucky escape; but if she refused him, he might as well be dead.

She didn't mean to, though. She wouldn't put him to all the

agony of suspense, hours of it, if she meant to refuse him. But perhaps she thought that it would be kinder that way. Couldn't bear to hurt him by telling him ... He walked on blindly, seeing nothing, hearing nothing and, before he knew anything about it, he was at his door.

Garland Square is one of those little squares that have been dropped like pools of quiet and comfort here and there about London. They say that they are doomed, that modern traffic, modern I-don't-know-what, must drive them away. If that is true, then some of the most beautiful things in the world are doomed.

Garland Square is small, and its railed-in garden is like a green napkin laid out between the old dove-grey houses. Round the green Square flowers blow according to the seasons, daffodils, purple and white lilac; it is best in the spring; in the summer such flowers as there are are hidden by the dark thick green of the trees and bushes. The trees are haunted by the birds who use the grass as their promenading ground by right immemorial. There is at one end the statue of an eighteenth-century gentleman in a tie-wig, with a cocked hat, and a handsome frill to his waistcoat. There are some green benches.

The inhabitants of the houses in the Square have, of course, a key to the garden—no one else in the world—and the old gardener who has a beard just like his broom regrets bitterly that, in these days, the inhabitants of the houses have gone down so dreadfully in 'class.' He belongs to the fine old days when 'class' mattered, when a gentleman *was* a gentleman. Now everybody is a gentleman, or nobody if you look at it his way.

Frederick's house was Number Ten and had been, like several others, divided into flats. They were not flats of the splendid West End order. There was no lift; you walked up the fine eighteenth-century stone staircase and then, if your room was high up, as Frederick's was, a further smaller staircase, and then a small corkscrew staircase most difficult to manœuvre if, like Mr. Bendish in the room opposite to Frederick, you came back early in the morning, wine having made your heart so glad that you sang aloud and disturbed everyone. Poor Bendish! He didn't care for wine, as he often told Frederick. He didn't care very much for whisky, but what were you to do when you were all alone in the world and one girl after another refused to marry you? He had proposed, he told Frederick, to twenty within the last year. It wasn't true (what the newspapers were always saying) that an Englishwoman would marry any man who asked her.

Frederick's room could not, by any sort of courtesy, be called a flat. It was simply a bed-sitting-room, and a woman (Mrs. Marl) came in the morning, gave him his breakfast, and cleaned up. He shared her with Bendish and the Russell Greens.

He could have afforded quite easily a real flat, but the house was so grand, the Square so beautiful and so quiet, the neighbourhood so good, and old Lady Cannon (who lived on the ground floor and whose house it was) so aristocratic, that he was lucky to be there. He loved his room, his view, his neighbourhood; only marriage with Lily would persuade him to depart.

He was standing now, his window flung up, looking out over the Square. Behind him his room told him that it was glad that he was back. He had two Chinese rugs, some good pieces of old furniture, and three pictures—an oil by Paul of a lady with a white face and a green nose, a sketch by Duncan Grant and a drawing of a music-hall by Sickert. He had had no taste when he had first come to this room five years ago, but the picture-gallery had educated him, educated him, Lily said, to liking everything that was ugly. She couldn't understand the lady with the green nose. After all, people didn't have green noses, whatever light you saw them in. It was their only real difference of opinion.

But he was not thinking of that now. As he leaned out of the window there came to him quite unmistakably the scent of lilac. It could not in reality be. There was no lilac in bloom in the gardens, and yet he smelt the lilac and seemed, as he leaned out, to see through the grey-moth-like evening the sky above the Square broken into soft shreds and patches of blue, and bushes of dim purple lilac staining the air with its colour, a cloud of shadowy radiance.

He knew that he was cheating himself and yet he urged himself to be cheated. The belief acting against knowledge that the lilac was there seemed to be linked with his dramatic anticipation of his fate. His heart was thumping, his throat hot and dry, his body suddenly tired with a rather pleasant fatigue; he was in short like a man waiting for his sentence of execution. And yet surely nothing very terrible could happen to him on so lovely an evening as this. All the world was beautiful, and the Rodin Balzac which he had so successfully sold, the soft Duncan Grant landscape (amber and rose its colouring), the Square with its sense of spring, its scent of lilac, all these beautiful things seemed to come together and assure him that his fate must be a kind one.

He was aware of the door opening and, turning, saw Bendish there.

Bendish was a large, stout, rumpled man with little blue eyes, grey untidy hair, and a small pouting mouth. He seemed to be always asking for your indulgence, wondering whether you would scold him or no. There was something eternally unsatisfactory about him, which was perhaps why girls had so often refused to marry him. Their maternal feelings were roused by his helplessness, their practical self-protection alarmed by his irresponsibility, and so he was still a bachelor.

'I say, have you got a hammer?' he asked.

'Yes,' said Frederick, turning back into the room. 'I think so.' As he turned back he was convinced that Lily would accept him, and the room blazed with light and the pictures danced.

'You look as though you'd come into a fortune,' said Bendish rather resentfully. Anstey, after all, was a very ordinary little fellow and yet he seemed to be always in luck, while himself . . .

Frederick rummaged in the cupboard, standing on his toes because he was short and the hammer was probably on the top shelf. Bendish, looking at his broad back, the strong sturdy strain of his body as he raised his arms, and something gay and independent about the set of his round, closely cropped bullet-head, suddenly liked him very much and, liking him, felt happier.

He had himself a decision that he must, that evening, come to a decision that all the week he had been evading. To escape from the thought of it he had come in to borrow a hammer (it was true that there *was* a hunting picture to hang). Now he was more cheerful, and when Frederick, the hammer in his hand, turned and showed his rosy, flushed face, he said quite amiably: 'Thanks. Lovely evening, isn't it?'

They both turned to the window.

'Bit nippy with the window open,' said Bendish.

'Funny thing,' said Frederick, 'I've been thinking I could smell lilac. Of course it's impossible. But an evening like this makes you imagine things.'

Bendish never imagined anything, so he said nothing.

'Made a good sale this afternoon,' the little man went on. 'Head of Balzac by Rodin. Sold it to that fellow Litehouse, the big tobacco man. He's collecting pictures and things. Doesn't know anything about art, but we look after him—see he doesn't get anything rotten, you know.'

'Much better,' said Bendish gloomily, 'if he gave his money to children's hospitals or something like that.'

'Oh, I don't know,' said Frederick, suddenly irritated because nothing exasperated him so much as this very popular sentiment, 'it would be an awful world if there weren't any beautiful things in it, and who'd go on making beautiful things if nobody ever bought them?'

'I don't see that,' said Bendish. 'Pictures are only a luxury.'

But he couldn't quarrel with Frederick; there was something in his easy, quite uncomplacent good-nature that made him difficult to quarrel with. Frederick, on his side, had a very strong impulse to tell Bendish all about Lily. Lily was around him, inside him, everywhere. His heart was still hammering, his cheeks were hot, his throat was dry. It would be a relief to tell Bendish and ask him what he thought of the chances, to gain encouragement perhaps in opposition to his own fears. But no, it was no use to tell Bendish anything. He was only interested in himself.

Bendish looked at him curiously. 'I believe you've been making money at racing,' he said. 'You do have all the luck. I've noticed it before.' He felt, himself, a temptation to tell Anstey about his problem. There was something about Anstey tonight.... But Anstey would only advise him to do what he didn't want to do.

'No,' said Frederick, 'I never have any luck with horses. I always lose.' Never any luck? Would he have luck with Lily? Even now she was making up her mind. It might be that she was, at this very moment, writing her letter.

'Dear Fred, I want to tell you—'

His heart seemed to knock him right over. It wouldn't have surprised him at all to find himself flat on the floor! To steady himself, he put his hand on Bendish's arm. At the touch the two men seemed to come into some new relation with one another. Bendish was a lonely fellow. No one ever seemed to need him or put themselves out to see him. Bendish was greatly moved. But all he said was, gruffly: 'Well, I must go and hang that picture.' By the door he added: 'Thanks for the hammer.'

Frederick said: 'That's all right. Come in any time you like.'

He was alone again: the house was utterly still about him.

Bendish had done something to him; he had made him see how desperate, how abandoned, how hopelessly ruined he would be did Lily refuse him. He would be like Bendish, only worse. Bendish's loose, stout, uncared-for figure seemed to be a prophecy of his later self refused by Lily. He would go down and down . . .

Standing now in the middle of his room he saw nothing. The room seemed to be filled with a warm, clinging, smelly fog. Deserted by Lily all the little devils that were always waiting in attendance (he could see them, hideous naked little demons squatting on their hams) would have their way with him. And their way would be a bad one. He was no saint (he little knew how few his sins were in comparison with many of his companions') and he would yield, he would yield. . . . He would go over to Paris with Prentiss or Solomon. He would take Miss Geary (what Miss Geary wanted of him had always been perfectly obvious) out to supper. He would . . .

He pressed his hands to his forehead, sat down, wretched misery overwhelming him. He could not smell any lilac now, but the room was so stuffy that he must go out. He must go out or his head would burst and scatter his brains (such as they were) about the floor. If he went out (the temptation suddenly came to him) he might in another moment be at Lily's door. A taxi would take him there in no time. But that he must not do. It would be breaking all the rules of restraint that he had ever formulated for himself and, worse than that, he would be driving Lily to some sort of forced decision which would in all probability be exactly the wrong one. But the temptation was fearful. It was exactly as though a little devil in a shiny top-hat and a frock-coat were leading him (he could feel the touch of the little pudgy hand) straight out of his door.

He got his hat, his coat and his stick and went out. He stood in the little passage and listened. No sound. Not even Bendish knocking nails into his wall. But he knew instinctively that Bendish had not really wanted the hammer. What he had wanted was Frederick's help about something. He had come in for company. He had his own especial troubles. Yes, after all, we were all alike. All in the soup together and the best thing that we could do was to help one another. He went carefully down the corkscrew staircase—he seemed to be slightly drunk—and, in the lower passage, almost collided with someone. It was dark here almost always, but this evening something of this miraculous spring had pushed through.

A faint pale glow suffused everything, the shabby yellowed print of Victoria receiving the news of her Succession, an umbrella stand, an old chair with a red-plush seat to it. Standing near to the chair, her hand resting upon it as though to support herself, was young Mrs. Russell Green. The Russell Greens were acquaintances of Frederick rather than friends. A very young couple who loved one another apparently but were for ever quarrelling. They had been quarrelling now, it seemed, for at once Mrs. Russell Green, on seeing Frederick, whispered: 'Oh, Mr. Anstey, I can't stand any more of it. I can't, indeed. I'm going to my mother this very night.'

She was, he saw, in a very agitated state, her hand to her heart, her eyes furious and miserable, staring at him as though she couldn't see him at all.

'What's the matter?' he asked. Their conversation had the oddest urgency and whispering conspiracy about it, as though they were, the two of them, plotting to murder someone.

'The matter is,' she whispered frantically, 'that he's just insulted me more than I can stand. Yes, more than I can stand. I've stood enough. I didn't marry him for this sort of thing. I've told him often enough that if he did it again I'd leave him. And now he's done it.'

'What's he done?' Frederick asked. He could smell the lilac once more. Certainly it was lilac. Coming in from the Square and stealing up the stairs.

'He's been out with that Marchmont girl again. All last evening when he said that he was with the Berys. He wasn't with the Berys at all. He's confessed it.'

Frederick understood, as though some special agent had whispered it to him, that this was really serious. If she went off now, in her hat and coat as she was, out of the house, she might never return. A burst of temper and jealousy and the Russell Green life was ruined for ever. He must persuade her into the flat again. He must, if it cost him his life. Once more, as with the Balzac and poor old Bendish, there seemed a fateful omen in this —if Mrs. Russell Green left the house Lily would refuse him.

'I shouldn't take it too seriously,' he whispered. 'You know he loves you, whatever he does. I don't suppose he meant any harm.'

'Harm! What do you call harm? If that Marchmont girl ... And lying to me, too! I've told him again and again I'll stand anything, but not lies. No, never!'

He touched her arm with his hand. She was trembling, but his touch seemed to steady her. She leant a little towards him. She liked him. She had always liked him. Nice kind little man. She realised him now, stolid and kind, wanting to help her. And realising him, she liked men better. She saw her own Walter with a little bit of Frederick Anstey stuck on to him.

'I shouldn't,' Frederick said, 'do anything drastic on such a lovely evening.'

Lovely evening! That was about the silliest thing she had ever heard! Nevertheless, there was something in it. She was a sentimental girl, and she loved Walter Russell Green more than all the world and everything in it. She caught Frederick's hand.

'What does he tell me lies for?' she went on in an agonised whisper. 'That's what I want to know. I could stand anything but that. And such silly lies. He's always found out and he knows it.'

'Everyone tells lies,' whispered Frederick. 'One can't help it. We all do. And what does it matter when you know he loves you? Anyone can see it.'

Yes, he did. Of that she was quite sure. At the thought of

the way that he loved her, of his past goodness, tenderness and incredible childish charm, she softened. She wanted to soften. She had wanted it all the time.

'Go back,' said Frederick. 'Don't leave to-night. See how it is in the morning.'

She looked at the door, sniffed, sighed.

'Very well, then. I'll give him another chance. But it's the last.' She nodded, pushed her Yale key into the door and vanished.

He shook his head. Perhaps in a moment she would be out again. He waited, half expecting the door to open and a furious figure to emerge, but nothing happened. Silence and the spring evening. He went down to the main hall which had still, at the bottom of its stone staircase, an air and a grandeur. The floor was paved in black and white squares; there was a large empty fireplace, and over it hung what Frederick had always supposed to be a young ancestor of Lady Cannon's—a handsome boy in a blue suit with a fine gold sword at his side.

'I wonder,' thought Frederick, looking at him, 'whether you ever proposed to a lady who couldn't make up her mind if she'd accept you or no.... I'm sure you did not.... You are too good-looking. Any woman would have accepted you at sight.'

He still hesitated, glancing at the door as though it held special temptation for him. He must not go out: he would be off at once to Lily. That would anger her. Everything would be ruined....

But the door pulled at him! Its strong dark face seemed to urge him: 'Come and open me! Slip outside. It is such a delicious evening.'

Then the door, to his astonishment, opened. The light spread softly towards him, he saw the white stone steps, the shining surface of the pavement, the dark trees beyond. Old Lady Cannon stood there, leaning against the door, as though she would fall.

He went quickly towards her, and she said with a little gasping sigh: 'Oh, Mr. Anstey.... I'm a little faint ... please.'

He supported her, standing there by the open door, and it was strange to him, having her in his arms, to feel the absolute frailty of her body, something so sparse and fragile that it was difficult to believe that it could still exist. She always wore the same clothes, a black bonnet, a shiny black dress, a round silver locket on her heart, long black gloves, all very old-fashioned and quaint; she was a figure that everyone stared at in the street.

She was very small in stature, with a little white peaked face in which were set large anxious eyes. Frederick did not know her very well. She could be haughty and superior. She let the rooms of her house through an agent, and Frederick might never have known her at all had it not been that she had asked his advice on two occasions about family pictures that she wished to sell. One of them, a very charming little Romney, had fetched an excellent price.

He had never entered the rooms where she lived. He was to enter them now.

She gave him the oddest, dry little smile. 'I'm sorry,' she said. 'I beg your pardon. I fear that I shall have to ask you to assist me. I'm not very well. My maid is out.' Then she added, speaking with great difficulty: 'They want so much freedom in these days.'

He almost carried her across the hall: she felt in the pocket of her black dress and gave him the key. They went through the little passage into a vast cold drawing-room, and here he placed her in an old deep chair covered with faded brocade near the wide empty fireplace. How cold the room was and, after he had settled her and looked about him, how empty and desolate!

He could see on the faintly yellow walls the marks where pictures had been hanging. There were still some pictures left, faint and beautiful under the electric light.

She said: 'Will you please turn the light off again? ... And my smelling salts, if you please. On that table!'

He switched the light off and at once the great room was beautiful. From the high wide windows a lake of pale colour spread over the old red carpet, the little tables, the old shabby gilt chairs. A clock struck the hour with a lovely silver tone as though it welcomed the evening.

She lay back, her bonnet on the table beside her, sniffing at the salts, her head turned away from him. He could not see her face. He was sitting stiffly on a gilt chair near to her.

'Can't I get you some brandy?' he asked gently. 'Is there something I can do for you?'

But she did not answer. Her thin arm in its long black glove had fallen to her side. He waited. He did not wish to disturb her. A certain deference that he had been trained from his babyhood to feel for the English aristocracy kept him silent. Our English snobbery, and yet not quite that. He felt, in the presence of an old lady like this, all the romance and colour of the English past. They said that the past didn't matter any more, that even to think of people belonging to this class or another was vain and empty-headed. Well, he *was* empty-headed then! This old lady had something that neither he nor Lily would ever have, and it was some beautiful thing with dignity, history, courage in it. Courage! The old lady needed it, he was sure. Looking cautiously about the dim empty room he felt an air of poverty and hardship. She should not be poor, receiving the rents for all the rooms in her house, and yet she was poor. There was some mystery here. He sat there, not venturing to move. He would stay there a little while, lest she needed somebody. He thought that she was asleep.

The door was a little open, and the farther door was open too. He could hear the chatter of the old clock in the hall.

He fell asleep. . . .

When he awoke he was fearfully cold. For a moment he could not remember where he was. Then it all came to him. At once his heart began to hammer again in his breast. Suppose that a letter had come while he slept. He could still see the figure in the chair, quite motionless. She also was sleeping.

Confusedly, things crowded about him—the Balzac, old Bendish, Mrs. Russell Green, the old lady. All omens for Lily; omens of life, too. All these ways life could go—the artist perfecting his beautiful work and then selling it to a man like Litehouse who cared for it only because it cost him money; if Lily refused him, the aimless, decaying life of Bendish; if Lily accepted him, perhaps the quarrelling, jealous life of marriage; and at last, at the end, this old age, nothing left save the past, all gone, all empty, all the fire and stress as though it had never been. Those were the ways that life could take.

But he was no very great philosopher. For an instant only the fantasy of this strange mystery had danced before his eyes. Now it was gone. Lily. Lily . . . Oh, Lily, my darling, darling!

He got up very carefully from his chair, stole across the floor, moved into the dusky hall. There was the letter-box hanging like a malicious chin from the dark surface. Trembling so that he could scarcely stand he went, opened it. There, shimmering white, was a letter. He saw that it was addressed to himself and was in Lily's handwriting.

Now his agony was upon him. He had to summon to his rescue every power that he had ever known. His forehead was damp with sweat. He took out his handkerchief and mopped it. He tore the envelope, letting it fall to the ground. In her big, sprawling handwriting, so precious to him, he read:

DEAREST FRED,

I want you to know that I love you and will marry you to-morrow, if you want me to. My mind was made up this afternoon (it has always really been made up), but I wouldn't tell you in that hurry, and then father . . .

He read no more. All the world was singing. He flung open the hall door and a great flood of lilac seemed to salute him and in the dusk he saw the clustered bushes burning purple.

THE OLDEST TALLAND

Mrs. Comber explained to Miss Salter that, although she had been living in Cornwall all these years, she was only now, during this stay at Rafiel, beginning truly to appreciate it.

'You see, my dear, a school's a school, and it does somehow rather take the edge off an appreciation of beauty, having to keep the little boys clean and ordering the mutton, although I must say that our matron is a thoroughly capable woman—she comes from Marlborough, where she was for a term, but couldn't endure it because—— Well, I'm wandering from the subject— what I mean is that one *does* see things on a holiday that one hasn't quite time for perhaps during term-time.'

Rafiel was all the more beautiful for the five days' rain that had but now submerged and obscured it. It was incredible after the dirty grey that it had so recently presented that it could now, so transcendently, glitter and shine. Mrs. Comber had watched it first from the heights of Sea View Villa. From that point it lay huddled, packed together between the hills, with its boats drawn up in rows together inside its square little harbour. Seen thus on a fine day, it caught blue from the sea and green from the hills, and wrapped its slates and stones in reflected lights. From a height it was something that might at any moment be over-whelmed by the sea—something pretty but insignificant.

How different in the heart of it! Mrs. Comber, as she picked her way along the tiny cobbled streets, exclaimed at every step that she took. At first the place offered you a straight and some-what dingy street, with nothing very different from other streets in other Cornish towns. One or two little shops suggested to the hungry visitor saffron buns, apples and peppermints, and for the untidy inhabitant there were bootlaces, buttons and pins. There was also a Methodist chapel.

But it was when the village had tumbled so far as the post office that it suddenly made up its mind that it would, from that moment, be as incredible, as haphazard, as beautiful as water, bricks and Nature would allow it to be. Three little streets went dancing into the sea, little streets with shapeless roofs, steps leading up to green-painted doorways that hung in mid-air, streets with cobbles and dark, mysterious caverns and bursting, bulging windows, and across these three little streets a river ran for no reason at all, except that it gave an opportunity for more hanging balconies and green-and-blue reflections of painted doors and shutters. And then the streets and the river were, in an instant, pulled up by the little harbour—a square, shimmering space of blue water—with all the brown-and-blue-masted boats riding upon it like hounds in leash, and the grey stone pier blocking it from the sea.

The whole village hangs over this blue square and is reflected in it; the sky is painted there, and also the hills. Every mood, every glory, every temper of the place is to be found there. Beyond the stone wall there is the Atlantic, with sharp, jagged rocks (they are called the Peaks) as gateways on either side. All of this is within the compass of five minutes; it is as ancient as it can be, as crooked and unexpected and childish. There are wilder seas here than anywhere on the English coast, save, perhaps, on the Land's End, and the saffron buns, the buttons and the peppermints are very often in danger of being swept away altogether.

And meanwhile on the face of that little square harbour every mood of earth and sky is reflected.

Mrs. Comber took it, on her first vision of it, into the arms of her most extravagant enthusiasm. Her enthusiasms were always perfectly genuine affairs, for, although she always liked to have someone with whom they might be shared, she demanded no audience for their exhibition.

She nearly filled one of the three merry little streets, her cheeks blazing with excitement, a hard black hat slipping, it seemed, from her head, her hair threatening descent, her green skirt, short and showing thick square-toed shoes, her large, good-natured mouth and black, laughing eyes.

Full of health, good temper and colour she was, and she seemed to push back the street from her on both sides with her strong arms.

The natives looked at her, as they looked at all tourists, with a friendly indifference that was ready at any moment to develop into friendly attention if pounds, shillings and pence were in the air. The Rafiel citizens are not mercenary, but as most of them are supporting families on something approaching forty pounds a year, 'tourists' may often make considerable difference to personal comfort. Friendliness, moreover, is invited, and as, again, most of the aforesaid citizens have never in their lives penetrated farther into the heart of the world than St. Tryst, a town seven miles away (many of them have never seen a train), conversation with visitors is instructive and entertaining.

At the same time, be it understood, there is never intimacy.

Of these things Mrs. Comber knew nothing. You may be the wife of a schoolmaster in Cornwall for a number of years without knowing anything about Cornwall. The school had always swallowed up all possible backgrounds. This was the first time that Cornwall was considered for itself, and Mrs. Comber, in the burning joy of her enthusiasm, determined to take the inhabitants of Rafiel entirely to her heart.

Here she was, staying at a dull *pension,* and her husband away on the golf links all day—why, of course, the only thing to do was to get to know the place and the people. Anything more attractive than the people were, too! How readily they all said 'Good-day,' how pleasantly they smiled, how amiably they chattered with one another on their bright little doorsteps! As the sun shone and the cobbles glittered, and the sky was blue upon blue and then blue upon that again, Mrs. Comber could have kissed the old fishermen one by one, and the old ladies one after another.

As a matter of fact, the thing that she did do, in the heat of her enthusiasm, was to trample with one of her square-toed shoes upon a small and dirty girl, to send the little thing sprawling, to pick her up with a thousand exclamations, to kiss her dirty mouth, and to carry her, after explanations, back to her family.

Her family, as Fate would have it, was the Talland family.

The Tallands and the Tresennens divide Rafiel between them. They have so divided it ever since that legendary day when the first of the Tallands stood on one of the Peaks and flung rocks at the first of the Tresennens, who stood on the other of the Peaks and did his best to respond in kind.

Relations are outwardly friendly enough between the two families (there is very little bad temper in Rafiel), but through all the centuries there has been no intermarriage between them, and the rivalry is unremitting, never forgotten, never allowed to lapse.

At the head of the Tallands at this time there ruled an old lady of mythical age. She was so old that the next oldest inhabitant in Rafiel (and he was over ninety) was supposed to be a child to her. Nobody knew how old she was, and she was popularly supposed to have had no beginning; and it was expected that death would never succeed in catching her. As far as appearance went, there was nothing of her face to be seen except a sharp nose, a sharper chin, and two eyes sharper still. The nose and the chin met, and the eyes blazed. These blazing eyes stared at you from the blackness of a dark and low-roofed kitchen. Huddled amongst cushions she faced the world from her corner by the fireplace—faced the world and cursed the Tresennens.

The Talland stronghold was a crooked and uneasy house perched behind the post office, a little way up the hill, and resting there, as it seemed, on one foot, and leering down at the post office and the harbour with a wink and a snigger; with every wind it threatened collapse. The Tallands had lived there now for a very long time, and it had the advantage of being higher in position than the chief castle of the Tresennens, although the Tresennens, from their windows, could see everyone who went in and out of the Talland doorway.

Here in her dark corner old Mrs. Talland, like the most sinister and patient of spiders, had been sitting for years and years and years.

A long time ago—ten or fifteen years back, it might be— something had happened to the old lady's throat, and her voice disappeared.

The family had at first looked on this event as an unmixed blessing, and some of the younger branches had suggested that the occasion ought to mark the end of the old lady's rule. Little these youngsters knew. After the accident Mrs. Talland's power was redoubled. Now that she could speak no more, her eyes, always fierce enough, had twice their former power. She attained a kind of mystical splendour that had been absent before, and, with the exception of her hard-faced youngest daughter, a maiden lady of some sixty years, who washed and fed her, the family trembled before her glance. Her eldest son, the greatest bully in Rafiel, quailed when she looked at him, and during these years of her rule the Tresennen family did not dare set their feet within a stone's throw of the Talland house.

And it was of the Tresennen family that Mrs. Talland was always thinking. In the days of her youth—and the number of years ago that was only Mrs. Talland knew—she had been concerned in strange happenings up on the windy hill with old Mother Perith, happenings that were connected with broomsticks and wax dolls and fires and skulls and strange weeds from the hedges.

She had not forgotten anything that she had learnt then. Brooding there in her fireplace, she knew the things that she could do to the Tresennens, if she needed. But it was a long time now since she had called those powers to her aid.... Scornfully she thought to herself that the Tresennens could be kept in their proper place without any need for such assistance.

Fiercely, with furious determination, she bent her will to keeping herself free, independent from any assistance in this world or the next. Clergymen, visitors, doctors had forced upon her, from time to time, their officious presences.... She had sent them all packing. They had fled before her glance.

Let her once, her old heart fiercely determined, give in to anyone, and her power would be gone and the Tresennens triumph.

There in her stronghold she kept back the world. Then into the kitchen, noisily, with friendship shining about her and in and out of her, Mrs. Comber burst.

The Tresennens, from their windows, marked her entry.

Mrs. Comber stood, smiling, in the doorway, holding tightly by the hand the youngest of the Tallands. Gathered in a little group by the fireplace were other Tallands, a number of them, and huddled amongst her cushions, with her hands shaking a little on her lap and her eyes flaming, was the oldest of them all. Behind her chair stood the gaunt, bony Janet Talland, whose duty it was to keep her mother clean and fed.

The room was very close, as it had every reason to be, because the street door was generally shut, and the little diamond-paned window never opened. The air was heavy with the odour of fish, dying geraniums, saffron buns and tobacco.

Mrs. Comber addressed herself to Miss Janet Talland.

'I do hope I'm not in any way interrupting or interfering, but I was silly enough—careless, perhaps I ought to say—to knock over your little girl; at least, they tell me this is her home. And how I came to do it I can't think, except that I was admiring your beautiful town and didn't really notice where I was going, which is a silly trick that I really must try——' She broke off and patted the head of the youngest of the Tallands. 'I don't think I hurt you, dear, did I? She cried just a little at first, but it was more fright than anything else, being knocked down suddenly——'

The Tallands had had strange tourists within their castle before, but never any tourist like this tourist. Mrs. Comber, so glowing with colour, so voluble, so eager, froze them into silence. Old Mrs. Talland leaned forward in her chair, and her dry fingers rattled together on her lap.

'Come 'ere, Annie,' said Miss Janet Talland. 'What be 'ee at, gettin' in the lady's way?'

Annie disengaged herself from Mrs. Comber's grasp and shuffled across the floor, whimpering.

'I do hope——' began Mrs. Comber. She stopped because she was bewildered by the sudden, sweeping disappearance of most of the Talland family through the street-door. Only the old lady and her grim-faced daughter remained. 'I do hope,' went on Mrs. Comber, more cheerfully than ever, 'that you won't visit the accident on poor little Annie. It wasn't in the least poor Annie's fault. If I'd only looked where I was going——'

It was then that Mrs. Comber noticed old Mrs. Talland. Nobody could have looked, to the outside observer, more helpless and ready for charity. 'Here,' said Mrs. Comber at once to herself, 'is a person to do good to. Here is the very interest that I have been wanting.'

'I hope you don't mind,' said Mrs. Comber gaily, 'my just

stopping a moment or two. I'm not interrupting you in anything, am I? Because just tell me if I am, and go on doing just the things that you'd do if I weren't here. Make me at home, you know.' She sat down in a chair by the fire quite close to Mrs. Talland.

The old woman leant forward still farther and stared at her. It was many months now since any visitor had braved her presence, but no visitor within her memory had braved her as this one did. The flaunting, highly coloured, bold-faced thing! Mrs. Talland always disliked seeing youth and vigour and energy—it made her feel old—but this noise and heartiness in one who was no longer young simply disgusted her. She would have liked to slap Mrs. Comber's red cheeks. She looked up at her daughter. Why was Janet not sending the woman to the rightabout, as she generally did? She was actually allowing her to sit there.

Janet had at first been taken aback by Mrs. Comber's energy, and then, as the minutes passed, her slow brain began to move. She knew well enough the things that her mother was thinking. She knew how she must hate the impertinence of this woman. But also she knew that for many, many years now she had served the old woman and received no return for it, had served her faithfully and obeyed her in everything. In the woman's heart, although she had not known it until now, for many years resentment had been growing. Supposing that she should disobey her now? A fierce, hot pleasure was in her breast at the thought of getting some revenge at last. Moreover, this woman, were she treated gently, would bring things into the house—jellies and fruits and custards. And oh, how the old tyrant would hate it!

'Sit you down, ma'am,' Janet said slowly. 'You aren't disturbing us, I assure 'ee. Mother can't tark—'er speech is gone this many a year.'

'Poor old woman! Poor old woman!' said Mrs. Comber, her voice full of compassion.

'But she ain't deaf, all the same,' said Miss Talland, fearful lest the tourist should drive her mother to some sudden frenzy. ''Er 'earing's arl right.'

Mrs. Comber was filled with the most genuine feelings of pity and tenderness. She hated anyone to be as feeble and desolate as this poor old lady. The room seemed to her dirty and uncared for.

And how terrible to be unable to speak and to be in the hands of that cruel-looking woman. Mrs. Comber felt that she would never sleep again did she not relieve in some way Mrs. Talland's condition.

'Oh, but I *am* sorry!' she cried, and her large black eyes were full of tenderness. 'How dreadful not to be able to talk! I don't know what I should do if such a thing were to happen to me. Although, perhaps,' she went on, laughing gaily, 'some people would say it was a good thing, because, you know, I do talk so much, too much; and it's a trick I've tried to break myself of ever since I was a girl and I've never been able to.'

Mrs. Talland's hands rapped against each other in an agony. What was this horrible thing, and what, above all, was Janet about? It was then that, flinging a sharp glance at her daughter, she caught a first glimpse of the thoughts that were passing behind those cold eyes. Janet stood, gaunt and severe, with her hands folded in front of her, and about her mouth there lingered the suspicion of a grim smile.

'Yes,' she said, 'it do be 'ard for mother, for she was always one to love a good tark, and now she must sit there and listen, as you might say.'

'Oh dear, dear, I *am* sorry,' said Mrs. Comber. She found it so difficult to force herself to remember that Mrs. Talland was not deaf as well as dumb. 'But, really, Mrs. Talland, I want to do everything I can to help you.' Here Mrs. Talland's hands were more frantic than ever. 'Yes, I will, indeed. If there's anything I can do. Perhaps, Miss Talland, you can suggest——'

'Well,' said Miss Talland slowly, 'mother du have a likin' to jellies and them soup squares, as you *are* so kindly askin'. The doctor 'asn't been in for a long time, but the last day 'e *was* 'ere I remember 'is sayin' that a drop o' soup *and* a little jelly——'

Surely about Mrs. Talland's ears the world must have seemed, at that moment, to be tumbling. In her breast there was a fierce, dogged determination to fight to the bitter end, but it was the first rebellion that she had had to meet for many a long year. . . . And then from Janet—Janet, the most faithful of servants.

She did what she could with her face, striving to fling into her eyes all the hatred and loathing and disgust that was in her heart.

Oh, if she could have spoken, what things she would have said!

'Well,' continued Mrs. Comber amiably, 'that's very good of you, Miss Talland, to tell me the kind of thing. But do you really mean to tell me that the doctor hasn't been here for a long time?'

'No, that 'e 'asn't.' Miss Talland did not add that, owing to the plain speaking of the Talland family on his last visit, he had uttered a solemn vow never to cross their threshold again.

'And he looks such a nice, kind man,' said Mrs. Comber. 'I really must speak to him, because a doctor can be such a help sometimes. I remember once when a little boy of mine was ill that I was in such trouble about him because he'd got a rash, but it might have been just from over-eating himself in the hot weather. But our doctor was so clever about him. Really, if he hadn't been there—well,' she continued brightly, getting up from her chair, 'I mustn't trouble you any longer, Miss Talland. I'm sure you must have heaps to do, and I must be getting along. But I *have* enjoyed this talk so much. It *is* so nice getting to know you all. Good-bye, Mrs. Talland. Be assured that I will do everything for you that's possible, and I'll speak to the doctor about coming to see you. I'll look in myself again in a little time. I'm *so* glad we've made one another's acquaintance. Good-bye.'

Mrs. Comber shook hands with the unresponsive Janet and was gone.

It must be confessed that, for a moment, as the two women faced one another, Janet's courage forsook her. Mrs. Talland had not established her rule during all these years for nothing. The old woman's eyes were living flames. As she sat up amongst her cushions her whole body was tense with hatred, horror, surprise, vindictive longing to get at someone and tear limb from limb.

Certainly, at that instant, those things that had belonged to Mother Perith many years ago might now have found themselves once more a home. Janet had often seen her mother look angry before, but she had never seen her anything like this. She faced her mother's eyes—drew fire from them during a long moment, and then, slowly stealing back her gaze, she smiled. Mrs. Talland knew then that the moment had come that she had dreaded ever since she had lost her voice. Her rule was threatened.

But, worse than that, from the Tresennen windows, eyes —eager, mocking eyes—were watching. They had seen that woman come. They would see her come again.

It was well, at that moment, for Mrs. Comber that she was not within reach of Mrs. Talland's long and grasping fingers.

Very shortly after this, Mrs. Comber, up at Sea View Villa, met the doctor, who had been invited in to bridge. She talked to him a great deal, and amongst other things she mentioned the Tallands.

'Of course, it's really no business of mine, doctor, but that poor old woman did look so uncared for there, with only that grim, ugly woman to look after her. She looked as though she needed company so badly, and I thought, perhaps, if you were to go in and just give her a bright word——'

'I'm afraid bright words, Mrs. Comber,' said the doctor, 'are not things that the Talland family care for very much. Last time I was there they were so rude to me that I vowed I'd never go again. But still—I promise you—I'll try once more.'

'Of course,' said Mrs. Comber, 'they're difficult.'

'Just as though,' the doctor said to his wife afterwards, 'she'd been visiting Cornish fishermen all her days.'

In her own mind Mrs. Comber concluded that the doctor had been rough with the poor people, and, of course, they didn't like that.

Nevertheless, the doctor kept his word and went, and, to his great surprise, was allowed by Janet to examine the old lady and to suggest medicines. Janet did not, indeed, say much to him during the visit; for the most part she remained, with her hands folded, grimly watching her mother, but the doctor was permitted to do what he would.

'Really, Mrs. Comber,' he said after his visit, 'you're a wonderful person. I don't know what you've done to them, but a month ago it was as much as my life was worth to go inside their door.'

And Mrs. Comber was pleased. She now paid a visit every afternoon, and sat there sometimes for half an hour talking to Mrs. Talland. She did not in the least mind the fact that Mrs. Talland was unable to answer her. She liked to have someone to whom she might talk without interruption.

Then she brought the vicar's wife, who brought tracts and left them on Mrs. Talland's table. And from their windows the Tresennens watched it all....

And Mrs. Comber was really happy, and spent much more than she could afford on jellies and soups and chickens.

The younger Tallands had watched these things with dumb, gasping amazement. They had always left the treatment of the head of the family in Janet's capable hands. Janet had invariably good reasons for everything that she did, and it was to be supposed, therefore, that she had good reasons for what she did now. Slowly some inkling of the truth stole in upon them. Very, very slowly they understood.

Meanwhile, what old Mrs. Talland suffered no human being will ever know. She wrote desperately words on the slate that she was given for expressing her desires. But her old fingers were very shaky now.

'Burn,' 'Woman,' 'Hate,' 'Hell,' could be deciphered.

If eyes could have slain, Janet would long ago have been dead. When the washing, dressing and undressing periods arrived, Mrs. Talland would have bitten or strangled or torn her daughter had she been able, but Janet was a very strong woman.

Had only a week passed since this horrible creature's first arrival? Already the other Tallands, the sons, the daughters-in-law, paid less attention to her. No longer did they come in with soft step 'lest Granny should be sleepin'.' They pretended not to hear her when she rattled her slate-pencil at them.

They did not often come to her now and amuse her with the gossip of the town.

She could do nothing—she could do nothing.

Her doom had come upon her.

At last the definite moment of defeat came. Little Annie, who had always, until now, been in the utmost terror of her great-grandmother, was left in charge whilst Janet was busily employed with shopping.

The girl looked at the old woman and then defiantly, if just a little timidly, began to whistle between her teeth in a way that she had always understood was abominable to an older person.

Mrs. Talland rattled her pencil against her slate.

Annie continued to whistle.

Mrs. Talland stamped with her foot (it was a very feeble tap); she clapped her hands together, gnashed her two teeth.

Annie paused a moment, her legs apart, facing the chair.

'Shan't!' she said, and then, appalled by her daring, ran from the room.

The old woman was alone. Shaking from head to foot, she did what she had not done for many years: she got up from her chair. Leaning on her stick, she tottered to a drawer that was near. From this she extracted something, then tottered back to her place.

With her cap off her head, the cushions tumbling about her, muttering, she began to turn and twist the thing that she had in her hands. It was a piece of old, soiled, grimy wax.

Her brain was fiery with thoughts of that red-faced woman who had ruined her life.

She turned the wax, muttering.

But it would not twist; it was so hard and old. It fell from her nerveless fingers and lay amongst the ashes in the hearth. Her last resort was gone. The old world had faded, the old gods and devils had fled. There was a new order now, a new world.

The end of her life had come. Tired, thin tears trickled slowly down the dried furrows of her cheeks.

Twenty-four hours later she was dead.

'Poor thing,' said Mrs. Comber when she heard of the funeral. 'But I'm glad that I did a little something to brighten her last hours.'

THE LITTLE GHOST

Ghosts? I looked across the table at Truscott and had a sudden desire to impress him. Truscott has, before now, invited confidences in just that same way, with his flat impassivity, his air of not caring whether you say anything to him or no, his determined indifference to your drama and your pathos. On this particular evening he had been less impassive. He had himself turned the conversation towards spiritualism, séances, and all that world of humbug, as he believed it to be, and suddenly I saw, or fancied that I saw, a real invitation in his eyes, something that made me say to myself: 'Well, hang it all, I've known Truscott for nearly twenty years; I've never shown him the least little bit of my real self; he thinks me a writing money-machine, with no thought in the world besides my brazen serial stories and the yacht that I purchased out of them.'

So I told him this story, and I will do him the justice to say that he listened to every word of it most attentively, although it was far into the evening before I had finished. He didn't seem impatient with all the little details that I gave. Of course, in a ghost story, details are more important than anything else. But was it a ghost story? Was it a story at all? Was it true even in its material background? Now, as I try to tell it again, I can't be sure. Truscott is the only other person who has ever heard it, and at the end of it he made no comment whatever.

It happened long ago, long before the war, when I had been married for about five years, and was an exceedingly prosperous journalist, with a nice little house and two children, in Wimbledon.

I lost suddenly my greatest friend. That may mean little or much as friendship is commonly held, but I believe that most Britishers, most Americans, most Scandinavians, know before they die one friendship at least that changes their whole life experience by its depth and colour. Very few Frenchmen, Italians or Spaniards, very few Southern people at all, understand these things.

The curious part of it in my particular case was that I had known this friend only four or five years before his death, that I had made many friendships both before and since that have endured over much longer periods, and yet this particular friendship had a quality of intensity and happiness that I have never found elsewhere.

Another curious thing was that I met Bond only a few months before my marriage, when I was deeply in love with my wife, and so intensely preoccupied with my engagement that I could think of nothing else. I met Bond quite casually at someone's house. He was a large-boned, broad-shouldered, slow-smiling man with close-cropped hair turning slightly grey, and our meeting was casual; the ripening of our friendship was casual; indeed, the whole affair may be said to have been casual to the very last. It was, in fact, my wife who said to me one day, when we had been married about a year or so: 'Why, I believe you care more for Charlie Bond than for anyone else in the world.' She said it in that sudden, disconcerting, perceptive way that some women have. I was entirely astonished. Of course I laughed at the idea. I saw Bond frequently. He came often to the house. My wife, wiser than many wives, encouraged all my friendships, and she herself liked Charlie immensely. I don't suppose that anyone disliked him. Some men were jealous of him; some men, the merest acquaintances, called him conceited; women were sometimes irritated by him because so clearly he could get on very easily without them; but he had, I think, no real enemy.

How could he have had? His good-nature, his freedom from all jealousy, his naturalness, his sense of fun, the absence of all pettiness, his common sense, his manliness, and at the same time his broad-minded intelligence, all these things made him a most charming personality. I don't know that he shone very much in ordinary society. He was very quiet, and his wit and humour came out best with his intimates.

I was the showy one, and he always played up to me, and I think I patronised him a little and thought deep down in my subconscious self that it was lucky for him to have such a brilliant friend, but he never gave a sign of resentment. I believe now that he knew me, with all my faults and vanities and absurdities,

far better than anyone else, even my wife, did, and that is one of
the reasons, to the day of my death, why I shall always miss him
so desperately.

However, it was not until his death that I realised how close
we had been. One November day he came back to his flat, wet
and chilled, didn't change his clothes, caught a cold, which
developed into pneumonia, and after three days was dead. It
happened that that week I was in Paris, and I returned to be
told on my doorstep by my wife of what had occurred. At first
I refused to believe it. When I had seen him a week before he
had been in splendid health; with his tanned, rather rough and
clumsy face, his clear eyes, no fat about him anywhere, he had
looked as though he would live to a thousand, and then when I
realised that it was indeed true I did not during the first week or
two grasp my loss.

I missed him, of course; was vaguely unhappy and discontented; railed against life, wondering why it was always the best
people who were taken and the others left; but I was not actually aware that for the rest of my days things would be different, and that that day of my return from Paris was a crisis in my
human experience. Suddenly one morning, walking down Fleet
Street, I had a flashing, almost blinding, need of Bond that was
like a revelation. From that moment I knew no peace. Everyone
seemed to me dull, profitless and empty. Even my wife was a
long way away from me, and my children, whom I dearly loved,
counted nothing to me at all. I didn't, after that, know what was
the matter with me. I lost my appetite, I couldn't sleep, I was
grumpy and nervous. I didn't myself connect it with Bond at all.
I thought that I was overworked, and when my wife suggested a
holiday, I agreed, got a fortnight's leave from my newspaper, and
went down to Glebeshire.

Early December is not a bad time for Glebeshire. It is just
then the best spot in the British Isles. I knew a little village
beyond St. Mary's Moor, that I had not seen for ten years, but
always remembered with romantic gratitude, and I felt that that
was the place for me now.

I changed trains at Polchester and found myself at last in a
little jingle driving out to the sea. The air, the wide open moor,

the smell of the sea delighted me, and when I reached my village, with its sandy cove and the boats drawn up in two rows in front of a high rocky cave, and when I ate my eggs and bacon in the parlour of the inn overlooking the sea, I felt happier than I had done for weeks past; but my happiness did not last long. Night after night I could not sleep. I began to feel acute loneliness and knew at last in full truth that it was my friend whom I was missing, and that it was not solitude I needed, but his company. Easy enough to talk about having his company, but I only truly knew, down here in this little village, sitting on the edge of the green cliff, looking over into limitless sea, that I was indeed never to have his company again. There followed after that a wild, impatient regret that I had not made more of my time with him. I saw myself, in a sudden vision, as I had really been with him, patronising, indulgent, a little contemptuous of his good-natured ideas. Had I only a week with him now, how eagerly I would show him that I was the fool and not he, that I was the lucky one every time!

One connects with one's own grief the place where one feels it, and before many days had passed I had grown to loathe the little village, to dread, beyond words, the long, soughing groan of the sea as it drew back down the slanting beach, the melancholy wail of the sea gulls, the chattering women under my little window. I couldn't stand it. I ought to go back to London, and yet from that, too, I shrank. Memories of Bond lingered there as they did in no other place, and it was hardly fair to my wife and family to give them the company of the dreary, discontented man that I just then was.

And then, just in the way that such things always happen, I found on my breakfast-table one fine morning a forwarded letter. It was from a certain Mrs. Baldwin, and, to my surprise, I saw that it came from Glebeshire, but from the top of the county and not its southern end.

John Baldwin was a Stock Exchange friend of my brother's, a rough diamond, but kindly and generous, and not, I believed, very well off. Mrs. Baldwin I had always liked, and I think she always liked me. We had not met for some little time, and I had no idea what had happened to them. Now in her letter she told

me that they had taken an old eighteenth-century house on the
north coast of Glebeshire, not very far from Drymouth, that
they were enjoying it very much indeed, that Jack was fitter than
he had been for years, and that they would be delighted, were I
ever in that part of the country, to have me as their guest. This
suddenly seemed to me the very thing. The Baldwins had never
known Charlie Bond, and they would have, therefore, for me no
association with his memory. They were jolly, noisy people, with
a jolly, noisy family, and Jack Baldwin's personality was so robust
that it would surely shake me out of my gloomy mood. I sent a
telegram at once to Mrs. Baldwin, asking her whether she could
have me for a week, and before the day was over I received the
warmest of invitations.

Next day I left my fishing village and experienced one of
those strange, crooked, in-and-out little journeys that you must
undergo if you are to find your way from one obscure Glebeshire
village to another.

About midday, a lovely, cold, blue December midday, I discovered myself in Polchester with an hour to wait for my next
train. I went down into the town, climbed the High Street to
the magnificent cathedral, stood beneath the famous Arden
Gate, looked at the still more famous tomb of the Black Bishop,
and it was there, as the sunlight, slanting through the great east
window, danced and sparkled about the wonderful blue stone of
which that tomb is made, that I had a sudden sense of having
been through all this before, of having stood just there in some
earlier time, weighed down by some earlier grief, and that nothing that I was experiencing was unexpected. I had a curious sense,
too, of comfort and condolence, that horrible grey loneliness that
I had felt in the fishing village suddenly fell from me, and for the
first time since Bond's death, I was happy. I walked away from
the cathedral, down the busy street, and through the dear old
market-place, expecting I know not what. All that I knew was
that I was intending to go to the Baldwins' and that I would be
happy there.

The December afternoon fell quickly, and during the last part
of my journey I was travelling in a ridiculous little train, through
dusk, and the little train went so slowly and so casually that

one was always hearing the murmurs of streams beyond one's window, and lakes of grey water suddenly stretched like plates of glass to thick woods, black as ink, against a faint sky. I got out at my little wayside station, shaped like a rabbit-hutch, and found a motor waiting for me. The drive was not long, and suddenly I was outside the old eighteenth-century house and Baldwin's stout butler was conveying me into the hall with that careful, kindly patronage, rather as though I were a box of eggs that might very easily be broken.

It was a spacious hall, with a large open fireplace, in front of which they were all having tea. I say 'all' advisedly, because the place seemed to be full of people, grown-ups and children, but mostly children. There were so many of these last that I was not, to the end of my stay, to be able to name most of them individually.

Mrs. Baldwin came forward to greet me, introduced me to one or two people, sat me down and gave me my tea, told me that I wasn't looking at all well, and needed feeding up, and explained that Jack was out shooting something, but would soon be back.

My entrance had made a brief lull, but immediately everyone recovered and the noise was terrific. There is a lot to be said for the freedom of the modern child. There is a lot to be said against it, too. I soon found that in this party, at any rate, the elders were completely disregarded and of no account. Children rushed about the hall, knocked one another down, shouted and screamed, fell over grown-ups as though they were pieces of furniture, and paid no attention at all to the mild 'Now, children' of a plain, elderly lady who was, I supposed, a governess. I fancy that I was tired with my criss-cross journey, and I soon found a chance to ask Mrs. Baldwin if I could go up to my room. She said: 'I expect you find these children noisy. Poor little things. They must have their fun. Jack always says that one can only be young once, and I do so agree with him.'

I wasn't myself feeling very young that evening (I was really about nine hundred years old), so that I agreed with her and eagerly left youth to its own appropriate pleasures. Mrs. Baldwin took me up the fine broad staircase. She was a stout, short woman, dressed in bright colours, with what is known, I believe, as an infectious laugh. To-night, although I was fond of her, and knew very well her good, generous heart, she irritated me, and for some reason that I could not quite define. Perhaps I felt at once that she was out of place there and that the house resented her, but in all this account, I am puzzled by the question as to whether I imagine now, on looking back, all sorts of feelings that were not really there at all, but come to me now because I know of what happened afterwards. But I am so anxious to tell the truth, the whole truth, and nothing but the truth, and there is nothing in the world so difficult to do as that.

We went through a number of dark passages, up and down little pieces of staircase that seemed to have no beginning, no end, and no reason for their existence, and she left me at last in my bedroom, said that she hoped I would be comfortable, and that Jack would come and see me when he came in, and then paused for a moment, looking at me. 'You really don't look well,' she said. 'You've been overdoing it. You're too conscientious. I always said so. You shall have a real rest here. And the children will see that you're not dull.'

Her last two sentences seemed scarcely to go together. I could not tell her about my loss. I realised suddenly, as I had never realised in our older acquaintance, that I should never be able to speak to her about anything that really mattered.

She smiled, laughed and left me. I looked at my room and loved it at once. Broad and low-ceilinged, it contained very little furniture, an old four-poster, charming hangings of some old rose-coloured damask, an old gold mirror, an oak cabinet, some high-backed chairs, and then, for comfort, a large armchair with high elbows, a little quaintly-shaped sofa dressed in the same rose colour as the bed, a bright crackling fire, and a grandfather clock. The walls, faded primrose, had no pictures, but on one of them, opposite my bed, was a gay sampler worked in bright colours of crimson and yellow and framed in oak.

I liked it, I loved it, and drew the armchair in front of the fire, nestled down into it, and before I knew, I was fast asleep. How long I slept I don't know, but I suddenly woke with a sense of comfort and well-being which was nothing less than exquisite. I belonged to it, that room, as though I had been in it all my days.

I had a curious sense of companionship that was exactly what I had been needing during these last weeks. The house was very still, no voices of children came to me, no sound anywhere, save the sharp crackle of the fire and the friendly ticking of the old clock. Suddenly I thought that there was someone in the room with me, a rustle of something that might have been the fire and yet was not.

I got up and looked about me, half smiling, as though I expected to see a familiar face. There was no one there, of course, and yet I had just that consciousness of companionship that one has when someone whom one loves very dearly and knows very intimately is sitting with one in the same room. I even went to the other side of the four-poster and looked around me, pulled for a moment at the rose-coloured curtains, and of course saw no one. Then the door suddenly opened and Jack Baldwin came in, and I remember having a curious feeling of irritation as though I had been interrupted. His large, breezy, knickerbockered figure filled the room. 'Hullo!' he said, 'delighted to see you. Bit of luck your being down this way. Have you got everything you want?'

II

That was a wonderful old house. I am not going to attempt to describe it, although I have stayed there quite recently. Yes, I stayed there on many occasions since that first of which I am now speaking. It has never been quite the same to me since that first time. You may say, if you like, that the Baldwins fought a battle with it and defeated it. It is certainly now more Baldwin than—well, whatever it was before they rented it. They are not the kind of people to be defeated by atmosphere. Their chief duty in this world, I gather, is to make things Baldwin, and very good for the world too; but when I first went down to them the house was still challenging them. 'A wee bit creepy,' Mrs. Baldwin confided to me on the second day of my visit. 'What exactly do you mean by that?' I asked her. 'Ghosts?'

'Oh, there are those, of course,' she answered. 'There's an

underground passage, you know, that runs from here to the sea, and one of the wickedest of the smugglers was killed in it, and his ghost still haunts the cellar. At least that's what we were told by our first butler, here; and then, of course, we found that it was the butler, not the smuggler, who was haunting the cellar, and since his departure the smuggler hasn't been visible.' She laughed. 'All the same, it isn't a comfortable place. I'm going to wake up some of those old rooms. We're going to put in some more windows. And then there are the children,' she added.

Yes, there were the children. Surely the noisiest in all the world. They had reverence for nothing. They were the wildest savages, and especially those from nine to thirteen, the cruellest and most uncivilised age for children. There were two little boys, twins I should think, who were nothing less than devils, and regarded their elders with cold, watching eyes, said nothing in protest when scolded, but evolved plots afterwards that fitted precisely the chastiser. To do my host and hostess justice, all the children were not Baldwins, and I fancy that the Baldwin contingent was the quietest.

Nevertheless, from early morning until ten at night, the noise was terrific and you were never sure how early in the morning it would recommence. I don't know that I personally minded the noise very greatly. It took me out of myself and gave me something better to think of, but, in some obscure and unanalysed way, I felt that the house minded it. One knows how the poets have written about old walls and rafters rejoicing in the happy, careless laughter of children. I do not think this house rejoiced at all, and it was queer how consistently I, who am not supposed to be an imaginative person, thought about the house.

But it was not until my third evening that something really happened. I say 'happened,' but did anything really happen? You shall judge for yourself.

I was sitting in my comfortable armchair in my bedroom, enjoying that delightful half-hour before one dresses for dinner. There was a terrible racket up and down the passages, the children being persuaded, I gathered, to go into the schoolroom and have their supper, when the noise died down and there was nothing but the feathery whisper of the snow—snow had been falling all day—against my window-pane. My thoughts suddenly turned to Bond, directed to him as actually and precipitately as though he had suddenly sprung before me. I did not want to think of him. I had been fighting his memory these last days, because I had thought that the wisest thing to do, but now he was too much for me.

I luxuriated in my memories of him, turning over and over all sorts of times that we had had together, seeing his smile, watching his mouth that turned up at the corners when he was amused, and wondering finally why he should obsess me the way that he did, when I had lost so many other friends for whom I had thought I cared much more, who, nevertheless, never bothered my memory at all. I sighed, and it seemed to me that my sigh was very gently repeated behind me. I turned sharply round. The curtains had not been drawn. You know the strange, milky pallor that reflected snow throws over objects, and although three lighted candles shone in the room, moon-white shadows seemed to hang over the bed and across the floor. Of course there was no one there, and yet I stared and stared about me as though I were convinced that I was not alone. And then I looked especially at one part of the room, a distant corner beyond the four-poster, and it seemed to me that someone was there. And yet no one was there. But whether it was that my mind had been distracted, or that the beauty of the old snow-lit room enchanted me, I don't know, but my thoughts of my friend were happy and reassured. I had not lost him, I seemed to say to myself. Indeed, at that special moment he seemed to be closer to me than he had been while he was alive.

From that evening a curious thing occurred. I only seemed to be close to my friend when I was in my own room—and I felt more than that. When my door was closed and I was sitting in my armchair, I fancied that our new companionship was not only Bond's, but was something more as well. I would wake in the middle of the night or in the early morning and feel quite sure that I was not alone; so sure that I did not even want to investigate it further, but just took the companionship for granted and was happy.

Outside that room, however, I felt increasing discomfort. I

hated the way in which the house was treated. A quite unreasonable anger rose within me as I heard the Baldwins discussing the improvements that they were going to make, and yet they were so kind to me, and so patently unaware of doing anything that would not generally be commended, it was quite impossible for me to show my anger. Nevertheless, Mrs. Baldwin noticed something. 'I am afraid the children are worrying you,' she said one morning, half interrogatively. 'In a way it will be a rest when they go back to school, but the Christmas holidays is their time, isn't it? I do like to see them happy. Poor little dears.'

The poor little dears were at that moment being Red Indians all over the hall.

'No, of course, I like children,' I answered her. 'The only thing is that they don't—I hope you won't think me foolish—somehow quite fit in with the house.'

'Oh, I think it's so good for old places like this,' said Mrs. Baldwin briskly, 'to be woken up a little. I'm sure if the old people who used to live here came back they'd love to hear all the noise and laughter.'

I wasn't so sure myself, but I wouldn't disturb Mrs. Baldwin's contentment for anything.

That evening in my room I was so convinced of companionship that I spoke.

'If there's anyone here,' I said aloud, 'I'd like them to know that I'm aware of it and am glad of it.'

Then, when I caught myself speaking aloud, I was suddenly terrified. Was I really going crazy? Wasn't that the first step towards insanity when you talked to yourself? Nevertheless, a moment later I was reassured. There *was* someone there.

That night I woke, looked at my luminous watch and saw that it was a quarter past three. The room was so dark that I could not even distinguish the posts of my bed, but there was a very faint glow from the fire, now nearly dead. Opposite my bed there seemed to me to be something white. Not white in the accepted sense of a tall, ghostly figure; but, sitting up and staring, it seemed to me that the shadow was very small, hardly reaching above the edge of the bed.

'Is there anyone there?' I asked. 'Because, if there is, do speak to me. I'm not frightened. I know that someone has been here all this last week, and I am glad of it.'

Very faintly then, and so faintly that I cannot to this day be sure that I saw anything at all, the figure of a child seemed to me to be visible.

We all know how we have at one time and another fancied that we have seen visions and figures, and then have discovered that it was something in the room, the chance hanging of a coat, the reflection of a glass, a trick of moonlight that has fired our imagination. I was quite prepared for that in this case, but it seemed to me then that as I watched the shadow moved directly in front of the dying fire, and delicate as the leaf of a silver birch, like the trailing rim of some evening cloud, the figure of a child hovered in front of me.

Curiously enough the dress, which seemed to be of some silver tissue, was clearer than anything else. I did not, in fact, see the face at all, and yet I could swear in the morning that I had seen it, that I knew large, black, wide-open eyes, a little mouth very faintly parted in a timid smile, and that, beyond anything else, I had realised in the expression of that face fear and bewilderment and a longing for some comfort.

III

After that night the affair moved very quickly to its little climax.

I am not a very imaginative man, nor have I any sympathy with the modern craze for spooks and spectres. I have never seen, nor fancied that I had seen, anything of a supernatural kind since that visit, but then I have never known since that time such a desperate need of companionship and comfort, and is it not perhaps because we do not want things badly enough in this life that we do not get more of them? However that may be, I was sure on this occasion that I had some companionship that was born of a need greater than mine. I suddenly took the most frantic and unreasonable dislike to the children in that house. It was exactly as though I had discovered somewhere in a deserted part of the

building some child who had been left behind by mistake by
the last occupants and was terrified by the noisy exuberance and
ruthless selfishness of the new family.

For a week I had no more definite manifestation of my little
friend, but I was as sure of her presence there in my room as I was
of my own clothes and the armchair in which I used to sit.

It was time for me to go back to London, but I could not
go. I asked everyone I met as to legends and stories connected
with the old house, but I never found anything to do with a little
child. I looked forward all day to my hour in my room before
dinner, the time when I felt the companionship closest. I sometimes woke in the night and was conscious of its presence, but, as
I have said, I never saw anything.

One evening the older children obtained leave to stay up
later. It was somebody's birthday. The house seemed to be full of
people, and the presence of the children led after dinner to a perfect riot of noise and confusion. We were to play hide-and-seek
all over the house. Everybody was to dress up. There was, for that
night at least, to be no privacy anywhere. We were all, as Mrs.
Baldwin said, to be ten years old again. I hadn't the least desire
to be ten years old, but I found myself caught into the game, and
had, in sheer self-defence, to run up and down the passages and
hide behind the doors. The noise was terrific. It grew and grew
in volume. People got hysterical. The smaller children jumped
out of bed and ran about the passages. Somebody kept blowing a
motor-horn. Somebody else turned on the gramophone.

Suddenly I was sick of the whole thing, retreated into my
room, lit one candle and locked the door. I had scarcely sat down
in my chair when I was aware that my little friend had come. She
was standing near to the bed, staring at me, terror in her eyes. I
have never seen anyone so frightened. Her little breasts panting beneath her silver gown, her very fair hair falling about her
shoulders, her little hands clenched. Just as I saw her, there were
loud knocks on the door, many voices shouting to be admitted,
a perfect babel of noise and laughter. The little figure moved,
and then—how can I give any idea of it?—I was conscious of
having something to protect and comfort. I saw nothing, physically I felt nothing, and yet I was murmuring, 'There, there, don't

mind. They shan't come in. I'll see that no one touches you. I understand. I understand.' For how long I sat like that I don't know. The noises died away, voices murmured at intervals and then were silent. The house slept. All night I think I stayed there comforting and being comforted.

I fancy now—but how much of it may not be fancy?—that I knew that the child loved the house, had stayed so long as was possible, at last was driven away, and that that was her farewell, not only to me, but to all that she most loved in this world and the next.

I do not know—I could swear to nothing. What I am sure of is that my sense of loss in my friend was removed from that night and never returned. Did I argue with myself that that child companionship included also my friend? Again, I do not know. But of one thing I am now sure, that if love is strong enough, physical death cannot destroy it, and however platitudinous that may sound to others, it is platitudinous no longer when you have discovered it by actual experience for yourself.

That moment in that fire-lit room, when I felt that spiritual heart beating with mine, is and always will be enough for me.

One thing more. Next day I left for London, and my wife was delighted to find me so completely recovered—happier, she said, than I had ever been before.

Two days afterwards, I received a parcel from Mrs. Baldwin. In the note that accompanied it, she said:

I think that you must have left this by mistake behind you. It was found in the small drawer in your dressing-table.

I opened the parcel and discovered an old blue silk handkerchief, wrapped round a long, thin wooden box. The cover of the box lifted very easily, and I saw inside it an old, painted wooden doll, dressed in the period, I should think, of Queen Anne. The dress was very complete, even down to the little shoes, and the little grey mittens on the hands. Inside the silk skirt there was sewn a little tape, and on the tape, in very faded letters, 'Ann Trelawney, 1710.'

MRS. LUNT

'Do you believe in ghosts?' I asked Runciman. I had to ask him this very platitudinous question more because he was so difficult a man to spend an hour with than for any other reason. You know his books, perhaps, or more probably you don't know them —*The Running Man, The Elm Tree,* and *Crystal and Candlelight.* He is one of those little men who are constant enough in this age of immense overproduction of books, men who publish every autumn their novel, who arouse by that publication in certain critics eager appreciation and praise, who have a small and faithful public, whose circulation is very small indeed, who when you meet them have little to say, are often shy and nervous, pessimistic and remote from daily life. Such men do fine work, are made but little of in their own day, and perhaps fifty years after their death are rediscovered by some digging critic and become a sort of cult with a new generation.

I asked Runciman that question because, for some unknown reason, I had invited him to dinner at my flat and was now faced with a long evening filled with that most tiresome of all conversations, talk that dies every two minutes and has to be revived with terrific exertions. Being myself a critic, and having on many occasions praised Runciman's work, he was the more nervous and shy with me; had I abused it, he would perhaps have had plenty to say—he was that kind of man. But my question was a lucky one: it roused him instantly, his long, bony body became full of a new energy, his eyes stared into a rich and exciting reminiscence, he spoke without pause, and I took care not to interrupt him. He certainly told me one of the most astounding stories I have ever heard. Whether it was true or not I cannot, of course, say: these ghost stories are nearly always at second or third hand. I had, at any rate, the good fortune to secure mine from the source. Moreover, Runciman was not a liar: he was too serious for that. He himself admitted that he was not sure, at this distance of time, as to whether the thing had gained as the years passed. However, here it is as he told it.

'It was some fifteen years ago,' he said. 'I went down to Cornwall to stay with Robert Lunt. Do you remember his name? No, I suppose you do not. He wrote several novels; some of those half-and-half things that are not quite novels, not quite poems, rather mystical and picturesque, and are the very devil to do well. De la Mare's *Return* is a good example of the kind of thing. I had reviewed somewhere his last book, and reviewed it favourably, and received from him a really touching letter showing that the man was thirsting for praise, and also, I fancied, for company. He lived in Cornwall somewhere on the sea-coast, and his wife had died a year ago; he said he was quite alone there, and would I come and spend Christmas with him; he hoped I would not think this impertinent; he expected that I would be engaged already, but he could not resist the chance. Well, I wasn't engaged; far from it. If Lunt was lonely, so was I; if Lunt was a failure, so was I; I was touched, as I have said, by his letter, and I accepted his invitation. As I went down in the train to Penzance I wondered what kind of a man he would be. I had never seen any photographs of him; he was not the sort of author whose picture the newspapers publish. He must be, I fancied, about my own age—perhaps rather older. I know when we're lonely how some of us are for ever imagining that a friend will somewhere turn up, that ideal friend who will understand all one's feelings, who will give one affection without being sentimental, who will take an interest in one's affairs without being impertinent—yes, the sort of friend one never finds.

'I fancy that I became quite romantic about Lunt before I reached Penzance. We would talk, he and I, about all those literary questions that seemed to me at that time so absorbing; we would perhaps often stay together and even travel abroad on those little journeys that are so swiftly melancholy when one is alone, so delightful when one has a perfect companion. I imagined him as sparse and delicate and refined, with a sort of wistfulness and rather childish play of fancy. We had both, so far, failed in our careers, but perhaps together we would do great things.

'When I arrived at Penzance it was almost dark, and the snow, threatened all day by an overhanging sky, had begun gently and timorously to fall. He had told me in his letter that a fly would be at the station to take me to his house; and there I found it—a funny old weather-beaten carriage with a funny old weather-beaten driver. At this distance of time my imagination may have created many things, but I fancy that from the moment I was shut into that carriage some dim suggestion of fear and apprehension attacked me. I fancy that I had some absurd impulse to get out of the thing and take the night train back to London again—an action that would have been very unlike me, as I had always a sort of obstinate determination to carry through anything that I had begun. In any case, I was uncomfortable in that carriage; it had, I remember, a nasty, musty smell of damp straw and stale eggs, and it seemed to confine me so closely as though it were determined that, once I was in, I should never get out again. Then, it was bitterly cold; I was colder during that drive than I have ever been before or since. It was that penetrating cold that seems to pierce your very brain, so that I could not think with any clearness, but only wish again and again that I hadn't come. Of course, I could see nothing—only feel the jolt over the uneven road—and once and again we seemed to fight our way through dark paths, because I could feel the overhanging branches of the trees knock against the cab with mysterious taps, as though they were trying to give me some urgent message.

'Well, I mustn't make more of it than the facts allow, and I mustn't see into it all the significance of the events that followed. I only know that as the drive proceeded I became more and more miserable: miserable with the cold of my body, the misgivings of my imagination, the general loneliness of my case.

'At last we stopped. The old scarecrow got slowly off his box, with many heavings and sighings, came to the cab door, and, with great difficulty and irritating slowness, opened it. I got out of it, and found that the snow was now falling very heavily indeed, and that the path was lighted with its soft, mysterious glow. Before me was a humped and ungainly shadow: the house that was to receive me. I could make nothing of it in that darkness, but only stood there shivering while the old man pulled at the door-bell with a sort of frantic energy as though he were anxious to be rid of the whole job as quickly as possible and return to his own place. At last, after what seemed an endless time, the door opened, and an old man, who might have been own brother to the driver, poked out his head. The two old men talked together, and at last my bag was shouldered and I was permitted to come in out of the piercing cold.

'Now this, I know, is not imagination. I have never at any period of my life hated at first sight so vigorously any dwelling-place into which I have ever entered as I did that house. There was nothing especially disagreeable about my first vision of the hall. It was a large, dark place, lit by two dim lamps, cold and cheerless; but I got no particular impression of it because at once I was conducted out of it, led along a passage, and then introduced into a room which was, I saw, as warm and comfortable as the hall had been dark and dismal. I was, in fact, so eagerly pleased at the large and leaping fire that I moved towards it at once, not noting, at the first moment, the presence of my host; and when I did see him I could not believe that it was he. I have told you the kind of man that I had expected; but, instead of the sparse, sensitive artist, I found facing me a large burly man, over six foot, I should fancy, as broad-shouldered as he was tall, giving evidence of great muscular strength, the lower part of his face hidden by a black, pointed beard.

'But if I was astonished at the sight of him, I was doubly amazed when he spoke. His voice was thin and piping, like that of some old woman, and the little nervous gestures that he made with his hands were even more feminine than his voice. But I had to allow, perhaps, for excitement, for excited he was; he came up to me, took my hand in both of his, and held it as though he would never let it go. In the evening he apologised for this. "I was so glad to see you," he said; "I couldn't believe that really you would come; you are the first visitor of my own kind that I have had here for ever so long. I was ashamed, indeed, of asking you, but I had to snatch at the chance—it means so much to me."

'His eagerness, in fact, had something disturbing about it; something pathetic, too. He simply couldn't do too much for me: he led me through funny crumbling old passages, the boards creaking under us at every step, up some dark stairs, the walls hung, so far as I could see in the dim light, with faded yellow photographs of places, and showed me into my room with a deprecating agitated gesture as though he expected me at the first sight of it to turn and run. I didn't like it any more than I liked the rest of the house; but that was not my host's fault. He had done everything he possibly could for me: there was a large fire flaming in the open fireplace, there was a hot bottle, as he explained to me, in the big four-poster bed, and the old man who had opened the door to me was already taking my clothes out of my bag and putting them away. Lunt's nervousness was almost sentimental. He put both his hands on my shoulders and said, looking at me pleadingly: "If you only knew what it is for me to have you here, the talks we'll have. Well, well, I must leave you. You'll come down and join me, won't you, as soon as you can?"

'It was then, when I was left alone in my room, that I had my second impulse to flee. Four candles in tall old silver candlesticks were burning brightly, and these, with the blazing fire, gave plenty of light; and yet the room was in some way dim, as though a faint smoke pervaded it, and I remember that I went to one of the old lattice windows and threw it open for a moment as though I felt stifled. Two things quickly made me close it. One was the intense cold which, with a fluttering scamper of snow, blew into the room; the other was the quite deafening roar of the sea, which seemed to fling itself at my very face as though it wanted to knock me down. I quickly shut the window, turned round, and saw an old woman standing just inside the door. Now every story of this kind depends for its interest on its verisimilitude. Of course, to make my tale convincing I should be able to prove to you that I saw that old woman; but I can't. I can only urge upon you my rather dreary reputation of probity. You know that I'm a teetotaller, and always have been, and, most important evidence of all, I was not expecting to see an old woman; and yet I hadn't the least doubt in the world but that it was an old woman I saw. You may talk about shadows, clothes hanging on the back of the door, and the rest of it. I don't know. I've no theories about this story, I'm not a spiritualist, I don't know that I believe in anything especially, except the beauty of beautiful things. We'll put it, if you like, that I fancied that I saw an old woman, and my fancy was so strong that I can give you to this day a pretty detailed account of her appearance. She wore a black silk dress, and on her breast was a large, ugly gold brooch; she had black hair, brushed back from her forehead and parted down the middle; she wore a collar of some white stuff round her throat; her face was one of the wickedest, most malignant and furtive that I have ever seen—very white in colour. She was shrivelled enough now, but might once have been rather beautiful. She stood there quietly, her hands at her side. I thought that she was some kind of housekeeper. "I have everything I want, thank you," I said. "What a splendid fire!" I turned for a moment towards it, and when I looked back she was gone. I thought nothing of this, of course, but drew up an old chair covered with green faded tapestry, and thought that I would read a little from some book that I had brought down with me, before I went to join my host. The fact was that I was not very intent upon joining him before I must. I didn't like him. I had already made up my mind that I would find some excuse to return to London as soon as possible. I can't tell you why I didn't like him, except that I was myself very reserved and had, like many Englishmen, a great distrust of demonstrations, especially from another man. I hadn't cared for the way in which he had put his hands on my shoulders, and I felt perhaps that I wouldn't be able to live up to all his eager excitement about me.

'I sat in my chair and took up my book, but I had not been reading for more than two minutes before I was conscious of a most unpleasant smell. Now, there are all sorts of smells—healthy and otherwise—but I think the nastiest is that chilly kind of odour that comes from bad sanitation and stuffy rooms combined; you meet it sometimes at little country inns and decrepit town lodgings. This smell was so definite that I could almost locate it; it came from near the door. I got up, approached the door, and at once it was as though I were drawing near to somebody who, if you'll forgive the impoliteness, was not accustomed to taking too many baths. I drew back just as I might had an actual person been there. Then quite suddenly the smell was gone, the room was fresh, and I saw, to my surprise, that one of the windows had opened and that snow was again blowing in. I closed it and went downstairs.

'The evening that followed was odd enough. My host was not in himself an unlikable man; he did his very utmost to please me. He had a fine culture and a wide knowledge of books and things. He became quite cheerful as the evening went on; gave me a good dinner in a funny little dining-room hung with some admirable mezzotints. The serving-man looked after us—a funny old man, with a long white beard like a goat—and, oddly enough, it was from him that I first recaught my earlier apprehension. He had just put the dessert on the table, had arranged my plate in front of me, when I saw him give a start and look towards the door. My attention was attracted to this because his hand, as it touched the plate, suddenly trembled. My eyes followed, but I could see nothing. That he was frightened of something was perfectly clear, and then (it may, of course, very easily have been fancy) I thought that I detected once more that strange unwholesome smell.

'I forgot this again when we were both seated in front of a splendid fire in the library. Lunt had a very fine collection of books, and it was delightful to him, as it is to every book-collector, to have somebody with him who could really appreciate them. We stood looking at one book after another and talking eagerly about some of the minor early English novelists who were my especial hobby—Bage, Godwin, Henry Mackenzie, Mrs. Shelley, Mat Lewis and others—when once again he affected me most unpleasantly by putting his arm round my shoulders. I have all my life disliked intensely to be touched by certain people. I suppose we all feel like this. It is one of those inexplicable things; and I disliked this so much that I abruptly drew away.

'Instantly he was changed into a man of furious and ungovernable rage; I thought that he was going to strike me. He stood there quivering all over, the words pouring out of his mouth incoherently, as though he were mad and did not know what he was saying. He accused me of insulting him, of abusing his hospitality, of throwing his kindness back into his face, and of a thousand other ridiculous things; and I can't tell you how strange it was to hear all this coming out in that shrill piping voice as though it were from an agitated woman, and yet to see with one's eyes that big, muscular frame, those immense shoulders and that dark-bearded face.

'I said nothing. I am, physically, a coward. I dislike, above anything else in the world, any sort of quarrel. At last I brought out, "I am very sorry. I didn't mean anything. Please forgive me," and then hurriedly turned to leave the room. At once he changed again; now he was almost in tears. He implored me not to go; said it was his wretched temper, but that he was so miserable and unhappy, and had for so long now been alone and desolate that he hardly knew what he was doing. He begged me to give him another chance, and if I would only listen to his story I would perhaps be more patient with him.

'At once, so oddly is man constituted, I changed in my feelings towards him. I was very sorry for him. I saw that he was a man on the edge of his nerves, and that he really did need some help and sympathy, and would be quite distracted if he could not get it. I put my hand on his shoulder to quiet him and to show him that I bore no malice, and I felt that his great body was quivering from head to foot. We sat down again, and in an odd, rambling manner he told me his story. It amounted to very little, and the gist of it was that, rather to have some sort of companionship than from any impulse of passion, he had married some fifteen years before the daughter of a neighbouring clergyman. They had had no very happy life together, and at the last, he told me quite frankly, he had hated her. She had been mean, overbearing, and narrow-minded; it had been, he confessed, nothing but a relief to him when, just a year ago, she had suddenly died from heart failure. He had thought then that things would go better with him, but they had not; nothing had gone right with him since. He hadn't been able to work, many of his friends had ceased to come to see him, he had found it even difficult to get servants to stay with him, he was desperately lonely, he slept badly—that was why his temper was so terribly on edge. He had no one in the house with him save the old man, who was, fortunately, an excellent cook, and a boy—the old man's grandson. "Oh, I thought," I said, "that that excellent meal to-night was cooked by your housekeeper." "My housekeeper?" he answered. "There's no woman in the house." "Oh, but one came to my room," I replied, "this evening —an old lady-like-looking person in a black silk dress." "You were mistaken," he answered in the oddest voice, as though he were exerting all the strength that he possessed to keep himself quiet and controlled. "I am sure that I saw her," I answered. "There couldn't be any mistake." And I described her to him. "You were mistaken," he repeated again. "Don't you see that you must have been when I tell you there is no woman in the house?" I reassured him quickly lest there should be another outbreak of rage. Then there followed the strangest kind of appeal. Urgently, as though his very life depended upon it, he begged me to stay with him for a few days. He implied, although he said nothing definitely, that he was in great trouble, that if only I would stay for a few days all would be well, that if ever in all my life I had had a chance of doing a kind action I had one now, that he couldn't expect me to stop in so dreary a place, but that he would never forget it if I did. He spoke in a voice of such urgent distress that I comforted him as I might a child, promising that I would stay, and shaking hands with him on it as though it were a kind of solemn oath between us.

II

'I am sure that you would wish me to give you this incident as it occurred, and if the final catastrophe seems to come, as it were, accidentally, I can only say to you that that was how it happened. It is since the event that I have tried to put two and two together, and that they don't altogether make four is the fault that mine shares, I suppose, with every true ghost story.

'But the truth is that after that very strange episode between us I had a very good night. I slept the sleep of all justice, cosy and warm, in my four-poster, with the murmur of the sea beyond the windows to rock my slumbers. Next morning too was bright and cheerful, the sun sparkling down on the snow, and the snow sparkling back to the sun as though they were glad to see one another. I had a very pleasant morning looking at Lunt's books, talking to him, and writing one or two letters. I must say that, after all, I liked the man. His appeal to me on the night before had touched me. So few people, you see, had ever appealed to me about anything. His nervousness was there and the constant sense of apprehension, yet he seemed to be putting the best face on it, doing his utmost to set me at my ease in order to induce me to stay, I suppose, and to give him a little of that company that he so terribly needed. I dare say if I had not been so busy about the books I would not have been so happy. There was a strange eerie silence about that house if one ever stopped to listen; and once, I remember, sitting at the old bureau writing a letter, I raised my head and looked up, and caught Lunt watching as though he wondered whether I had heard or noticed anything. And so I listened too, and it seemed to me as though someone were on the other side of the library door with their hand raised to knock; a quaint notion, with nothing to support it, but I could have sworn that if I had gone to the door and opened it suddenly someone would have been there.

'However, I was cheerful enough, and after lunch quite happy. Lunt asked me if I would like a walk, and I said I would; and we started out in the sunshine over the crunching snow towards the sea. I don't remember what we talked of; we seemed to be now quite at our ease with one another. We crossed the fields to a certain point, looked down at the sea—smooth now, like silk—and turned back. I remember that I was so cheerful that I seemed suddenly to take a happy view of all my prospects. I began to confide in Lunt, telling him of my little plans, of my hopes for the book that I was then writing, and even began rather timidly to suggest to him that perhaps we should do something together; that what we both needed was a friend of common taste with ourselves. I know that I was talking on, that we had crossed a little village street, and were turning up the path towards the dark avenue of trees that led to his house, when suddenly the change came.

'What I first noticed was that he was not listening to me; his gaze was fixed beyond me, into the very heart of the black clump of trees that fringed the silver landscape. I looked too, and my heart bounded. There was, standing just in front of the trees, as though she were waiting for us, the old woman whom I had seen in my room the night before. I stopped. "Why, there she is!" I said. "That's the old woman of whom I was speaking—the old woman who came to my room." He caught my shoulder with his hand. "There's nothing there," he said. "Don't you see that that's shadow? What's the matter with you? Can't you see that there's nothing?" I stepped forward, and there was nothing, and I wouldn't, to this day, be able to tell you whether it was hallucination or not. I can only say that, from that moment, the afternoon appeared to become dark. As we entered into the avenue of trees, silently and hurrying as though someone were behind us, the dusk seemed to have fallen so that I could scarcely see my way. We reached the house breathless. He hastened into his study as though I were not with him, but I followed and, closing the door behind me, said, with all the force that I had at command: "Now, what is this? What is it that's troubling you? You must tell me! How can I help you if you don't?" And he replied, in so strange a voice that it was as though he had gone out of his mind: "I tell you there's nothing. Can't you believe me when I tell you there's nothing at all? I'm quite all right.... Oh, my God!—my God! ... don't leave me! ... This is the very day—the very night she said.... But I did nothing, I tell you—I did nothing—it's only her beastly malice...." He broke off. He still held my arm with his hand. He made strange movements, wiping his forehead as though it were damp with sweat, almost pleading with me; then suddenly angry again, then beseeching once more, as though I had refused him the one thing he wanted.

'I saw that he was truly not far from madness, and I began myself to have a sudden terror of this damp, dark house, this great, trembling man, and something more that was worse than they. But I pitied him. How could you or any man have helped it? I made him sit down in the armchair beside the fire, which had now dwindled to a few glimmering red coals. I let him hold me close to him with his arm and clutch my hand with his, and I repeated, as quietly as I might: "But tell me; don't be afraid, whatever it is you have done. Tell me what danger it is you fear, and then we can face it together." "Fear! fear!" he repeated; and then, with a mighty effort which I could not but admire, he summoned all his control. "I'm off my head," he said, "with loneliness and depression. My wife died a year ago on this very night.

We hated one another. I couldn't be sorry when she died, and she knew it. When that last heart attack came on, between her gasps she told me that she would return, and I've always dreaded this night. That's partly why I asked you to come, to have some-one here, anybody, and you've been very kind—more kind than I had any right to expect. You must think me insane, going on like this, but see me through to-night and we'll have splendid times together. Don't desert me now—now, of all times!" I promised that I would not. I soothed him as best I could. We sat there, for I know not how long, through the gathering dark; we neither of us moved, the fire died out, and the room was lit with a strange dim glow that came from the snowy landscape beyond the uncur-tained windows. Ridiculous, perhaps, as I look back at it. We sat there, I in a chair close to his, hand in hand, like a couple of lovers; but, in real truth, two men terrified, fearful of what was coming, and unable to do anything to meet it.

'I think that that was perhaps the queerest part of it; a sort of paralysis that crept over me. What would you or anyone else have done—summoned the old man, gone down to the village inn, fetched the local doctor? I could do nothing but see the snow-shine move like trembling water about the furniture and hear, through the urgent silence, the faint hoot of an owl from the trees in the wood.

III

'Oddly enough, I can remember nothing, try as I may, between that strange vigil and the moment when I myself, wak-ened out of a brief sleep, sat up in bed to see Lunt standing inside my room holding a candle. He was wearing a nightshirt, and looked huge in the candlelight, his black beard falling intensely dark on the white stuff of his shirt. He came very quietly towards my bed, the candle throwing flickering shadows about the room. When he spoke it was in a voice low and subdued, almost a whis-per. "Would you come," he asked, "only for half an hour—just for half an hour?" he repeated, staring at me as though he didn't know me. "I'm unhappy without somebody—very unhappy." Then he looked over his shoulder, held the candle high above his

head, and stared piercingly at every part of the room. I could see
that something had happened to him, that he had taken another
step into the country of Fear—a step that had withdrawn him
from me and from every other human being. He whispered:
"When you come, tread softly; I don't want anyone to hear us."
I did what I could. I got out of bed, put on my dressing-gown
and slippers, and tried to persuade him to stay with me. The fire
was almost dead, but I told him that we would build it up again,
and that we would sit there and wait for the morning; but no,
he repeated again and again: "It's better in my own room; we're
safer there." "Safe from what?" I asked him, making him look at
me. "Lunt, wake up! You're as though you were asleep. There's
nothing to fear. We've nobody but ourselves. Stay here and let
us talk, and have done with this nonsense." But he wouldn't
answer; only drew me forward down the dark passage, and then
turned into his room, beckoning me to follow. He got into bed
and sat hunched up there, his hands holding his knees, staring at
the door, and every once and again shivering with a little tremor.
The only light in the room was that from the candle, now burning low, and the only sound was the purring whisper of the sea.

'It seemed to make little difference to him that I was there.
He did not look at me, but only at the door, and when I spoke to
him he did not answer me nor seem to hear what I had said. I sat
down beside the bed and, in order to break the silence, talked on
about anything, about nothing, and was dropping off, I think,
into a confused doze, when I heard his voice breaking across
mine. Very clearly and distinctly he said: "If I killed her, she
deserved it; she was never a good wife to me, not from the first;
she shouldn't have irritated me as she did—she knew what my
temper was. She had a worse one than mine, though. She can't
touch me; I'm as strong as she is." And it was then, as clearly as
I can now remember, that his voice suddenly sank into a sort of
gentle whisper, as though he were almost glad that his fears had
been confirmed. He whispered: "She's there!" I cannot possibly
describe to you how that whisper seemed to let Fear loose like
water through my body. I could see nothing—the candle was
flaming high in the last moments of its life—I could see nothing; but Lunt suddenly screamed, with a shrill cry like a tortured

animal in agony: "Keep her off me, keep her away from me, keep her off—keep her off!" He caught me, his hands digging into my shoulders; then, with an awful effect of constricted muscles, as though rigor had caught and held him, his arms slowly fell away, he slipped back on to the bed as though someone were pushing him, his hands fell against the sheet, his whole body jerked with a convulsive effort, and then he rolled over. I saw nothing; only, quite distinctly, in my nostrils was that same fœtid odour that I had known on the preceding evening. I rushed to the door, opened it, shouted down the long passage again and again, and soon the old man came running. I sent him for the doctor, and then could not return to the room, but stood there listening, hearing nothing save the whisper of the sea, the loud ticking of the hall clock. I flung open the window at the end of the passage; the sea rushed in with its precipitant roar; some bells chimed the hour. Then at last, beating into myself more courage, I turned back towards the room. . . .'

'Well?' I asked as Runciman paused. 'He was dead, of course?'

'Dead, the doctor afterwards said, of heart failure.'

'Well?' I asked again.

'That's all.' Runciman paused. 'I don't know whether you can even call it a ghost story. My idea of the old woman may have been all hallucination. I don't even know whether his wife was like that when she was alive. She may have been large and fat. Lunt died of an evil conscience.'

'Yes,' I said.

'The only thing,' Runciman added at last, after a long pause, 'is that on Lunt's body there were marks—on his neck especially, some on his chest—as of fingers pressing in, scratches and dull blue marks. He may, in his terror, have caught at his own throat. . . .'

'Yes,' I said again.

'Anyway'—Runciman shivered—'I don't like Cornwall—beastly county. Queer things happen there—something in the air. . . .'

'So I've heard,' I answered.

SENTIMENTAL BUT TRUE

Mrs. Comber had no idea where it came from. She had been sitting on the green, sloping cliff at Rafiel, a fishing village on the south coast of Cornwall, looking at the sea, and suddenly it came up to her.

'Came' is perhaps an inaccurate word—'rolled' or 'tumbled' would describe more nearly its motion, although even then one conveys no sense of its sudden, abrupt halt, a check so sharp that it seemed as though the dog must, by the force of it, be tumbled backwards.

It had come so suddenly from nowhere that Mrs. Comber of course expected that, in a moment, someone (its master or mistress) would turn the corner and summon it down the hill. But the minutes passed and no one came, and the sun continued to blaze out of burning blue into burning blue, and little Rafiel lay on its back down in the valley behind the hill and simmered, and the dog sat there motionless, frozen into amazement at the vision of Mrs. Comber.

Mrs. Comber knew very little about dogs, but she knew enough to be sure that there was no other dog in the world quite like this one.

He might have been, were he smaller, a Yorkshire terrier, or, were he very, very much larger, a sheepdog. He had, too, a dash of Skye. He was small but remarkably square, so square that he bore a distinct resemblance to the popular conception of a sea-captain. Hair that was turned up at the ends of it into little curls by the wind fell all about him—over his eyes, spreading into an American sharp-pointed beard under his chin, making his legs like the legs of an Eskimo, waving in frantic agitation all round his stump of a tail. His nose, like a wet black button, and his mouth, with an under-lip that went back in rather a melancholy curve, were his most certain features, but his eyes, when his hair allowed you to see them, were a beautiful melting brown.

Perhaps the most amazing thing about him was that the

second half of his body was quite different from the first half, being broader and thicker, so that he seemed to have been the complete result of two divided dogs—and these two had been rather badly glued together.

He looked at Mrs. Comber and then he laughed. He gave two short, sharp barks and wagged his stump of a tail.

Mrs. Comber was large and highly coloured. Her face was stout and good-natured; her eyes appealed to you as though they said, 'I know that I'm silly and stupid and scatter-brained, but do try to find something to like in me.'

She liked to wear purple or bright green or red; she always looked untidy and a little dusty; she was always in a breathless hurry, hastening to do something that she had forgotten, and so forgetting something that she ought already to have done. She loved to be liked, and therefore seized at any sign of goodwill, but she always made advances too quickly, was flung back, and, with tears, determined that she'd never make advances to anyone again, and then made them again immediately.

Her husband was stupid, conventional, self-opinionated, and an entirely self-satisfied man, who took his wife for granted, and thought she was lucky to be allowed to serve his wants. He was a master at Moffatt's, a school not far from Rafiel, and there he had been during twenty years of his life, and would be in all probability for twenty years more. He liked food and golf and bridge and arguments and putting people in their places. He despised his wife in her sentimental moments and disliked her in her careless ones, but on the whole he found her useful.

Mrs. Comber had felt lonely and just a little depressed. Certainly this fine weather was very wonderful, and it was a great deal better—oh, yes! a *great* deal better—than that miserable wet time that they had had during their first days in Rafiel, but it *did* mean that her husband disappeared every morning with his golf-clubs and was no more seen until the evening, when he was too tired to talk.

No one, up at the *pension* where they were staying, appealed to her except a girl, Miss Salter, who was at the present moment occupied with a young man who was expected very shortly to propose.

So, in spite of her protestations, Mrs. Comber was lonely. Up at the villa she said, 'I can't tell you how delightful it is just pottering about by myself all about the little place. One gets to know the villagers so well. They are always so glad to see one, so friendly, it's quite like home. I've never enjoyed myself so much.'

But the honest truth was that Mrs. Comber longed for company. As the wife of a schoolmaster she had during the greater part of the year more than enough of her fellow creatures. One might have supposed that solitude would be pleasant for a little time. So in theory it was. During the heat and battle of term-time, to be alone seemed the most fortunate of destinies. But now in practice—now!

Mrs. Comber looked at the blue sea and the green cliffs and longed for conversation, affection, the positive proof that there was someone in the world—scoundrel or vagabond, it did not matter—who was at that moment desiring her company.

Well, the dog desired it. Of that there could be no possible doubt. His brown eyes, through the tangled hair, gazed at Mrs. Comber with the utmost devotion. Then, his whole body quivering, his lip drew back and he grinned, the most pathetic, urgent, wheedling grin.

Down upon the black rocks far below, the gulls, like flakes of snow, hovered and wheeled, rose and fell. The sea broke into crisp patterns along the shore; its lazy murmur mingled with the hum of bees behind her, among the honeysuckle.

Round the point the Rafiel fishing-boats, with their orange sails, stole as though bent on some secret, nefarious business.

Mrs. Comber, who was emotional and completely at the mercy of fine weather and a coloured world, felt that her heart was full. She drew the dog towards her.

II

Seven o'clock struck suddenly down in the valley, and Mrs. Comber ceased her conversation with the dog and pulled herself together.

Meanwhile, she had told the dog everything. She had explained to him that apparently hopeless paradox that, although one was longing for peace and quiet, yet nevertheless one hated solitude. She explained to him all the disadvantages of having to do with schools most of one's life, and at the same time gave him to understand that she was not complaining, and that many poor people had much worse times, and that most of her troubles came from the difficulties of her own temperament, from her impetuosity and clumsiness and bad memory for detail.

The dog understood every word of it.

He had a way of sitting with one of his back legs stretched out in a straight line from his body, so that he seemed more certainly than ever to be compounded of two different dogs. His brown eyes gazed sadly out to sea, but every now and again he bent forward and licked her hand. She had now no sense, when she had finished her impetuous disclosures, of shame because she had been too garrulous, too intimate, too confiding. The dog could have listened to a great deal more.

He followed closely at her side as she walked down the hill. She had still, at the back of her brain, a confused sense that his master would suddenly appear round the corner. She would be very sorry when he was taken away from her.

He ran on in front of her, ran back, jumped upon her, showed himself in every way delighted at the afternoon's events. When he ran, he ran like a rabbit with his stump of a tail in the air, his head down, his ears flapping, and his legs scattering.

The evening scents stole out upon the air. The little square harbour was starred and crossed with reflected lights—blue and brown and grey. The crooked streets flung voices from one corner to another and one evening star came out.

Mrs. Comber climbed the opposite hill up to Sea View Villa, and still the dog was with her.

At one of the little cottages she stopped for a moment to speak to Mr. Tregatta, known in the village by the title of 'Captain.' Captain Tregatta, although he was sixty-two, looked not a day more than forty. He was short and square, with the compact, buttoned look that years in the navy give a man. He had retired now and received a small pension weekly.

He lived for two things—his son and music—and he had

talked a good deal to Mrs. Comber about both of these things. His son was in a hosier's in Bristol, and he had not, during the last five years, found time to come and pay his father a visit, and had quite plainly expressed his wish that his father should not come and visit him. So his father had waited, and now, as Mrs. Comber knew, the son was at last coming home.

'To-morrer,' said the captain, as he gave Mrs. Comber good evening, 'to-morrer the lad's comin', bless 'is 'eart. "Inconvenient, dad, though it is," 'e writes to me, "I wouldn't disappoint 'ee"— no, nor 'e wouldn't, bless 'ee.'

'I'm sure I'm very glad,' said Mrs. Comber, a little doubtfully, wondering whether the reality of this reluctant son from a Bristol hosier's would be quite so glorious as the anticipation. She liked the little captain better than anyone in Rafiel. He had a mild blue eye, a most sentimental heart, and he was lonely.

'That's a nice little dawg,' eyeing Mrs. Comber's shaggy admirer, who was sitting now with his leg out and his lip in.

'Yes,' said Mrs. Comber eagerly. 'I don't know whom it belongs to. It just came along and attached itself to me. Dogs are so confiding, aren't they? And, really, it's a nice little creature. Yes —well, if you hear of anyone who's lost one, Captain Tregatta. Good-night.'

She climbed the hill and did hope, as she went, that the son would not turn out too dreadfully disappointing—five years in a hosier's shop could make such a difference.

It was then, as the hideous front of Sea View Villa shone horribly before her, that she first seriously confronted the question of the dog. He, she could perceive, had no question at all as to what she would do with him, and his confidence alone would have made it difficult for her to dismiss him.

But she knew, assuredly, without any question of his attitude to her, that she could not leave him. It might be only for to-night. Probably in the morning someone would come and claim him. But to-night she must keep him.

Then, as she drew nearer Sea View Villa, she knew that she would need all her courage. Had she been of the type that per-petually accuses Fate she would have taken this moment as only another instance of the way that she was for ever driven into the ludicrous. Other human beings passed through life gathering what they desired, achieving their aims, always, to the end, preserving their dignity. But she——

Years ago, when she had first married Freddie Comber, she had told herself that, whatever happened, for his sake as well as her own, she must henceforth never be absurd.

And since then, beyond her agency, without any action on her part, she was driven again and again into ridiculous situations. She was always being driven into them. Things that others could achieve without danger were, for her, beset with difficulties. Always the laughing audience, always that amused anticipation 'that Mrs. Comber would put her foot into it.'

Well, for herself, she might perhaps endure it, but Freddie did hate it so. He hated it, and he showed her that he hated it.

Now, once again, when an ordinary person could arrive with perfect security at a *pension* with a strange dog, Mrs. Comber knew that, for herself, it would be a position of danger and insecurity. Freddie liked dogs—of his own discovering—but he would hate this one. The others, with the exception of Miss Salter, would see in it 'another of Mrs. Comber's funny ways.' Mrs. Pentaglos, the head of Sea View Villa, would be kind and polite, but she would disapprove.

For an instant Mrs. Comber hesitated. Then, remembering that long exchange of intimacies on the cliff, she marched boldly forward.

III

She had hoped that, on this one occasion, Fortune would favour her, would permit her to creep round at the back with the dog and put him in the outhouse, then gradually, at her own time, she might explain to them his presence. But no. How like Fortune's treatment of her! There, to her horror, she saw them all, taking their last glimpse at a magnificent sunset, sitting in the little green strip of garden.

She could not escape them. Freddie, just returned from golf, was standing, in radiant glow from the sunset, enormous, important, in the fullest of plus fours.

She heard him say, 'You can take my opinion for what it is worth, Mrs. Cronnel. I don't pretend to be one of these brainy fellows.'

She'd heard him say that so often before. Mrs. Cronnel, always fat and yellow, but now under the sunset positively golden, was filling a large easy-chair and was looking up into Freddie Comber's face with rapt attention. Miss Bride and Miss Salter, two young ladies who were rivals for the hand of Mr. Salmon, the only bachelor resident at Sea View Villa, were saying bitter things to one another in a sprightly and amiable manner.

All these people turned at the sound of Mrs. Comber's feet upon the gravel and saw her, flushed, untidy, agitated, with a strange dog at her side. Mrs. Cronnel, who for obvious reasons hated Mrs. Comber, cried, with a shrill scream, 'Oh! a dog!'

Otherwise there was silence.

Mrs. Comber, laughing nervously, came forward.

'Oh! I didn't know you'd all be here; that is, I might have guessed that you'd all be looking at the sunset—so natural—but here you all are. Yes, I've found a dog, such a dear little thing, and it would come all the way with me, although I did try to send it back. I *did* really. But you know what dogs are, Mrs. Cronnel.' (Mrs. Cronnel, who detested dogs, obviously, from her expression, declined to have any knowledge of them whatever.) 'I hadn't the heart, I hadn't really. Isn't he jolly? A Yorkshire, I think, only he's rather large. He's so hairy I think I shall call him Rags.'

Mrs. Comber paused.

Mrs. Cronnel said, with a cruel little smile, 'Rather a common-place name for a dog, Mrs. Comber.'

Mrs. Comber laughed nervously. 'Oh, do you think so? Perhaps it is.'

Then there was a long pause. The dog looked at them all and understood at once that he was not likely to be very popular there. But he had, in all probability, been received doubtfully before on other occasions. He was brave; he smiled at them all, wagged his tail, went into the middle of them, pretended to see an enemy, growled; rolled on his back, finally sat up, and, with one ear back, lifted his blackberry nose towards Mr. Comber with the most amiable of interrogations.

Freddie Comber looked at him, then across at his wife. 'What a cur!' he snapped, and vanished.

Mrs. Comber slowly coloured, and a little smile, intended for bravery, but too struggling and fugitive for success, came and passed.

They all saw it, and even in Mrs. Cronnel's dry heart there was sympathy. Miss Salter fell on her knees before the dog.

'You darling! You really are! Oh, Mrs. Comber, how splendid of you to find him! I know Mrs. Pentaglos won't mind. He can be kept in the stable. And he looks as good as gold. I *know* he's adorable.'

To all the women, as they stood there with the dusk coming up about them, there came the thought that men were beasts, that women must band together, that no woman in the world could ever be as cruel as Mr. Comber had been. For the moment they came together—Miss Bride and Miss Salter, Mrs. Comber and Mrs. Cronnel.

'I knew you'd all love him,' said Mrs. Comber, in an ecstasy.

IV

Freddie Comber was one of those men who say a thing by accident and then afterwards cling to what they have said as though it were the key-note of their lives. He liked dogs—he had always liked them.

Had Mrs. Cronnel found the dog, or had even his own Mrs. Comber brought it to him at a propitious moment—when he was flushed with success at golf or billiards or argument—he would in all probability have taken the dog to himself, acclaimed it as his own find, petted and indulged it.

But his wife had arrived at a moment when he was explaining the world to sympathetic listeners, she had looked foolish and frightened—the dog had been condemned.

He had called the dog a cur in public, therefore must the dog always be a cur. His wife had been foolish about the dog in the beginning, therefore must she always be considered foolish. The dog was a nuisance, his wife was a fool—so must things remain.

He regarded Rags, therefore, with exceeding disgust, and the secret affection that he felt for him in his heart only spurred him to further obstinate exhibitions of his disgust.

At any rate, the dog must be a wastrel of the very worst description, because nobody came to claim him. It was obvious to any intelligent person that his former owner had desired anxiously to be rid of him. Probably the dog had some horrible disease or infirmity. Probably he had a vicious temper and bit children and horses. Drowning was much the best thing.

'I know a bit about dogs,' he would say a hundred times a day, 'and if ever there was a cur——'

Secretly, in his heart, he admired it. With the other inhabitants of Sea View Villa Rags had instantly won his way.

He was a dog of the most engaging character in the world and of an amazing intuition. He realised, for instance, that what Mrs. Cronnel liked was for people to be deferential to her, to listen and to admire. He therefore lay at her feet and looked up at her golden locks with the burning eyes of a devout adorer. He never practised upon her his humour, of which he had a vast store. She did not understand humour.

He kept his humour for Miss Salter, in whom it lay dormant, waiting for encouragement. Miss Salter had been too anxiously engaged in landing Mr. Salmon to see anything in a very humorous light, but Rags restored to her the funny side of things and was never serious with her for a moment.

To Mrs. Pentaglos he paid the deference that is due to the head of an establishment, to one who may dismiss you in an instant into an outhouse if she so pleases. He was always very staid and respectful to Mrs. Pentaglos.

But it was to Mrs. Comber only that he gave his heart.

The two of them discovered during the weeks that they were together a thousand things that they had in common. They were really very alike in many ways, except that the dog had far more tact, adapted himself much more swiftly to the atmosphere about him. Mrs. Comber herself perceived this. She saw that the dog at Sea View Villa was a very different dog from the dog down in Rafiel. At the villa he was ordinary, amusing on the surface. He did little tricks; he played in an amiable manner on the grass; he allowed himself to be petted by Miss Salter or Mrs. Pentaglos. Down in the narrow little streets of the village he was a dog of importance and also a dog of mysterious perceptions and intuitions.

Mrs. Comber felt that, with the dog at her side, she was more at home among those cobbles, bending roofs, sudden glimpses of blue water, and clustered fishing-boats than she ever was alone. Rags knew every inhabitant; he selected the good from the bad, the worthy from the unworthy; he was treated with a deference by the other dogs of the place that was remarkable indeed, for the dogs of Rafiel were a wild and savage race.

To Mrs. Comber the effect of it all was astonishing—it was as though the dog were, through all these weeks, explaining the place to her. She felt it—the mysterious, subtle life of it—so poignantly that the knowledge that in another week or two she must be uprooted from it all and go back to her commonplace, workaday Moffatt's—little boys, mutton underdone, Freddie overdone—seemed to her, through these glorious hours, an incredible disaster.

She couldn't go back—she couldn't go back. Then, coming to herself, she laughed. Had she not lived that life for all these past years? Could one always expect holiday?

Then also, perhaps, if the dog had so lightened this place for her he would also lighten Moffatt's in the same way. She must take him back—she *must* take him back. Would Freddie allow it? He *must* allow it. This time she would have her way.

Of all the Rafiel natives Rags liked best Captain Tregatta. The little man had an affection for all animals, but perhaps it was because he represented more truly than any other inhabitant the Rafiel spirit that Rags liked him so much. They had always, when they were together, an air of the most complete understanding. Captain Tregatta did not find it necessary to speak to Rags as he would to an ordinary dog. Words were not needed.

Mrs. Comber, indeed, almost resented a feeling that she had when she was with them both that she was 'out of it.'

Rags did not like young Tregatta from Bristol. He would go nowhere near him. He would neither bark nor smile, wag nor quiver. He would cut him dead.

Mrs. Comber did not like the young man either. He was thin, with lank black hair, watery eyes and a pallid cheek. His ears stood out from his head like wings. He patronised and sneered at his father. He always 'washed his hands' as he came towards Mrs. Comber, and obviously found it very difficult to refrain from saying, 'And what can I do for you today, madam?'

They stood, all four, outside Captain Tregatta's cottage. Young Tregatta said:

'Well, it 'as been a fine day, ma'am.'

'Yes,' said Mrs. Comber, who was always at her most voluble when she was in company that she disliked. 'It has—really wonderful; so much colour and sun. I——'

'My boy's had a fine outing to-day, haven't yer, John? We went and picnicked up along to Durotter, us and the Simpsons and Mrs.——'

'All right, father,' the young man interrupted. 'Stow it. Stupid day, I call it.'

He caught Rags's eye. Rags was regarding him with a cold and haughty malevolence. He bent down and snapped his fingers. '*Goo*' dog—*goo*' doggie! Come along then.'

Rags did nothing, but continued to stare. Mrs. Comber wished them good-night and passed up the hill. How she disliked the young man! The captain had a wistful look; she was sure that the son had been a great disappointment. What a horrid mess towns could make of a man!

v

And now was she horribly driven in upon her climax. Never in all her married life before had she so eagerly desired a request to be granted by Freddie. Never before had she faced the approaching moment of demand with such sinkings of the heart.

They had only another three days before they must return to Moffatt's, and with every instant of the swiftly vanishing time the spell of Rafiel increased. Could she take Rags back with her to her daily life, then she would seem to be taking with her some of the adorable things that belonged to Rafiel. He would remind her of some of the most precious moments of her life.

But, indeed, of himself now he had contrived to squeeze himself into her heart. Whatever part she might play to herself, God knew that for many years that heart had been empty. But Rags had wanted it and had taken it.

She watched Freddie's every movement now to give her a clue to his probable answer. Golf had been well with him during these last days; he was in a good temper. Had Mrs. Comber been able to hide her feelings, had she managed to surprise him suddenly with her request, at the last moment, on the eve of departure, she might have won. But she was no diplomatist. She showed him by her fluttering agitation that there was something that she wanted to ask him, and she showed him that she was afraid, already, lest he should refuse.

That determined him at once. He *would* refuse. These little opportunities of displaying his authority were of great value. Every husband ought to refuse his wife at least once a month. He would certainly refuse.

The moment came. It was the last night but one of their holiday, and Freddie was undoing his collar before the looking-glass. The head of the stud had allowed itself to be bent and the collar refused to move.

Of course, Mrs. Comber chose this unpropitious moment for her petition. It was odd that she should feel seriously about it, but her throat was quite dry and her heart was beating furiously.

'Freddie!'

'Yes? Con—found it!'

'Freddie!'

'Well?'

'I wonder—I've been thinking—it's occurred to me——'

The stud broke, the collar was off, but what was one going to do in the morning? There was no other stud with a large enough head, and on the very day when there would be so much to see to——

'Hang it! Well?'

'I'm so sorry, dear. Perhaps I'll be able to find another. What I was going to say, to ask you, was whether—if you wouldn't very much mind—whether—he wouldn't be in the way, really no trouble at all, and it would make such a difference to me—and I

think you'd like him after a time; it would be so nice for the boys,
too, and there *is* that kennel——'

'What *are* you talking about?'

He had turned and faced her, his cheeks still flushed with the
exertion of the stud.

'Well'—Mrs. Comber's voice trembled a little—'it's only
Rags. I thought, if you didn't dreadfully mind, if I might—if we
might—take him back with us to Moffatt's; it would make *such*
a difference to me. I've got to love this place so, you know, and
you'll think it very silly of me, but if I had Rags with me at Moffatt's—well, I know you'll think it just like my usual silliness, but
I should feel as though I had taken a bit of this place with me.'

Freddie had said no word, only stood there, staring at her, and
fingering, absent-mindedly, his stud. Her allusion to the place
had suddenly surprised some curious feeling, right down deep in
him, that he too had loved this Rafiel, had had the best of days
here, would be immensely sorry to leave it. And this sudden feeling angered him. What was he doing with feelings of that kind?

He was quite ashamed, and resenting his shame, laid the discomfort of it to his wife's charge, and beyond her to the dog. The
dog! The mongrel!

His wife wanted the dog at Moffatt's. She was terrified lest
he should refuse. He was master. He was a man. No more of this
miserable sentiment for him. He would show her.

'Once for all,' he said, glowering at her, 'you can put that out
of your mind. I've hated the dog from the first; it's a beastly mongrel, and the sooner it's drowned the better.'

'But, Freddie——'

'Not another word will I utter. I'm a man who means what he
says.'

'Please, just listen. He——'

'No more. I've got to get undressed. You must get rid of the
dog.'

She saw that it was final—that, and how much else? For, as he
stood there, denying her this simple thing, as he looked at her so
angrily, so cruelly, she knew, once and for all, that all her love for
him was gone, had been gone indeed for many years past. She
would in the future care for him in a protecting, motherly way;

she would always be a good wife to him, but no more passion, no more colour, no more poetry.

She turned away and lay by his side that night as though he were suddenly a stranger. In the morning it was almost more than she could bear, the joy that Rags, coming to meet her, flung upon her. He curved round until his tail was nearly in his mouth; he bared his teeth; his stump of a tail, with hair branching out of it on every side until it looked like a Christmas-tree, almost wagged itself from his body. It was very early, before breakfast. Down the hill they went into the little village, all sparkling with morning freshness, the little quay reeking with fish, the cobbles glittering with silver scales.

She turned the corner and came out on to the path that runs above the little harbour. The boats, blue and green, lay in rows and, beyond and above them, the little white cottages stole up the hill into all the misty brightness of a summer morning. A haze was over the sea, so that it came quite suddenly out of nowhere, white and blue, on to the rocks.

The abandon and reality of the beauty of it all came up to Mrs. Comber, but she seemed to have no place in it. The future of her life, how dreary, how purposeless! Not even Rags to comfort her! For the first time since her marriage she rebelled—hotly, fiercely rebelled. Why should she not leave Freddie? Why should she be the only one in the world to do without things? Why *need* she suffer so? It was the hardest, sharpest, cruellest moment of her life.

Little Captain Tregatta turned the corner. Rags ran forward to meet him, jumped upon him, licked his hand. But Captain Tregatta's face was sad, his shoulders drooped, he looked old.

'Good-marnin', ma'am.'

'Good-morning,' said Mrs. Comber.

'Lovely day. Yes, indeed, if you're in tune for it; but there's nothing like lovely weather for making you melancholy if you're out of sorts.'

His distress touched her at once.

'I'm sorry if something's the matter,' she said.

'Oh! it's silly. Only my boy. 'E goes back to Bristol to-day, and 'e's glad to go. Yes, 'e is—I knaws it. And 'e'll never come back,

I knaws that, too. All this time I've been 'appy thinking that 'e cared for me—maybe 'e was a bit busy, but 'e cared all the same— and now I knaws 'e doesn't—I knaws it; and now all the day will be without somethin', always. It's a long time to be waitin', doing nothing, thinking of nothing.'

Rags, with his back legs before his front ones, sat hunched up, looking at the sea.

As she felt the glory of the morning the idea came to her—it flashed upon her.

'Captain Tregatta,' she said hurriedly, 'I'm going away to-morrow—I can't take the dog with me. It wouldn't do in a school, you know. Would you look after him for me? Keep him here with you so that he'll be here when I come back next summer. I've loved Rafiel so, and I feel that if I knew you were both here together I would feel as though I'd got a link with the place— both of you together here.'

'I will, ma'am,' he said. 'Certainly I will. 'E'll be 'ere for yer when yer come back to us, as I hope yer will.' Then, with a little sigh of satisfaction, 'Yes. That's of it.'

Mrs. Comber thanked him. She waited, tried to say more, but failed.

They all three looked out to sea. Cries and bells came up to them from the village. Suddenly Mrs. Comber, very red in the face, caught Rags's body in her arms, gave him one hug, and then thrust him into the captain's hands.

'There—take him—take him. You two together will be splendid to think of. Good-bye—good-bye. I'm feeling too silly for words. Good-bye—good-bye—good-bye.'

She went, almost running, down into the flashing village, past the fish, the smells, the gossip, the cobbles—up the hill to Sea View Villa.

She did not turn or stay, but in her heart there was that picture of the dog and the man—both of them wanting her to come back.

She had staked her claim in Rafiel after all.

PORTRAIT IN SHADOW

Mr. K—— told me this story one wet day in Cumberland. He did not tell it me all in one piece: the first part of it I had as we walked in soaking rain from Braithwaite to Buttermere, the second part that same evening over a fire in the Buttermere Inn, and he finished it for me next day on our tramp under a mellow September sun into Ennerdale. We had met three days before in Keswick; we were both looking for the right kind of companion. The week that we then spent together seemed to promise a good and strong friendship but, alas, K—— died in the following year, of pneumonia. I have concealed his name because he would himself have wished it. He had a charming and most original talent, but some kind of delicacy and mistrust of himself, also, I fancy, a constitutional ill-health which all his life pursued him, and thirdly a comfortable income, prevented him from making the mark that he should have done. In all his forty-eight years he published only three little books; one of them, a slight but most brilliant Venetian story, had some success.

However, in these days, with the rush, roar and confusion of letters, a very delicate and fugitive talent such as his has not, I fear, a great chance of survival.

In appearance K—— was tall, slim, and fragile. He had eyes of a very bright blue and eyebrows that were almost white, so faint in colour were they. He had a charming nervous smile and never seemed to be quite sure what to do with his legs and his arms.

But it was his voice that was beautiful. How can I describe it? Anyone who knew it will hear the echo of it so long as life lasts. It had a cadence of reminiscence as though it were best pleased to speak of the past. The timbre was marvellous, very lightly pitched and yet as clear as a bell across water. He was the least affected of men, yet he had a way of lingering over a beautiful word as though he hated to let it go. His shyness, his humour, good-fellowship, almost childish gratitude for being liked, all these things made up his charm, and yet there was more than these—some special goodness of spirit, perhaps, that put him a little apart from other men.

This was his story. I have tried to give it as though he were himself telling it. The point about it is that it should have happened to K—— of all people in the world. There are men I know to whom such an incident would have been nothing at all. It would have been forgotten as soon as it occurred. To K—— it was epochal, transforming. The man with the air *en brosse,* the room with the picture, these were part of his life for ever after.

It happened (said K——) more than twenty years ago. Before the war—the way we date everything now. I had come down from Oxford and was very uncertain as to my next step. I had some means of my own, you see, and I was an orphan. I have been an orphan nearly all my life.

I had been brought up by an uncle who lived in Leeds, but he died while I was at Oxford, and it was then that an aunt of mine became my friend. The odd thing about this aunt was that she was only some five years older than myself. She was my father's youngest sister, fifteen years younger than he. My father married when he was twenty, and I was his only child. I did not see much of this aunt until my uncle died. She lived with a rather tyrannical, selfish father in London. Then at almost the moment when my uncle died her father died also, and that seemed to bring us together. We were both quite alone in the world.

But she was in a worse position than I, for she had almost no means. She was perfectly charming. I can't possibly give you any idea of her charm. She was slight, fair, most delicately made, full of zest for life, a zest that she had never been able to fulfil. She had always had the very dullest time.

She was a child in many ways, taking everything with an eager intensity and quite surprisingly ignorant of the world. As a matter of fact, I was that also. I had never been strong, had been driven by a quite invincible shyness into a remote life of my own. I wanted to make friends but did not know how to make them. So, when we discovered one another, it was wonderful for both of us. Almost the first thing I wanted to do was to take her abroad and give her a splendid holiday. She had never been out of England.

The thought of the holiday excited her tremendously. I can see her now, sitting in a dingy room of the London house, leaning on the table after breakfast, her fragile body shaking with enthusiasm, a fog slurring the lines of the street beyond the window, the sordid remains of the meal all about her, as she cried:

'Oh, but how wonderful! . . . France, Spain, Italy . . . !'

In the end it was Spain, and, of all mad things, the north of Spain in August. I know that we were crazy, and you may be sure that everyone told us that we were. The north of Spain! August! and you must remember that before the war Spain was by no means the sanitary and clinical paradise that its splendid 'Turismo' has lately succeeded in making it.

Yes, everyone said that we were mad, but it was the Sun that we both wanted. We found that we were completely agreed about that. My aunt had never had any Sun at all. She had never been really warm. Northern Spain in August—yes, we would be certain to be warm!

So off we went. What an enchanting journey we had! We found that we were perfect travelling companions. The perfect travelling companion! Isn't he or she practically an impossibility? As with marriage, you may compromise, and nine out of ten times you do. Is it your fault or the other's? Surely not your own, for you start out with such splendid confidence as to your own character. And, to the very last, it isn't your own character that seems to have failed. Aside from one or two little irritabilities you have been perfect, but the other——! You had no idea before you started of the weaknesses, the selfishness, the odd, exasperating tricks, the refusal to agree to the most obvious course, the insistence on unimportant personal rights! No, it has most certainly *not* been your fault; and yet, in retrospect, are there not suddenly exposed certain flecks, little blemishes in your own personality that you had never suspected?

Forgive me for emphasising the obvious, but this very question of companionship plays its important part in the little story. For my aunt and myself were the most perfect companions. We simply found, as the days passed and all those little accidents, upsets, surprises, turned up their innocent faces, as they always do on such an expedition, that we were only more and more suited to one another. We liked the same things but had our different points of view, we were amused by the same nonsense, exhilarated by the same drama, enriched by the same beauty.

My aunt's sure perception and lovely sense of humour threw a light about her as a flower is lit by the shaking glitter of a neighbouring fountain. She had that iridescence, that eternal possibility of some beautiful surprise. And yet what a child she was! She had indeed seen nothing of life at all, and every moment of her day was a wonder and an amaze.

Well, we reached San Sebastian, and the heat was terrific. It was then that for the first time I knew a moment of alarm. This was indeed heat as I had never known it, and I lay, that first night in the San Sebastian hotel, naked on my bed while the sweat poured in streams off my body. My aunt, however, I discovered next morning, was in no way inconvenienced by it. She was ready, she declared, for anything!

I was determined to discover some small place by the sea that should be for us characteristically Spanish but quiet and beautiful. Quiet, you know, is not Spain's most eminent characteristic! I asked the porter of the hotel, and he spoke to me at once of the little resort of Z——, a charming place, he said, over the hills, quiet and beautiful. Strange to think that it was from the round plump features of the porter of that San Sebastian hotel that, in such commonplace words, I first heard of a spot that would never, from that moment, leave me again!

I spoke of it to my aunt and she enthusiastically agreed! How little we both of us knew to what we were going!

At that time a small clumsy railway ran over the mountains to the sea. Into the fearfully hot, exceedingly democratic carriage we climbed! We had chosen an evening train that we might escape the heat of the day. We were embedded in a cheerful clump of eager, friendly people, two priests, an old and a young one, three pretty girls, a stout farmer, a clerk. I can see them all now as though they were still with me, as perhaps they are! I knew some Spanish. There are no people at the same time so friendly and so uninterfering as the Spaniards! Their hospitality is prodigious, their pride and sensitiveness also. They are gay, but never to abandon, and one of their mysteries is that they should at the same time be so kind to children and so cruel to animals.

The heat, I suppose (for that carriage *was* hot!), sent me into a kind of trance. I saw my companions after a while as trees walking, and the coloured haze that fell in an ever deepening purple bloom about the hills seemed to tell me that I was entering a new country.

There is little twilight in this country—soon all was dark beyond our windows, and when at last we had arrived we stepped down into mystery. About us, in the little station, I remember, was the sharp scent of some strange unknown flower and the dry sandy whisper of the sea. No breeze, and a sky stiff with the most silver stars I had ever seen.

But it was in the morning that, on waking, we realised the splendour into which we had stepped. It is the charm of Z—— that it lies, surrounded with woods, backed by mountains, in a kind of delicious privacy, as though that especial piece of sea were its own creation and separate possession. The beach is in fact large, but the black rocks that run out on either side to protect it give it a natural aristocracy, as though it were a beach preserved during many, many years by some lordly and beneficent owner for the pleasure of his friends.

Not that it was deserted or sacred with a sort of Crusoe loneliness. Far from it. As we looked out on it that morning (we had slept late) all the brilliantly striped tents—green, purple, red, yellow—were unfolding, and from every side, down the hill, the bathers, all wrapped in dressing-gowns as gay as flower-beds, were advancing. I believe that even now, you know, that Spanish custom of coloured dressing-gowns on the beaches is preserved.

Well, but when we saw it all more completely we had both the same sensation. Z—— was like a flower shining at the heart of dark leaves, for all the brilliance of light and colour was enfolded by the dark woods, darker than any woods that we had ever seen.

'It must be terrible in rain and storm,' said my aunt with a little shiver, and then I, looking more closely, fancied that some of the old houses that bordered the woods were of the order of the storm and the wind, old and green, with gardens along whose paths the leaves thickened and in whose hedges no birds sang. This light in this darkness! That was Z——!

Only this was curious—on that very first morning, the two of us walking out towards the beach together, I noticed, from all the others, the very house, the house that still so often seems to invite me within its doors—a gate, rather shabby, a garden-path, some beds thick with dark-red flowers, a front of faded brown, and a bright green door with a silver knocker. It was, I think, the bright green and the silver of the knocker that attracted me. The knocker sparkled in the sun, and even as we looked the door opened and an old lady and gentleman, the old lady in a large black hat and leaning on a stick, walked out. We passed on.

Reaching the beach, it seemed to our young and inexperienced souls that we had attained Paradise. The water came rolling in, trembling in crystal lights, green like a bird's wing; the tents of crimson and gold were grander and more lordly than anything that we had ever imagined for a beach.

Undressing under a rock on the Cornish coast was the nearest to them that we knew. Don't imagine, though, that there was anything stiff or ceremonial about the life here. For a week at least we were as happy and care-free as any two in the world. I knew some Spanish, my aunt could smile and nod her head and look the friend of all the world, which, for that moment, she was.

Yes, we had the happiest week of our lives. We had never conceived such a sun, such colour, such laughter, such freedom from interference, such willingness on the part of everyone that we should be at home.

Then, on a lovely morning, some time between seven and eight, bathing alone, I encountered a gentleman in the water. He was, judging by his head, a very jolly gentleman indeed.

He shouted that it was a lovely morning, that the water was perfect. I called back in my funny Spanish that he couldn't possibly say enough about it or do it any sort of justice.

It was, I think, my funny Spanish that won him, for, coming out of the sea at the same time as myself, he said that he supposed that I was English or American. Now that should have told me something, for the Spaniards, the *right* Spaniards, are the most courteous people in the world and never press into the privacy of anyone.

But I never gave that a thought. I liked him at once. Standing there in the new morning sun, the water dropping from him in crystal drops, he was as handsome a man as I've ever seen —more handsome, I sometimes think, than anyone else in the world. What was he like? I don't know, except that his hair stood up stiffly *en brosse*, even then when it was soaked with water. Its colour was raven black, his body bronze. He had a small mole underneath one eye. We talked, and he made me lose my accustomed shyness. He had always a great deal to say and he found everything amusing. He told me at once his name—Ramón Quintero. He was staying with relations. He had been here a fortnight. He liked English people. How well I spoke Spanish! Oh, yes, I did. My accent was very attractive.

At breakfast I told my aunt about him. Later that morning, while we sat under our crimson tent eating grapes, he was introduced to her. I know now that she fell in love with him at once, and that from that moment some thin, almost invisible cloud obscured our own relationship.

What a commonplace it is nowadays to remark that we are all as lonely in this life as Crusoe on his island, but it is true enough. On the instant that I introduced Ramón Quintero (robed, I remember, at the moment in a purple dressing-gown, his face of shining bronze, his blue eyes sparkling with an amusement that seemed always to be directed more against himself than anyone else) to my aunt, I lost for ever the only really close intimacy with another human being that I have ever known or, I fancy, ever will know.

Remember that my aunt and I had only reached any sort of true companionship during the last week; there had not been time enough for a real basis of trust, fond though we were growing of one another. Had fate given us another two months!—— But it did not. Does it not often seem to break something that is *almost* completed?—shrugging its shoulders, saying: 'Oh, well, this is disappointing. I thought it would turn out better. I'll smash this and start again.'

In any case she was not, I suppose, sure enough of herself. She fancied, perhaps, that I should think her foolish. . . . But I don't know. *I don't know.* That's what, after all this time, makes me so unhappy. Yes, even now. I'm telling you the story perhaps only that I may clear it up a little more to myself in the telling.

Such a child as she was, but not more of a child than I. Quintero must at once have put me right out of account as someone not worth considering. That is why the sequel must have astonished him!

I don't wonder now on looking back that she fell in love with him at sight. My only wonder is that I should have been such a fool as not to have noticed it, but I knew very little about life or human beings at that time. I was quite incredibly ignorant.

The other figure in the story now appears—Sancho Panza. He was obviously Sancho to anyone coming to Spain for the first time, although Ramón Quintero was most certainly no Don Quixote. He was round and fat like a tub, with a jolly laughing face, and he had all Sancho's proper equipment of proverbs, love of food and drink, a passion for display, a wife, to whom he was apparently devoted, very much in the background, and a passionate affection for his friend and master, Quintero. He was supposedly Quintero's secretary, although he never wrote any letters so far as I could see. He did everything for him—a great many things of which I was probably at the moment not in the least aware. He ran messages, endured every kind of insult, was Quintero's utterly faithful hound.

On the very first day of our acquaintanceship he mentioned my sister.

'My aunt,' I said.

'Your aunt? Impossible!'

I explained.

He spoke only Spanish. Quintero spoke only Spanish. That was one reason why I never dreamed of an intimacy between himself and her. How could there be? Which showed how little, how sadly little, I knew about love and lovers. Quintero was teaching her Spanish on that very first day.

Then Sancho said:

'So lovely and unmarried!'

'Yes,' I said.

'And rich? All the English are rich.'

'Rolling,' I answered. It was a joke, my answer, and, as it turned out, a deadly one.

I should have resented his impertinence, but it was impossible to resent anything that Sancho said or did. He meant so well to everyone.

The next thing that occurred was that we visited the house. I see now—oh, how many things I see!—that that had been arranged by the two of them. I can see her now as, coming over to me on the verandah of the hotel, laying her hand on my shoulder, she said:

'Mr. Quintero has asked us to go to tea to-morrow afternoon!'

'How do you know?' I said, laughing. 'You can't understand a word he says.'

'Oh yes, I can,' she answered.

I should have known by the way she said that that she had already moved worlds away from me. With what a speed, with what force of a sweeping whirlwind, this thing must have caught her! She was not one, as the sequel shows, to love idly or lightly. Had she been, there would have been no story in this. This was the way, I can see now, that she had always dreamt that love would come—in a foreign land, colour and loveliness on every side of her, and the handsomest, kindest, tenderest hero at her feet! Any girl's dream! How often in that ugly London house, with a cross father inside and the rain outside, she must have cherished just such dreams! Unlike Desdemona, she could not listen to his tales of peril and adventure, but with every word of Spanish that he taught her she crept closer to him, he had her in his possession more securely.

'Of course we'll go,' I said. 'Quintero's a good fellow. I like him. Where does he live?'

Well, he was staying in that very house with the bright green door and the silver knocker! As we walked up the garden path the world closed in darkly about us. Spain is a noisy country; this house was as still as the grave. But my impressions of that first visit are an odd conflict of silence and sound. The background did not accord with the actors in front of it. In an old room hung with a green wall-paper painted with golden bees we had tea. The two old people, relations of Quintero's, were there, Sancho Panza, my aunt and myself. Quintero was 'the life of the party.' He was brilliant; he was perfect. Merry, kind, full of ridiculous stories, considerate of everyone. How we laughed! We sang songs to an old cracked piano while the two old people sat and nodded their heads with approval like two gentle and very ancient mandarins. To all the noise the house made no response. Beyond the windows were the shadows of the trees, and through the trees the glory of the summer sun came so dimly that it flung a pale glow. Somewhere a bird twittered in a cage.

Then they said that we must see 'The Picture.' We climbed a fine old staircase that creaked with our steps, passed ghostly cabinets crowded with ghostly china, and then found ourselves in a room hung with red curtains, containing only a bookcase, a table, an old green silk settee, and some chairs as furniture, and there, the only ornament of the walls, was an amazing picture. I don't know how good a picture it was. I am no connoisseur. It represented a young man in eighteenth-century dress, standing against a dark background of porticoes, a fountain, shadowy trees. With head erect he stood smiling. His smile was as fascinating and as mysterious as the Gioconda's. He was young, fiery with energy and the pride of life. He was on tip-toe for any adventure. His beauty (for he was beautiful) resided in his eagerness, his almost impertinent self-confidence. While I looked I thought to myself, 'What a splendid friend to have!' and then, moving to another part of the room, the light changed for me, there came some twist in the lip, some evil glint in the eyes, and I said: 'He is a rogue, a rascal—I wouldn't trust him a yard.' Then, moving back again, all my confidence in him returned.

'That's odd,' I remember saying, but, looking round, found only the stout and smiling Sancho with me.

'Where are the others?'

'They have gone into the garden.'

I thought nothing of that. I was absorbed by the picture. I stayed there twenty minutes looking at the picture. Friend or rogue? Good man or base? To be trusted or to be fled from?

I did not know then. I do not know now.

We went to the house on many more occasions. We had tea and dinner there. Many of Quintero's friends came. Time passed with enchanting swiftness. The weather was lovely. The waves turned with caressing, loving lightness on the gold sand. The beach was covered with the brilliant shining tents, with hundreds of naked bronze babies; the women walked selling their biscuits, offering lottery tickets, crying the delights of the Tombola; evening after evening sank from crystal blue into grape-dark skies, and the mornings glittered like fire.

But suddenly I wasn't happy. Why? I didn't know. I wanted to go away, but my aunt grew pale at the hint. She had never been so happy anywhere in her life as here. I detected in her a strange kind of fierceness. I realised with a flash why I was unhappy. She and I had lost touch with one another. We were never alone any more. We had no longer any confidences. I brooded sometimes, but I was too young, too inexperienced, to find a solution —I knew that we loved one another as deeply as ever. What had occurred?

Then I began to hear things about Quintero. Speaking Spanish, I made friends easily, friends outside the Quintero circle. I found that Quintero was not approved of. He was a waster, an adventurer, something of a rascal. Oh, a jolly fellow of course! Grand company. But not to be trusted. Beware of him. Don't lend him money. A dangerous man about money. And yet there was nothing very definite. They told me frankly that there was nothing actually against him. Perhaps he was not bad, only— what was his occupation? On what did he live? And there were stories from Madrid. . . .

I wanted to speak to her about him and I had not the courage. She was so happy. She moved like the spirit of good fortune. I noticed—poor fool that I was—a kind of ecstasy of happiness in her eyes, in her laughter. But I guessed nothing. I only knew that we were never alone together, and I wanted to go away. . . .

Then, in a moment, in a blinding second of revelation, the catastrophe crashed. Blinding! That is my only excuse, that I had no chance of preparation, no time for thought.

One lovely morning I went down alone to the beach and came, without warning, upon Quintero and Sancho Panza. I came upon them in the middle of a fearful and appalling row.

I caught a glimpse—as you see a face in a flash of lightning—of Quintero in a temper. It was a fine sight, something grand and elemental about it. He looked as though he could have caught the beach, tents and babies and all, into his fist and thrown it, crumpled to nothing, into the sea. He gave me one glance and, without a word, strode off.

Sancho was in a rage too. He was quivering like a jelly in his bathing-dress, a very ludicrous sight. He was too angry to measure his words. With real foreign abandon he flung himself on me. There were no words adequate for Quintero. Had he not slaved for him, endured every insult, served him as no other man? ... and now to be cheated ... money ... fair wages ... I caught here and there fragments of his fury.

'And you look out!' He grasped my arm. 'You say she's your aunt. Well, whatever she is, he's got her. In another day or two he'll be off with her, money and all. . . . What will *you* look like, my friend?'

I gazed at him bewildered. I had, I remember, a *sticky* sense of being bogged. I felt perhaps as a fly may feel when, dancing aimlessly, its spidery feet catch the fly-paper, its shrill buzz like the twanging of a thin wire. . . . But I didn't utter a sound. I simply stared at him. His contempt for me was boundless, aided perhaps by the consciousness of his coming contempt for himself for giving his beloved friend away. He had wondered how long it would be before I would see it. My aunt—or whatever she was— had been crazy about Quintero from the first instant. That was no new thing. Quintero was used to it. In ordinary he let them go. He was not in reality greatly interested in women. But this time it was different. He had liked her, she was pretty, only a child—and then he was low in funds. He had always intended to make a safe marriage. My aunt was 'rolling'—I had said so. It was myself, it seemed, who had been the trouble. At first she had said that she must tell me everything. At least that is what they thought that she meant, for one of the great difficulties throughout had been her ignorance of Spanish on one side and his of English on the other. But he had convinced her that it would be wiser to tell me after the deed was done. To warn me would only disturb me, burden me with a sense of responsibility. In any case, everything was arranged. In three days' time they were to be married in San Sebastian. . . .

'But she hasn't a penny!' was the cry on my lips. I don't know now what held me back. The beginning, maybe, of that uncertainty that has haunted me all my life after.

Well, I was in an agony of distress. I use that word deliberately. It *was* an agony, like the fiercest toothache or the first pain of a broken arm. For so many men it would have meant nothing at all. They would have gone to her and said: 'Look here, my dear, what's all this about your running away with a Spaniard? All nonsense. . . . He's a rogue and a vagabond. I'm not going to hear of it.' But it is the point of this story that neither she nor I could take anything lightly. This was the first big crisis of both our lives. If only it had come a little later when we knew one another better! But I walked down that beach simply feeling that I had been for ever and ever betrayed! I had lost, in one jeering glance from that Spaniard, the only loving intimacy I had ever known in my life. She might have told me. Oh! she might have told me!

And then, passion rising in me, my only thought was that I would at once prevent it. He was marrying her for her money— the old, old story—and she hadn't a penny! I had a wild, savage, childish, boyish pleasure in thinking that now I could have my revenge, that now I could make her unhappy. That wickedness— for such selfish angry cruelty is perhaps the wickedest thing our hearts can know—rose round the light and happiness of those last weeks as the dark trees closed in on the golden beach and the bright jade water. I would not waste an instant. I would show my power.

I was, of course, on the outside edge of the story, completely justified. Here was my poor little friend, ignorant utterly of life, in the hands of an adventurer, whom I, by a casual careless remark, had led into thinking her wealthy.

It was my plain duty to put things right. *That* on the outside —the *heart* of the affair was quite other.

Miserable, angry, blinded as though the sand had risen in a storm about my eyes, I hastened, almost running, to the house.

I remember the stillness and quietness when I had closed the gate and was alone on the garden-path. Something in that stillness made me pause as though a voice out of those thick trees whispered to me: 'This isn't what you think. Go back and wait! ... Go back!' It was all dim in that garden, the rumble of the sea rocking through the trees, the sunlight shimmering in shadow and little sudden patterns of brilliant light. That garden tried to hold me, but I wouldn't be held. I knocked on the silver knocker. When the servant came I asked for Quintero. He was an old bent man, that servant, with a bald patch on his head like a nutmeg-grater. He too seemed to say before he let me in: 'Won't you stop a moment, sir, and think it over.'

He took me up the old creaking stairs and led me into the room with the picture. Then went softly out, closing the door behind him. Well, left alone, I looked at the picture, looked at it as though I had never seen it before.

At first, standing in a kind of raging despair, wanting only to get at Quintero as quickly as might be, charge him with treachery, strike him in the face, do anything that would relieve me, I thought that the young man smiled at me. He was wearing cherry-coloured breeches and a coat of white satin. He smiled at me as a friend, and the whole bare room seemed to be warm with his young honesty. 'Trust me!' he seemed to say. 'This is fair. Give me my opportunity. I never meant anything so truly.'

Then, in my restlessness, moving to another part of the room, his face grew shifty, his eyes narrow, his mouth curled. He seemed to disdain my simplicity, to laugh at my poor attempt at good conduct. Sometimes I think that light can do everything with pictures. Maybe there is no final value in any work of art, it is only our view that gives the estimate.

In any case I moved back to my first position again and suddenly determined to leave the thing alone, at least to wait and judge it more quietly. His honest eyes looked in mine. He seemed to nod approval. 'You'll find that best,' he seemed to say.

And then, with another shift, I was back to the other view again. This was a rascal! You could see it in his shifting eyes, the narrowness of his forehead ... Why! Just the fellow to marry a poor girl for her money and then to discard her because she hadn't any!

The door opened, and Quintero came in.

He advanced to me, his hand out, his face all smiles. And I, seeing the picture in the bad light, behaved with all the melodrama that a boy can use.

'You blackguard!' I cried.

'I know. Of course I am,' he said. 'But why?'

It was then that, oddly enough, I had the impulse to leave them alone, let them do as they wished, and go. The picture was smiling at me. 'What right have you to interfere with other lives? And it may be that I am a finer fellow than you are!'

I think that at that time he may have been, and that she was finer too.

But I turned my back on the picture and told him what I thought of him. I used fine language. He was carrying off a young girl for her money. He didn't love her.

'How do you know that I don't love her?'

He seemed now to be years older than before, and his voice was cold with a sick distaste.

'Because it's only for her money that you are taking her.'

'How do you know?'

'Because I know what you are. Everyone knows.'

Then he threw himself on me. He literally fell on to me, caught my throat with his hands, and we began the silliest, most childish rough-and-tumble. We were both young and strong. We fell about the floor, knocking the chairs over. I tore his shirt open and grabbed at his bare flesh; his long sinewy hand was strangling me. We fell together. He lay on top of me, and our hearts thumped together. We lay there panting in a kind of truce, and at last I gasped out:

'But you don't know—the best of it—she hasn't a penny.'

He raised himself and stared down into my face. We looked at one another, calmly, quietly, as though we loved one another. Our hands rested, palm against palm. I think that I had an odd awareness then that this was all a mistake, that if I had let them go on with it, helped them, been their friend, it would have been the most tremendous success—and for all three of us. But it was too late. I had taken the step in the wrong direction. Even if I could draw back he would not. For, resting his hand on my heart, looking down on me, he said:

'So she lied.'

I swore, panting, that she had not, that it had been my own foolish joke.

But he got up. I also scrambled to my feet.

'She has nothing?'

I said nothing.

'My last chance gone.' And, oddly enough, I'll swear to you that I believed then, and I believe now, that it was not of money at all that he was thinking. Had she, in some innocent ingenuous way that he could not possibly understand, suggested to him that she was rich? Was it that he, like Hamlet with Ophelia, suddenly believed her treacherous, and that, believing in someone for the first time, he was for the first time deceived?

In any case I swear that it was not the money that disappointed him. Something deeper . . .

He looked at me with hatred and contempt. No one, before or since, has ever so utterly despised me.

He conducted a short cross-examination as a judge might with his prisoner.

'She told you—about us?'

'Not a word.'

'She did. You have been laughing at me—both of you.'

'I tell you that I had no idea. I never saw. I was blind.'

'Yes, you might be. You are too simple for anything. All the same—you are a pair. I have been a fool for the first time—to be taken in by two English . . .' He broke off and added to himself, as I well remember, 'And to believe in an idyll—to think that once—only five minutes ago—I thought life could be like that.'

And then he burst out:

'She has nothing—not a penny?'

'Not a penny.'

He stopped then, looking at me with a sombre brooding as though he were taking a last look at something very beautiful. Then he added: 'Too good for me—the whole thing. Sentimental. I always knew it.'

He tossed his head as though he had come to a decision.

'Wait here,' he said, like a master to a servant. He left the room. I remained, trying to tidy myself, but feeling that I had, in some way or another, committed some great treachery. He quickly returned. He gave me a letter.

'That is for her,' he said.

I went out.

Well, then, what do you make of it? I lost the only great thing in my life, a relationship in bud, promising every sort of beauty and friendship. I have been afraid, since then, of making a relationship.

My aunt loved him until she died five years later. When I gave her that letter she died, died to all the new life that was just beginning for her. She became an old maid. After our return to England she shut herself up in the country somewhere. She died in the second year of the war, of pneumonia.

And Quintero? That is the oddest thing. I saw him again only last year, in the rooms at Monte Carlo. He was fat, ugly, peevish. I recognised him by the little mole under his left eye. We talked a little in quite a friendly fashion. Only, at the very last, he said, looking over my shoulder into distance:

'You should have let us go away. It was my only chance. I loved her quite sincerely.'

'Why did you care for what I said? I was only a boy. And if you loved her, why did the fact that she had nothing make you let her go?'

'It was not that.' He looked at me oddly. It was as though he were uncovering, for a moment, his lost self. 'I had been all along afraid of my fine feelings—so unusual to me, you know. The only ones of my life. I've never had them again. You came in and gave me the opportunity to be my natural self. But she might have made me . . .' He laughed and turned away.

So she was lost and I was lost and he was lost. And if I had let her go? He was a rascal. He would have broken her heart. Or perhaps he would not. No one is altogether a rascal. And in any case she would have had her glorious time, a week, a month, a year . . .

What right have we ever to take things into our own hands? And how do we know? Rascal or no, doesn't it depend on where we ourselves stand?

BIARRITZ, *September* 11, 1930

THE SNOW

The second Mrs. Ryder was a young woman not easily frightened, but now she stood in the dusk of the passage leaning back against the wall, her hand on her heart, looking at the grey-faced window beyond which the snow was steadily falling against the lamplight.

The passage where she was led from the study to the dining-room, and the window looked out on to the little paved path that ran at the edge of the Cathedral green. As she stared down the passage she couldn't be sure whether the woman was there or no. How absurd of her! She knew the woman was not there. But if the woman was not, how was it that she could discern so clearly the old-fashioned grey cloak, the untidy grey hair and the sharp outline of the pale cheek and pointed chin? Yes, and more than that, the long sweep of the grey dress, falling in folds to the ground, the flash of a gold ring on the white hand. No. No. NO. This was madness. There was no one and nothing there. Hallucination . . .

Very faintly a voice seemed to come to her: 'I warned you. This is for the last time. . . .'

The nonsense! How far now was her imagination to carry her? Tiny sounds about the house, the running of a tap somewhere, a faint voice from the kitchen, these and something more had translated themselves into an imagined voice. 'The last time . . .'

But her terror was real. She was not normally frightened by anything. She was young and healthy and bold, fond of sport, hunting, shooting, taking any risk. Now she was truly *stiffened* with terror—she could not move, could not advance down the passage as she wanted to and find light, warmth, safety in the dining-room. All the time the snow fell steadily, stealthily, with its own secret purpose, maliciously, beyond the window in the pale glow of the lamplight.

Then unexpectedly there was noise from the hall, opening of doors, a rush of feet, a pause and then in clear beautiful voices the well-known strains of 'Good King Wenceslas.' It was the Cathedral choir-boys on their regular Christmas round. This was Christmas Eve. They always came just at this hour on Christmas Eve.

With an intense, almost incredible relief she turned back into the hall. At the same moment her husband came out of the study. They stood together smiling at the little group of mufflered, becoated boys who were singing, heart and soul in the job, so that the old house simply rang with their melody.

Reassured by the warmth and human company, she lost her terror. It had been her imagination. Of late she had been none too well. That was why she had been so irritable. Old Doctor Bernard was no good: he didn't understand her case at all. After Christmas she would go to London and have the very best advice ...

Had she been well she could not, half an hour ago, have shown such miserable temper over nothing. She knew that it was over nothing and yet that knowledge did not make it any easier for her to restrain herself. After every bout of temper she told herself that there should never be another—and then Herbert said something irritating, one of his silly muddle-headed stupidities, and she was off again!

She could see now, as she stood beside him at the bottom of the staircase, that he was still feeling it. She had certainly half an hour ago said some abominably rude personal things—things that she had not at all meant—and he had taken them in his meek, quiet way. Were he not so meek and quiet, did he only pay her back in her own coin, she would never lose her temper. Of that she was sure. But who wouldn't be irritated by that meekness and by the only reproachful thing that he ever said to her: 'Elinor understood me better, my dear'? To throw the first wife up against the second! Wasn't that the most tactless thing that a man could possibly do? And Elinor, that worn elderly woman, the very opposite of her own gay, bright, amusing self? That was why Herbert had loved her, because she was gay and bright and young. It was true that Elinor had been devoted, that she had been so utterly wrapped up in Herbert that she lived only for him. People were always recalling her devotion, which was sufficiently rude and tactless of them.

Well, she could not give anyone that kind of old-fashioned sugary devotion; it wasn't in her, and Herbert knew it by this time.

Nevertheless she loved Herbert in her own way, as he must know, know it so well that he ought to pay no attention to the bursts of temper. She wasn't well. She would see a doctor in London ...

The little boys finished their carols, were properly rewarded, and tumbled like feathery birds out into the snow again. They went into the study, the two of them, and stood beside the big open log-fire. She put her hand up and stroked his thin beautiful cheek.

'I'm so sorry to have been cross just now, Bertie. I didn't mean half I said, you know.'

But he didn't, as he usually did, kiss her and tell her that it didn't matter. Looking straight in front of him, he answered:

'Well, Alice, I do wish you wouldn't. It hurts, horribly. It upsets me more than you think. And it's growing on you. You make me miserable. I don't know what to do about it. And it's all about nothing.'

Irritated at not receiving the usual commendation for her sweetness in making it up again, she withdrew a little and answered:

'Oh, all right. I've said I'm sorry. I can't do any more.'

'But tell me,' he insisted, 'I want to know. What makes you so angry, so suddenly?—and about nothing at all.'

She was about to let her anger rise, her anger at his obtuseness, obstinacy, when some fear checked her, a strange unanalysed fear, as though someone had whispered to her, 'Look out! This is the last time!'

'It's not altogether my own fault,' she answered, and left the room.

She stood in the cold hall, wondering where to go. She could feel the snow falling outside the house and shivered. She hated the snow, she hated the winter, this beastly, cold dark English winter that went on and on, only at last to change into a damp, soggy English spring.

It had been snowing all day. In Polchester it was unusual to have so heavy a snowfall. This was the hardest winter that they had known for many years.

When she urged Herbert to winter abroad—which he could quite easily do—he answered her impatiently; he had the strongest affection for this poky dead-and-alive Cathedral town. The Cathedral seemed to be precious to him; he wasn't happy if he didn't go and see it every day! She wouldn't wonder if he didn't think more of the Cathedral than he did of herself. Elinor had been the same; she had even written a little book about the Cathedral, about the Black Bishop's Tomb and the stained glass and the rest ...

What was the Cathedral after all? Only a building!

She was standing in the drawing-room looking out over the dusky ghostly snow to the great hulk of the Cathedral that Herbert said was like a flying ship, but to herself was more like a crouching beast licking its lips over the miserable sinners that it was for ever devouring.

As she looked and shivered, feeling that in spite of herself her temper and misery were rising so that they threatened to choke her, it seemed to her that her bright and cheerful fire-lit drawing-room was suddenly open to the snow. It was exactly as though cracks had appeared everywhere, in the ceiling, the walls, the windows, and that through these cracks the snow was filtering, dribbling in little tracks of wet down the walls, already perhaps making pools of water on the carpet.

This was of course imagination, but it was a fact that the room was most dreadfully cold, although a great fire was burning and it was the cosiest room in the house.

Then, turning, she saw the figure standing by the door. This time there could be no mistake. It was a grey shadow, and yet a shadow with form and outline—the untidy grey hair, the pale face like a moon-lit leaf, the long grey clothes, and something obstinate, vindictive, terribly menacing in its pose.

She moved, and the figure was gone; there was nothing there, and the room was warm again, quite hot in fact. But young Mrs.

Ryder, who had never feared anything in all her life save the vanishing of her youth, was trembling so that she had to sit down, and even then her trembling did not cease. Her hand shook on the arm of her chair.

She had created this thing out of her imagination of Elinor's hatred of her and her own hatred of Elinor. It was true that they had never met, but who knew but that the spiritualists were right, and Elinor's spirit, jealous of Herbert's love for her, had been there driving them apart, forcing her to lose her temper and then hating her for losing it? Such things might be! But she had not much time for speculation. She was preoccupied with her fear. It was a definite, positive fear, the kind of fear that one has just before one goes under an operation. Someone or something was threatening her. She clung to her chair as though to leave it were to plunge into disaster. She looked around her everywhere; all the familiar things, the pictures, the books, the little tables, the piano were different now, isolated, strange, hostile, as though they had been won over by some enemy power.

She longed for Herbert to come and protect her; she felt most kindly to him. She would never lose her temper with him again —and at that same moment some cold voice seemed to whisper in her ear: 'You had better not. It will be for the last time.'

At length she found courage to rise, cross the room and go up to dress for dinner. In her bedroom courage came to her once more. It was certainly very cold, and the snow, as she could see when she looked between her curtains, was falling more heavily than ever, but she had a warm bath, sat in front of her fire and was sensible again.

For many months this odd sense that she was watched and accompanied by someone hostile to her had been growing. It was the stronger perhaps because of the things that Herbert told her about Elinor; she was the kind of woman, he said, who, once she loved anyone, would never relinquish her grasp; she was utterly faithful. He implied that her tenacious fidelity had been at times a little difficult.

'She always said,' he added once, 'that she would watch over me until I rejoined her in the next world. Poor Elinor!' he sighed. 'She had a fine religious faith, stronger than mine, I fear.'

It was always after one of her tantrums that young Mrs. Ryder had been most conscious of this hallucination, this dreadful discomfort of feeling that someone was near you who hated you —but it was only during the last week that she began to fancy that she actually saw anyone, and with every day her sense of this figure had grown stronger.

It was, of course, only nerves, but it was one of those nervous afflictions that became tiresome indeed if you did not rid yourself of it. Mrs. Ryder, secure now in the warmth and intimacy of her bedroom, determined that henceforth everything should be sweetness and light. No more tempers! Those were the things that did her harm.

Even though Herbert were a little trying, was not that the case with every husband in the world? And was it not Christmas time? Peace and Good Will to men! Peace and Good Will to Herbert!

They sat down opposite to one another in the pretty little dining-room hung with Chinese woodcuts, the table gleaming and the amber curtains richly dark in the firelight.

But Herbert was not himself. He was still brooding, she supposed, over their quarrel of the afternoon. Weren't men children? Incredible the children that they were!

So when the maid was out of the room she went over to him, bent down and kissed his forehead.

'Darling . . . you're still cross, I can see you are. You mustn't be. Really you mustn't. It's Christmas time and, if I forgive you, you must forgive me.'

'You forgive me?' he asked, looking at her in his most aggravating way. 'What have you to forgive me for?'

Well, that was really too much. When she had taken all the steps, humbled her pride.

She went back to her seat, but for a while could not answer him because the maid was there. When they were alone again she said, summoning all her patience:

'Bertie dear, do you really think that there's anything to be gained by sulking like this? It isn't worthy of you. It isn't really.'

He answered her quietly.

'Sulking? No, that's not the right word. But I've got to keep quiet. If I don't I shall say something I'm sorry for.' Then, after a pause, in a low voice, as though to himself: 'These constant rows are awful.'

Her temper was rising again; another self that had nothing to do with her real self, a stranger to her and yet a very old familiar friend.

'Don't be so self-righteous,' she answered, her voice trembling a little. 'These quarrels are entirely my own fault, aren't they?'

'Elinor and I never quarrelled,' he said, so softly that she scarcely heard him.

'No! Because Elinor thought you perfect. She adored you. You've often told me. I don't think you perfect. I'm not perfect either. But we've both got faults. I'm not the only one to blame.'

'We'd better separate,' he said, suddenly looking up. 'We don't get on now. We used to. I don't know what's changed everything. But, as things are, we'd better separate.'

She looked at him and knew that she loved him more than ever, but because she loved him so much she wanted to hurt him, and because he had said that he thought he could get on without her she was so angry that she forgot all caution. Her love and her anger helped one another. The more angry she became the more she loved him.

'I know why you want to separate,' she said. 'It's because you're in love with someone else.' ('How funny,' something inside her said. 'You don't mean a word of this.') 'You've treated me as you have, and then you leave me.'

'I'm not in love with anyone else,' he answered her steadily, 'and you know it. But we are so unhappy together that it's silly to go on . . . silly. . . . The whole thing has failed.'

There was so much unhappiness, so much bitterness in his voice that she realised that at last she had truly gone too far. She had lost him. She had not meant this. She was frightened, and her fear made her so angry that she went across to him.

'Very well then . . . I'll tell everyone . . . what you've been. How you've treated me.'

'Not another scene,' he answered wearily. 'I can't stand any more. Let's wait. To-morrow is Christmas Day . . .'

He was so unhappy that her anger with herself maddened her. She couldn't bear his sad, hopeless disappointment with herself, their life together, everything.

In a fury of blind temper she struck him; it was as though she were striking herself. He got up and without a word left the room. There was a pause, and then she heard the hall door close. He had left the house.

She stood there, slowly coming to her control again. When she lost her temper it was as though she sank under water. When it was all over she came once more to the surface of life, wondering where she'd been and what she had been doing. Now she stood there, bewildered, and then at once she was aware of two things: one that the room was bitterly cold and the other that someone was in the room with her.

This time she did not need to look around her. She did not turn at all, but only stared straight at the curtained windows, seeing them very carefully, as though she were summing them up for some future analysis, with their thick amber folds, gold rod, white lines—and beyond them the snow was falling.

She did not need to turn but, with a shiver of terror, she was aware that that grey figure who had, all these last weeks, been approaching ever more closely, was almost at her very elbow. She heard quite clearly: 'I warned you. That was the last time.'

At the same moment Onslow the butler came in. Onslow was broad, fat and rubicund—a good faithful butler with a passion for church music. He was a bachelor and, it was said, disappointed of women. He had an old mother in Liverpool to whom he was greatly attached.

In a flash of consciousness she thought of all these things when he came in. She expected him also to see the grey figure at her side. But he was undisturbed, his ceremonial complacency clothed him securely.

'Mr. Fairfax has gone out,' she said firmly. Oh, surely he must see something, feel something.

'Yes, madam!' Then, smiling rather grandly: 'It's snowing hard. Never seen it harder here. Shall I build up the fire in the drawing-room, madam?'

'No, thank you. But Mr. Fairfax's study . . .'

'Yes, madam. I only thought that as this room was so warm you might find it chilly in the drawing-room.'

This room warm, when she was shivering from head to foot; but holding herself lest he should see ... She longed to keep him there, to implore him to remain; but in a moment he was gone, softly closing the door behind him.

Then a mad longing for flight seized her, and she could not move. She was rooted there to the floor, and even as wildly trying to cry, to scream, to shriek the house down, she found that only a little whisper would come, she felt the cold touch of a hand on hers.

She did not turn her head: her whole personality, all her past life, her poor little courage, her miserable fortitude were summoned to meet this sense of approaching death which was as unmistakable as a certain smell, or the familiar ringing of a gong. She had dreamt in nightmares of approaching death and it had always been like this, a fearful constriction of the heart, a paralysis of the limbs, a choking sense of disaster like an anæsthetic.

'You were warned,' something said to her again.

She knew that if she turned she would see Elinor's face, set, white, remorseless. The woman had always hated her, been vilely jealous of her, protecting her wretched Herbert.

A certain vindictiveness seemed to release her. She found that she could move, her limbs were free.

She passed to the door, ran down the passage, into the hall. Where would she be safe? She thought of the Cathedral where to-night there was a carol service. She opened the hall door and just as she was, meeting the thick, involving, muffling snow, she ran out.

She started across the green towards the Cathedral door. Her thin black slippers sank in the snow. Snow was everywhere— in her hair, her eyes, her nostrils, her mouth, on her bare neck, between her breasts.

'Help! Help! Help!' she wanted to cry, but the snow choked her. Lights whirled about her. The Cathedral rose like a huge black eagle and flew towards her.

She fell forward and even as she fell a hand, far colder than the snow, caught her neck. She lay struggling in the snow and as she struggled there two hands of an icy fleshless chill closed about her throat.

Her last knowledge was of the hard outline of a ring pressing into her neck. Then she lay still, her face in the snow, and the flakes eagerly, savagely, covered her.

THE RUBY GLASS

Poor Cousin Jane (as she was for ever afterwards known) arrived on a visit to the Cole family in Polchester in the spring of Jeremy's eighth year. He remembered the day exactly, because on that afternoon he had bought a bunch of daffodils as a peace-offering for his mother. A peace-offering was badly needed, both on his own part and that of his dog, Hamlet, for they had both of late been repeatedly in disgrace.

On Tuesday of that week Jeremy in a temper had thrown ink at Mary, his sister; on Wednesday he broke the window of the bathroom with a cricket-ball; on Thursday he insulted Miss Jones, their governess, so brutally that she gave notice, and was only with the greatest difficulty persuaded to remain.

It was perhaps the spring—it was certainly the hard truth that it was time that he went to school.

Hamlet also was unfortunate. On Tuesday he brought two filthy bones into the drawing-room at the very moment when the Dean's wife was paying a call. On Wednesday he frightened Mrs. Cole by running out on her from a dark passage, and on Thursday he was horribly sick on the dining-room carpet.

They were both in disgrace; they were both punished. In fact, matters were in a very ticklish state indeed. So Jeremy bought some daffodils and prayed most fervently that Fate would leave him alone for a while.

He disliked to be in disgrace; he disliked to make his incomprehensible elders unhappy; most of all did he dislike it when people muttered concerning Hamlet, 'That dog must go. We really cannot *endure* him any longer.'

So he was walking on egg-shells when Poor Cousin Jane arrived.

They christened her that immediately. In the first place she was a miserable scrap of a thing. When she stood in the hall, covered with innumerable wraps, she did not appear to be there at all.

Only her very red (for it was April weather) sharply peaked

little nose and strange pepper-and-salt eyes, with their sandy eyebrows, were visible.

Unwrapped she was revealed as a thin little girl, with an untidy bow in her hair and wrinkled black stockings on her spindly legs.

But what struck Jeremy, Mary and Helen immediately on sight of her was her terror. She was shaking with fright; her eyes roamed the room as though she were a wild animal for the first time caged, and when her aunt who had brought her from her home in Drymouth left her she burst into floods of tears.

Now the Coles were not an unkind family. The Rev. Mr. Cole, Jeremy's father, could certainly be severe on occasion when he felt it his duty to be so, but Mrs. Cole was the soul of maternal comfort—a nicer woman didn't exist anywhere.

Her three children also were kindly intentioned, only, like all normal children, they were healthy savages in process of being civilised.

Mary in especial was sentimental and emotional, wanted a girl friend, and would willingly have romanticised Cousin Jane had she been given the opportunity.

However, the odd thing about this story is that the only person who from the first did romanticise Jane was Hamlet, and that was queer indeed, because he hated little girls and liked to snap at their legs when nobody in authority was near.

Jeremy disliked Cousin Jane from the start. He could not help it. He was easily touched by females in distress, he was at times both courteous and chivalrous, and he had a good heart—but Jane he could not abide.

There was something about her terror that revolted him. He was not touched by it because it was so complete. He was not old enough to understand how anyone *could* be such a coward and *could* be such a fool.

His sister Mary was often both a coward *and* a fool, but she made brave attempts to conquer her weak points. He understood that. He had weak points himself.

But Jane made no attempt to conquer anything. She was frightened of Mr. Cole, Mrs. Cole, Jeremy, Mary, Helen, Miss Jones, the cook, the housemaid, and terrified of Hamlet.

She started at the slightest sound, blinked with alarm if anyone addressed her, and sat in a corner, straight on a chair, waiting for someone to attack her.

But—strangest of all strange things—Hamlet adored her. When on her arrival she stood among them all, bitterly weeping, he smelt her black stockings, then lay down, his pointed beard flat on his paws, and waited for her to ask him to do something for her. She did, of course, nothing of the kind. No matter. He devoted himself to her service.

Now, from the very moment of her arrival, Jeremy felt that something awful would occur in connection with her. He felt also perhaps ashamed of himself for disliking her, although it is difficult to say what small boys of eight feel and what they do not.

On the first afternoon of her stay it poured with rain, and the children sat in the schoolroom trying to play games. Cousin Jane, however, was a blight on all the proceedings.

'I know!' said Jeremy. 'We'll play buffaloes. I'll be the buffalo. Jane shall be captured by the Indians, and Mary and Hamlet shall rescue her.'

Jane's eyes nearly split with terror.

'Wouldn't you like that, Jane dear?' asked Mary in her propitiatory, mother-visiting-the-sick-and-ailing voice.

'Oh no, no, no!' cried Jane.

'There's halma,' said Jeremy disgustedly.

But Jane could understand nothing. She sat at the schoolroom table staring in front of her.

'Mary shall play with you and show you how to move.'

But it was of no use. She had an awful way of whispering under her breath. She was probably saying that she wanted to go home, but nobody could be sure.

'Mary shall tell us a story,' said Jeremy, trying hard to be a perfect gentleman. They sat round the fire and Mary began (very quickly lest someone should stop her, for she loved telling stories).

'Once upon a time there was a king who had three lovely daughters. One had black hair, one yellow, and one was between the two, and one day when the king——'

But Jane interrupted by slipping off her chair and creeping away to the window-seat, where she sat desolately looking out on to the rain. This was as bad an insult as any author ever received!

This sense of misfortune that Jeremy had in connection with his weeping cousin grew in the following days. He was in no way a morbid child, his imaginings were healthy, he very rarely saw visions, but just now he had the sense of the world that it was waiting round the corner to catch him.

He had had nightmares after stolen cheese or too much toffee, and in these to move a step was to lose your life!

So it was now. Something would happen to plunge him into disgrace, and Cousin Jane would be the agent. He knew it. He felt it in all his bones.

On a certain morning he woke and at once knew that this was an Evil Day. There were Evil Days, there were Ordinary Days and Days of Delight, and the kind of Day it intended to be it began from the very first moment by being!

This day began badly because Hamlet was not there. Always at a quarter to eight Hamlet, released by the cook from his basket in the kitchen, his hair brushed, his beard in shape, rushed upstairs and scratched on Jeremy's door. He was admitted, and games followed.

To-day there was no scratching at the door. Jeremy knew at once what had occurred. He was scratching at Cousin Jane's door. What did he see in the girl? What was it that had softened his ironic heart?

She had, Jeremy would have supposed, no charms for dogs at all. She did not like dogs. She screamed whenever they came near her.

Jeremy, his heart torn by a jealousy that he was far too proud to admit, went down to breakfast. Here for a moment things took a better turn.

'What do you think, my dears?' cried Mrs. Cole (who, loving her children, had never realised how intensely Mary and Jeremy hated to be 'my deared '). 'Miss Willink has asked us all to tea on Friday.'

Now, Miss Willink was one of life's joys. She was an elderly lady living five miles out of Polchester in the middle of one of the loveliest gardens in the world. Her house was large and grand, but Jeremy never gave it a thought.

The point was the garden with its lawns, rockeries, ponds, terraces, shrubberies, conservatories and gigantic trees. Moreover, Miss Willink understood what children wanted—namely, food, freedom and fraternity. She was a jolly old lady.

'Oh, hurray!' cried Jeremy, wondering whether he had been wrong about the day's omens. But he had not.

'Now mind, Jeremy,' said his father, who had neuralgia that morning. 'I don't know what's been the matter with you this week. One thing after another. Take care, or Miss Willink's is not for *you*.'

He *would* take care, and it occurred to him that he would propitiate the fates by being nice to Cousin Jane. They were to go for a walk that morning, it being a lovely spring morning, with clouds like galleons, sunny and shining, stretches of sky like violet-fields, and excited birds in flight.

He would take Cousin Jane to his secret place in Conmer Wood, where the daffodils were so thick that they were like shadowed plates of gold.

Smiling, he suggested it to her. But she shook her head. They were standing together alone in the schoolroom, and Hamlet was watching the girl, his eyes soft with sentiment. Every once and again he snapped dramatically at an imaginary fly, but plainly his thoughts were only for his adored one.

Jeremy was so deeply irritated that it was all he could do not to pull her long and lanky hair, but, remembering the fates, he held himself in.

'Don't you want to go *anywhere*?' he cried disgustedly. 'Don't you want to do *anything*?'

Her under-lip trembled.

'I don't like daffodils,' was her amazing statement.

'Don't like daffodils? But you don't like *anything*! All the time you've been here you haven't liked a *thing*. We're all being as nice as nice. Don't you like being here?'

Upon which Cousin Jane burst into tears, and at the same moment Mrs. Cole came into the room.

'Now, Jeremy, what *have* you been doing to Jane? What *is* it, dear? ... Never mind. Come with me and I'll show you some pretty things. Jeremy, I don't know *what* has come over you lately. You're always doing something wrong. Your father is very vexed. Remember what he said about Miss Willink. Now, come along, dear. Dry your eyes. We'll see what we've got downstairs to show you.'

Hamlet attempted to follow his heroine, but that at least Jeremy prevented.

'What *has* come over you?' he asked him. 'You can't *like* her. You don't like girls and this is one of the worst. Besides, she *hates you.*'

These remarks had no effect whatever on Hamlet, who had the art of sulking when he *wanted* to sulk beyond any dog ever known. He would half close his eyes, bury his mouth in his beard, turn his head away and yawn lazily, impertinently.

'Now come on,' said Jeremy. 'We'll go out and enjoy ourselves.'

But Hamlet refused. He would *not* go out. He would not *budge.* He sat there, his feet firmly planted, his head obstinately screwed away from his master. Jeremy dragged at his collar; his paws seemed to stick to the carpet. Jeremy pulled him, however, as far as the passage, then bumped, breathless and exasperated, into his father.

'Really, Jeremy,' Mr. Cole, whose neuralgia was worse, cried, 'you must look where you are going, my boy. And what are you doing to the poor dog?'

'Oh, nothing.' And Jeremy, running downstairs, left dog, father and all to their proper destinies.

'Sulky,' thought Mr. Cole sadly. 'Sulky and ill-tempered. The boy will have to go to school.'

At luncheon another misfortune befell.

It happened that it was cold-beef day—cold beef and potatoes in their jackets. Now, Jeremy hated cold fat. So, apparently, did Cousin Jane. Her eyes filled with tears and she looked beseechingly at Mrs. Cole.

'Mother says I needn't eat fat when I feel sick,' she remarked. 'I feel sick now.'

'Very well, dear,' said Mrs. Cole, benevolently smiling.

A short while later Mr. Cole said cheerfully: 'Eat it up, Jeremy, my boy. You know what I've always told you. One day perhaps you will be glad——'

The injustice was more than he could bear.

'Jane didn't have to!' he said.

'Jeremy!'

'Well, father, Jane didn't——'

'Jeremy!'

'Well, but, father——'

He ate it, and most disgusting it was. He swallowed with splutterings a full glass of water. His eye rested on the splendid, tall, ruby glass that stood in the middle of a small table opposite him. This was the family pride.

It was, the children understood, Bohemian. There were little patterns of gold traced delicately over its crimson glories. Jeremy thought that it was laughing at him.

After luncheon he brooded miserably. Hamlet was nowhere to be seen. Even his sisters seemed to hold aloof from him. A hatred of his Cousin Jane stronger than any hatred that he had ever known for anyone possessed him.

He would like to torture her, to stick pins into her legs, to twist her arms, to pull her hair till she screamed.

Meanwhile, as the afternoon drew on, he felt catastrophe drawing nearer.

At tea-time he could have burst into tears, although he was not given to crying. The intensity of those moments in child-hood when one is deserted, helpless, under a curse that is eternal, is unknown to maturity.

It would be a miracle if he reached bedtime without disaster. Even the clocks seemed to say to him: 'Now—You—Are —Done—For—Little—Man. Now—You—Are—Done—For —Little—Man.' And indeed there is nothing more complacent and patronising than a moon-faced, stubborn clock.

The blow fell.

It was the pleasant Cole custom that one or two nights a week Mrs. Cole should read to the children for half an hour before bedtime. To-night the reading was to be in the dining-room, because a good fire was burning there. The book was *The Chaplet of Pearls*, by Charlotte Mary Yonge.

The children—Hamlet, Mary, Helen, Jeremy and Jane—
assembled and stood by the fire waiting. Hamlet sat, licking a
tangled foot and sniffing between licks. Jane showed a little ani-
mation. She began in her thin voice that was like a violin-string
struck just out of tune:

'We've got nicer things in our house than you have, Mary.'

'Oh no, you haven't,' said Mary, who was loyal if she was anything.

'Oh yes, we have.'

'Oh no, you haven't.'

'Oh yes, we have. We've got a clock with a Chinaman that
nods his head, and a picture as big as this room almost, and a rug
with a tiger's head, and——'

'You haven't,' said Mary slowly, pushing her spectacles
straight, 'anything as lovely as the ruby glass.'

'Oh yes, we have,' said Jane. But she was attracted nevertheless. The firelight danced on the deep colours, the thin tracery of
gold. She went to the table and picked it up.

'Oh, you mustn't!' cried Mary.

Jane heard the door opening, and, in alarm, dropped the glass.
It lay at her feet, 'smashed,' as the story-books have it, 'into a
thousand fragments.'

Mrs. Cole had entered. Her cry was an agonised one.

'Oh! My glass! My glass!'

Jeremy saw then terror as he was never in all his life again to
see it. Nothing, years later, in the Great War equalled it.

To say that Jane was 'frozen' with it says little; her face paled to
ash, her whole body was seized with a fearful trembling. It was as
though she saw the devil.

Something in that agony moved Jeremy to a revulsion of disgust. It was horrible, indecent. Eight years of age though he was,
he understood that there was something dreadful here that had
nothing to do with his own world—something from beyond
boundaries.

Mrs. Cole looked up from her knees.

'Oh, who——?' she began.

'I broke it,' said Jeremy.

'You were told never to touch it.'

He stared defiantly. None of the children spoke a word. Mary and Helen knew, as Jeremy knew, that Jane, dislike her as they did, must be protected. The door opened on the scene, and Mr. Cole entered:

'Well, children—' he began and then saw what had happened. 'The glass! ... Who touched it?'

'I did,' said Jeremy.

For the first time in his life Jeremy was locked in his bedroom. He was to have no supper. Miss Willink's garden would not, on this occasion, offer him a greeting.

He moved up and down, hot tears in his eyes, feeling sick, feeling utterly alone, deserted by all the world. Why had he done it? He did not know. He hated Cousin Jane. It would have given him joy to see her disgraced. Yet if it occurred again he would do as he had done.

He was a pariah (although he did not know what a pariah was). He would never be back any more in a world of sunshine, friendliness, good-will.

It was too much. He sat down by the dressing-table and burst into a passion of angry, desolated tears. Worst of all—oh, far, far worst of all—was Hamlet's desertion. That Hamlet should leave him for an ugly, stupid, miserable, little ...

He heard a sound. He choked down his sobs, raised his head and listened. There was a scratching at his door. Was he mistaken? He moved across the room. No, there was no mistake. The scratching continued. He went to the door and, pressing against it, whispered:

'Hamlet! Hamlet! Are you there?'

The scratching was eager, demonstrative, and then, quite beyond question, between the scratches, that sniff! That sniff of comradeship, of loyalty, of understanding.

'Hamlet, I can't get out. They've locked me in!'

He heard a soft thud. Hamlet had laid himself down, and nothing, no power, no authority, was going to move him.

Jeremy, smiling, himself again, all the curses and forebodings suddenly removed, turned to the table by the bed, found a pencil and a piece of paper, and, with wrinkled brow and lickings of the stubborn lead, began to draw pictures of Cousin Jane as a witch.

SPANISH DUSK

'The care with which the rain is wrong, and the green is wrong, and the white is wrong, the care with which there is a chair and plenty of breathing and the care with which there is incredible justice and likeness, all this makes a magnificent asparagus and also a fountain.'

So says Gertrude Stein. She may be right or she may be wrong, but she is right for me at least in this that, at this moment, looking out from my window on to the silver walls of rain that slash the Cumberland fields, that 'rain' is wrong and the green and the white are wrong too—for I am plunged back into memory, memory of twenty-five years ago. I love this scene as I love none other in the world, and even now the green shoulder of Cat Bells rises to reproach me, and I know that soon those clouds will break, the pale faint blue push its way, as tender as the leaves of a young lettuce, and the trees in my garden shake their glistening drops and raise their heads gratefully to heaven.

My memory for the moment rejects this world of beauty and claims the sun.

I here indulge myself, giving myself up to a breath, a flash of colour, hesitation on a staircase, a kiss from the first woman I ever loved.

It was my first adventure abroad. I was twenty-four years of age. I was to be a diplomat—that was the plan, and meanwhile because I had been always delicate and was an only child I was to be indulged.

My father was not a man given to the indulging of others. An ironical melancholy, native in him perhaps, but springing to action beside the death-bed of my mother (she died when I was ten years old: he had passionately worshipped her), kept him always from any very close contact with his fellows. Most men and many women feared him, and I, who was perhaps the only human being whom he truly loved, was only at affectionate ease with him in his absence.

As has been my own later case, he had from early days divided his sense of life, of beauty, of passion (if so warm a word may be used of him) between Spain and England. His books on Spanish life and literature, his *Cervantes,* his *Spanish Truth and Spanish Fiction,* his *Spanish Tragedy and Comedy,* are still read, I fancy. The *Cervantes* at least remains until the present the best work on that great writer. But he was never, as towards the end of his life he constantly told me, able to get on to paper what he really wanted to say.

He returned to Spain again and again, there seemed to be nothing there that he did not see (so far of course as a foreigner is able to see anything), and yet, he died a frustrated man.

He was physically more Spanish than English; short, slight, dark, with that quiet almost stern dignity that is so especially Spanish. He was an exile you might say in both countries, loving this Cumberland scene but sitting in the rain and longing for the dried land that quivers under the sun like a panting dog, and then back again under the snowy peaks of his beloved Nevadas, watching the olives smoking in the clear air, and praising the broken Cumberland sky, the ripple of light over Derwentwater, the thick green woods of Manesty.

It was a great occasion for both of us when I was to make my first Spanish journey. He said little—he was a man of few words —and, as was his way, what he did say was to counteract any kind of romantic notions that I might have formed.

And yet I was romantic. How could it be otherwise? From my babyhood I had understood that Spain was the very heart of romance. In the old Cumberland garden, on the English summer evenings filled with the sound of bees and the scent of roses, a boy to whom anything distant was lovely and anything unseen an adventure, I read Prescott—the old, faded red-crimson volumes, *Ferdinand and Isabella* and *Philip II.* and Irving's *Alhambra* and *Granada*—and how could it be but that Ponce de Leon and Alva and Don John clashed their silver armour about my ears, and the Moors cried from the watered gardens of Granada for vengeance on the accursed dog of a Christian?

Age did not sober me. Three years at Oxford did little to sophisticate me. I was an only child, shy, reserved, terrified of exposing my follies to the world, believing in my dreams more deeply than I dared confess to anyone.

The setting out on that journey was such an adventure as I never knew afterwards, as, alas! I shall never know again. Other journeys there have been, neither worthless nor sterile, but dry and barren indeed compared with that anticipation.

During the journey from Paris to Barcelona my father talked to me about women. He had never ventured on this subject before with me and I can realise now, with my later, older knowledge of him, what a difficult, embarrassing business it must have been for him. He spoke, I remember, with the embarrassment of a man confessing some shameful secret to another. He had, of course, himself no shameful secret to confess. He spoke of his love for my mother and told me that if I could I must hold myself sacred for just such a wonderful relationship. But if, on the other hand, I could not so keep myself, I was to ask his advice and remember that he was a man of the world. A man of the world! My poor father! I suppose no man was ever less of one! But I too, on my side, had no secrets to confess. I had ideals quite as beautiful, quite, if you please, as foolish as any that he could have wished for me. I confessed at last that I had never kissed a woman nor been kissed by one, save for my cousins who were to me female as the cow is female but with no more sex than that.

He was relieved, I fancy, but anxious too. He wanted me to be a man and found me, I fear, a good deal of a half-baked prig. In myself I had for some time now realised my own sad absence of experience and was most anxious to remedy it, but did not wish, more than any other boy, that my father should be witness of that part of my education.

He said no more and the barrier between us was increased rather than weakened by our halting little attempt at intimacy.

Nevertheless, his words only added to my already almost trembling excitement. Women! It needed only that word to complete the picture. I burned to have my first adventure, but so absurdly sensitive was I at that time to every minute impression that the smallest thing—a word, a gesture, a scent, a turn of the hand—could frighten my admiration, check my approval, cool my romance.

What I wanted was to be carried off my feet, to be flung, whether I wished or no, into that condition of worshipping adoration that asks no question. Then—so my pride assured myself —the lover that I could be! Poor boy—remote, touching, above all honest figure with motives clear as crystal and life as simple as a saint's Credo—how near and how far you are from me now. The rain is ceasing. All the trees glitter and the faint tender blue steals through the grey just as I knew it would, and the wing of a silver cloud flutters over the shadow of the Lake.

We arrived, I remember, in Barcelona at mid-day, and I can feel now, as I sit here, the fresh agony of my disappointment. Ponce de Leon in his silver armour, Alva stern and cruel on his coal-black horse—and here under a grey, gritty sky with a wind in it, the trams rattling, men as unromantically attired as though they were in Sheffield discussing business prices, the shops filled with vulgar clothes and the shabbiest of sham jewellery. I was sulky and silent. I could have wept. My father made what was for him so rare a thing, an affectionate gesture, pressing my arm with his hand.

'There are so many things in Spain,' he said, 'that are not as you expect them to be. Patience. Wait for something to happen. It always does here.'

Even that very afternoon I moved a step forward. Looking back now I seem to see clearly that all these little incidents were steps towards that one great moment that it is my wish here to recreate. In the middle of that afternoon my father left me on business, and I found my way into the Cathedral. Stepping into Barcelona Cathedral is tumbling into a well of blackness. There is no other Cathedral so dark. At first I groped my way about, but feeling already a certain pleasurable stir at the velvet pressure of the obscurity, the distant sound of echoing voices and the shadowed colour of high, richly deep windows. I stumbled at length to the lighter shadows before the High Altar and there at my back was the choir and in the choir the priests and boys busy over Vespers. It was all exciting and novel to me. Seated on the hard little bench, timidly twisting myself around so that I might see all that went on without appearing too rudely inquisitive, I watched everything as though it were a play. Soon the bells clashed and rattled, a door opened in the wall, the organ burst into what seemed to me a merry jig, and a little procession came out, an old man in a white wig and a rich crimson gown, two little boys bearing gigantic candlesticks with lighted candles, and behind them some four or five priests robed in gold and purple. They all hurried into the choir, and the organ played even more merrily and the prayers were chanted, and I was in an ecstasy. Under what seemed to my Protestant eyes a lectern, the old man with the white wig stood, the little boys on either side of him. I was yet more enchanted when I found the little boys pinching the wax off their candles and throwing it at one another while the old man, who had the rheumatics and moved restlessly from one foot to the other, reproached them gently and the little boys paid him no attention.

Then the organ played another tune, and out the little procession came again, hurrying once more for its very life, up to the altar, then down again with the incense, a minute child with a shock-head of untidy black hair swinging the censer with all his body and soul, down the precipitous steps to the mysterious candle-lit shrine beneath the altar. When they passed me and I was flooded with a cloud of incense, I was swung on that vibrating censer through the opening door into a magic world of light.

That was my first step towards that moment on the high gleaming staircase, the candles glimmering above my head, her hand resting for that immortal second on my forehead . . .

That same night we went to Madrid, and again, as in Barcelona, there was first disappointment and afterwards rapture. Here was no magic city, as I quickly perceived. Once more the trams clanged, shabby little men in dull clothes went about their business, and, for the women, I didn't see any. An hour or so and I was standing with my father in the Prado Gallery. It is one of my difficulties now to select out of all my later maturer experience the first naïveté of that original drama. That first shock of Velasquez (Greco was not for me until later), how can one ever recover it? Great painter, he becomes with one's passing maturity ever greater, but that leaping to one's eye of the splendour of Breda, of Las Meninas—and the others—what can one seize upon now but the vague heat of that excitement, the surging, fresh conviction of the nobility and immortality of the soul of man?

I knew at that time but little technically of painting; it had happened, though, that my father by an odd chance had been a friend of Sickert, Whistler, Spencer Gore and Stevens, through coincidence rather than deliberate purpose, and to our dreary empty house in London these men had occasionally come. Through their atmosphere I had caught some consciousness of French painting, and had, silently (because I was always afraid of betraying my ignorance), thought Manet 'marvellous,' Sisley 'wonderful,' Monet 'miraculous.' I had been perhaps in my secret soul conceited of my little knowledge and select preferences. At last now, in one enraptured instant of experience, my conceit fell from me. As my gaze, bewildered, passed from the glorious vitality of the God of Wine in the Borrachos to the fat, sinister malignity of the dwarf in Las Meninas, to the superb courtesy of the heroes of Breda, to the chill dignity of Philip, tears filled my eyes. I could not speak. I hated that my father should be at my side. It was as though my clothes had been suddenly stripped from me. I vowed myself there and then, in a glory of self-confidence, to the pursuit of Art, rejecting all but the finest, living a century of bare austerities in the ardour of my heroic chase.... Alas! alas! how ironically now Cat Bells tosses its shoulder at me beyond my window, laughing in the sunshine at the burnt stick that has fallen from that blazing star!

No matter. I lived in that great moment with all the heroes of the world! I may be said at that instant to have been baptized of Spain. I was never at least to lose touch with her again.

Two days later we were in Granada. I had had in my journey there an hour of the Sierra Morena at sunset, and the burning colour of that hour had brought me to the very edge of trembling anticipation....

Those colours—blood-red, purple, amber—lying over the sprawling grey hills like sheets of metal, and yet alive so that you could feel the soil breathe beneath their covering, had in their intensity given me a new sense of Light. I was not, in my present raptures, faithless to my own country. Looking back, it seems to me that that eager and ignorant boy was touchingly aware of the ties in his own soul that held him for ever to the English skies so faintly washed, the soil so gently coloured, but here, in this careless splendour of light, there was something savagely opulent and generous that had never been known before. I sat, in that train, staring from the window as though this were a new birth for me, and my father, his cap tilted over his eyes, soundly slept....

In Granada we drove up the hill through the archway under a sheet of stars. The hotel was filled with passengers from a Mediterranean cruise, but their noise, their absorption in their own affairs, could not rob me of my sense of my own drama—that I was stepping forward at once, without a moment's delay, into a great adventure.

Next day the Alhambra yet further reassured me. I had expected, from the pictures that I had seen of it, to find it large and gaudy, and was surprised with its gentleness, its colours of pigeon-grey and soft rose, the ceilings that hung in pointed clusters touched with flecks of blue, the fountains, the sounding waters, the views from every window of the town far below in patterns of silver-white against the hill—and above it all the Sierra Nevada with peaks of crystal that cut the blue. But it was all so gentle, so different from the fierce figures of old Muley Abu'l Hassan and the terrible Ez-Zagal.

Nevertheless, it completed my preparation. It whispered to me as the Nevadas flamed in sunset that my great moment was assured.

So far, looking back, I have been able to recover with some certainty my little history. From the Barcelona Cathedral to the Prado, from the Prado through the Sierra Morena to the Alhambra everything is clear like a geography book: 'The principal rivers of Spain are the Guadalquivir, the, etc., etc.' But now, with my father and myself seated next morning in the very rickety carriage that was to take us out to the house of my father's friend, romantic dimness comes down over the scene. Even the name of the house must be hidden. I have never seen it since that time, although on many occasions I might have done so. I have even refused to visualise it with any positive definition for myself. If

I call it anything it is the House of the Warrior, for reasons that will soon be plain.

It must be remembered too that there was, for me then, the added dimness of my complete ignorance of the Spanish language. I had been hitherto with my father in cosmopolitan hotels, but now I was to move in a world of strange voices, of sounds mingling and separating in the air like the waters of fountains, and even the sun itself was to look down upon me with a remote and foreign glow.

As we tumbled over the roads, muddy with February rains, with every kilometre of distance the country seemed to me to become stranger; the hills, speckled like English 'spotted dogs' with trees that, close to us, rolled their silver sides under the wind, gathered closer about us. The soil suddenly sprang out of its smoky grey into splashes of red streaked as though with blood, and shadows of angry clouds tore over the vast sky like huge birds obeying some god's command.

That vast sky flamed into purple, a great sun of arrogant gold stared from between the hills into our eyes, then dropped into dun, the dark world pressed upon us as though it would squeeze us flat, we laboured and groaned against the hill, night was everywhere, and we had arrived.

I felt, I remember, a thrill of mingled shyness and anticipation as I stepped timidly beside my father into the hall. It seemed to my first excited gaze to be filled with figures and with smoke. The smoke may have been simply the sudden illumination after the darkness of the carriage, but the candles were blowing in the breeze and there was a faint acrid haze from the logs that hissed and crackled in the big open fireplace. All at least was dim and to my excited fancy richly coloured. Men and women like figures in a play moved about me greeting my father, while I, awkward, embarrassed, hung behind him.

'This is my son,' he said in English, and a tall, hawk-nosed, black-eyebrowed gentleman, my very personification of a Spaniard, greeted me very kindly. I do not remember what he said. I stared through the blue haze at the white walls, the high carpetless staircase and a magnificent dark picture of a man in armour that hung half-way up the staircase. This was a grand warrior, this hero, with a black beard and armour of a dull gold, his gauntleted hand sternly set on his sword, and behind him the fires of a red sunset playing on the long silhouette of a dark mountain range.

It seemed to me a glorious picture, the romantic key that I needed, when, quite suddenly, as though she had descended upon us from the sky, standing in front of it was a lady in a white dress, a lace shawl of black silk over her shoulders, a bunch of dark purple violets at her breast. She had turned the corner of the stairs and then, seeing that there were new arrivals, hesitated. A moment later, moving, as it seemed to me, with the utmost grace, she had come down to us, and my father was being introduced to her. I was for the time forgotten until my father himself turning to me said something about our rooms, and we passed to the stairs.

With what startling, lightning vividness is that moment still with me, the dim hall on whose surface the Spanish words rose and fell, the wavering of the candles, the crackling of the logs, and the gentle low voice of that lady as we moved past her towards that golden-armoured warrior who commanded the stairway.

My room was vast, with a high purple canopy over the bed, dim portraits on the walls, and a beautiful triptych of the Virgin and Saints in faded red and blue over the stone fireplace. I was washing my hands when my father came in and spoke to me with that rough awkwardness that always came to him when he was wishing to show affection. With what sharp accuracy I remember his words!

'I hope you won't be lonely here. Several of the men speak English. In any case it will be a fine opportunity for you to observe Spanish life at first hand.'

'Oh no!' I answered eagerly. 'It is just what I hoped. It is the Velasquez pictures come to life.' Then, more timidly because I feared that he was laughing at my romanticism, 'Father, who is that lady?'

'Which lady? There were several.'

'The one who came down the stairs, to whom you were introduced.'

He told me. Her name? What does it matter? Whatever

name she had that night it was not destined to be hers for much longer. He told me that she was a guest there, that she was a lady with her husband from Segovia. He knew nothing at all about them.

That evening was spent by me in watching from my corner. No one, I fancy, paid me very much attention. A shy English boy who knew no Spanish would not be very entertaining company for them. Their Spanish courtesy did what was needful and no more. But indeed I asked for nothing more than to be left alone. Before that first evening was half over I was plunged fiercely, madly, wildly, breathlessly into the intoxicating waters of first love.

Everything maybe had been inevitably leading to this. My father's long intercourse with Spain, so that it had been for me so long the most romantic country in the world, this my first taste of it, the dark shadows of the Barcelona Cathedral, the paintings at Madrid, the violent burning colours of the sunlit Sierra, the tender light and running waters of the Alhambra, all had led me step by step to this moment.

My own life too had prepared me for it, shy and romantic, keeping always to myself my deepest thoughts, longing for love but resolving to know it only at its finest—yes, all the stage was prepared, the light had gone down that the little drama might begin.

But I like also to think that there was something in the beauty and grace of that lady herself. Was she beautiful in reality? How can I say? Reality, or rather realism, calm, cold, selective, had no part at all in this story.

She sat almost opposite to me at dinner, and on her right was a man, thick-set and strong but not dark like the other men, fair-haired, with blue eyes and a gentle rather indeterminate mouth. I noticed him although there was no especial reason then why I should. I think it was because he and she said no single word to one another throughout dinner. They did not look at one another. She was for the most part very silent, speaking only occasionally to the man on the other side of her; he, the fair-haired man, never spoke at all. Her face was grave, almost sad, and very white under the pile of her dark black hair. Her long white fingers played with the bread beside her plate. She ate and drank very little.

I noticed everything about her, watching her most secretly lest I should seem to be impertinent.

Oddly enough, that night my father, coming to my room to wish me good-night, spoke near to my thoughts. He spoke of Spanish ladies, how different from anything that we could imagine in England, how gay and pleasant their lives before marriage, watched and guarded of course, but designed only that they should be courted and flattered, every young man serving them, worshipping them, adoring them. Then, from the moment of marriage, imprisonment, the husband their jailer, never free, never alone, their only duty to obey their husband and bear children, the Priest over all.

Following I know not what train of thought, I asked my father of the fair-haired, blue-eyed man who had sat next to her at dinner. He was, it seemed, a Belgian, in Spain on some business. And her husband? Her husband was a gentleman, tall and thin and extremely dark, with a shining white hook of a nose. I had seen him talking after dinner gravely and with, I thought, a good deal of self-complacency with our host.

A prisoner! So she was a prisoner? All night (or so it seemed to me—I dare say that in reality I slept well enough) I lay tossing on my bed, thinking of her thus with that shining hooked nose hanging over her and the eyes behind ceaselessly watching her.

At last I slept, and when I awoke it was to a world of light. Standing at my window with only my English experiences to tell me, I could not believe that light, naked, piercing, sheeted light, could make a flood of glittering fire so cover the world. At the far distance the Sierra Nevada seemed to be built of white flame, and over the great tapestry of the valley the light played like a vast extended note of music. The valley was chequered with colour, the trees that peppered the grey hills, Granada that glittered like a heap of frosted pebble, fields of blood-red and saffron and emerald and the purple hills crusted in enamel. Every colour, but all subdued to this passionate light that was not angry nor cruel as I had heard that it was in the East, but radiating with conscious happiness and power.

It was into this light that my love was translated. Although we were only in early February, during all our stay at this place the light was there. Every morning I rose to it and every evening I bade it farewell.

'How lovely the dusk must be,' I remember thinking, but when that first evening came and I stood by the wall of the garden looking out to the snow hills, I had only an instant of it— one divine moment when the light fell lower, swinging down to purple shadow, and the thin pallor of the almond buds was blue. But it was only an instant caught in my eager hands between light and dark.

How strangely pathetic that first love is! One has learnt as yet no rules. The hot, biting emotions that tear one are so strange and new, so oddly compounded of shame and pride, of diffidence and boldness, hope and despair. One scarcely sees the beloved object; she is dimmed by the glory and worship that one flings over her.

So it was with her now. I scarcely saw her; she was part of the dusky hall, of the portrait of the warrior, of the first blossoming of the almonds, of the silver snow against the blue, the blood-red soil, three peasants moving down the field scattering the thin mist of the grain, of their sudden harsh cries, the lowing of the cattle, the boy singing as he laid the blue and yellow tiles for a new garden path.

Oddest of all, perhaps, that I should worship her so. I knew nothing at all about her. She never spoke to me, only smiled very gently as she passed me. She spoke indeed very little to anyone. Her husband was always with her and he became to me her grisly, fearsome jailer. I hated him and pictured him in my fancy torturing her.

Her face—how passionately I studied it when I thought that nobody watched me—was often sad, or I fancied so. Oh! If I could but speak her tongue or she mine! But I knew that she understood no English, and the few words that I now had in Spanish——!

At last on my third evening I plucked up heart to say 'Good-evening' to her in Spanish. She turned, smiled most sweetly, and answered me some Spanish words. I tried to say more, but alas!

'Good-day,' 'Good-night,' 'Thank you,' 'Breakfast,' 'Dinner'—
these were all my pitiful store. As she left me I stood there, my
heart beating so that my knees trembled.

Before the end of the week my imagination had created a
world for me. I saw her, alone, desolate, in that distant town of
Segovia, tyrannised by her hateful husband, longing for release.
Who knew but that she had noticed me, had begun to think of
me, even to care for me a little? I began—so mad and simple in
this early love—to fancy that she realised that there was some
especial relationship between us, that she felt my presence when
I was in the room with her, that she did not think of me as of the
others.

When I lay awake at night I created marvellous fictions in
which she made me understand that she loved me, that she hated
her bony-nosed husband, that she would escape with me to
England . . .

I rehearsed again and again the scene with my father. 'You
see, father, I love her. I have never loved before. I shall never love
again. And she loves me. She also has never loved before . . .'

Alas, alas, the two silver birches who guard now my library
door shake their leaves gently in derision of such folly, and there
is regret too perhaps because youth can never return.

But dreams are not folly. Reality sometimes pierces them and
they reality. So it was with my little story.

We had been guests a week and in another day or two would
be gone. I was determined now that somehow I would create my
link with her. Schemes chased one another through my brain. I
did not eat; I did not sleep; even my father—always unobservant
of my moods—was aware at last that something held me.

I need not have schemed; life itself brought me my climax.
So the moment came, the moment that still after so many years
and so many moments seems to speak of my experience—a flash
that lit more landscape than any that flamed for me afterwards.
I stood at my window knowing that the instant between daylight and dark that seemed too especially beautiful to me was
approaching.

My window was open. The garden shone as the light lowered;
the figures of the three sowers passing down the long red field

were softening into dark against the glow. I was of course thinking of her, wondering whether she would come perhaps into the
garden to catch a picture of that moment of dusk.

Three men passed across the gravel, quietly talking. One I
saw as her husband.

My bedroom door was ajar. I heard a step on the passage floor.
It hesitated and waited. Driven I know not by what inner certainty, I went to my door. She was standing in the darkening passage, staring into the wall. I saw her dark hair, her pale face, her
heaving breasts, and then—that she was crying. She did not try
to stop her tears, only stood there as though spellbound.

Her tears tore me with tenderness and love, yes, and triumph
too. If she was crying she was in trouble, and if she was in trouble
she needed me, and if she needed me——!

I drew her into my room. She came without any resistance. I
made her sit down in the tapestried chair by my bed, and then,
kneeling beside her, poured my heart out in a torrent of words.
What did I say? Would I recover the words if I could?

I told her that I loved her, that I had loved her from the first
moment of seeing her, that I could never love another woman,
but would adore her, worship her, serve her for ever. That her
husband was a tyrant as I knew, but that if she would come with
me out of Spain I would make her the most faithful of lovers
and husbands, only giving her my life, my service, my soul. . . .
And mingled all this with the light of the sky and the pictures of
Velasquez and the blood-red soil of Spain and all the new consciousness of life that had come to me.

She did not of course understand one word of it, but there,
allowing me to take her hand, her tears ceased to fall, she stared,
I remember, intently in front of her as though listening for some
sound. Then she put her hand for a moment on my forehead. At
that touch I was all on fire. I sprang to my feet and raised her to
hers. Then I held her in my arms and kissed her mouth. She did
not move, did not turn away from me. My mouth was on hers, I
took her fragrance and her softness into my soul and swam on
pinions of ecstasy into the most distant of heavens.

At last, very gently indeed, she disengaged herself. I tried to
say more, but something in her eyes forbade me. The last streak

of gold in the world lay on my floor in a broad bar of flame. In the passage above the stairs, where all was now dark, she laid her hand for a moment on my forehead, said something that I could not understand, and was gone.

I stayed motionless in my room.

Years afterwards I saw in London a play translated from, I think, the Hungarian, and in the course of it a boy loves a married woman, thinks that she will divorce her husband and marry him—and learns his lesson. Although the lesson that I learnt was very different from his, I sat in the theatre that night overcome with my own memories.

Even as that boy so was I. She loved me. Otherwise she would not have let me kiss her and hold her in my arms. She loved me and she would come with me to England and ... What matter that I was only twenty-four and she—I did not think of her age.

She was mine and I was hers for all, for all eternity! I stood there, once and again trembling with my happiness, for I know not how long. Then in the dark I found my way to my bed and, flinging myself down on it, lay there staring with burning eyes into the gloom.

Later—it must have been much later—I heard a great stir about the house. The sounds called me from my trance. Lights flashed beyond my windows, voices called, at last there was a rumble of carriage wheels on the path.

My door opened and my father came in, holding a lamp. I could see that he was gravely concerned.

He came to my bed, touched my arm. 'Are you asleep?' he asked.

'No,' I answered. And as I looked up at him I wondered, I remember, how he would take my news when he heard it. At first he would be very angry, cast me off perhaps; but afterwards, I was his only son, he loved me....

'Most unfortunate,' he said. 'Very inconvenient for us. We shall have to leave in the morning.'

Leave in the morning! Leave *her* in the morning? Oh, no! My heart beat fiercely.

'What is it?' I asked.

'The lady from Segovia—you know, you asked about her.

Senora S——.... She has run off with Mr. B——, the Belgian, the fellow with the fair hair and blue eyes. Three hours ago. They had a carriage waiting at the bottom of the road. They had been planning it, it seems, a long while. Señor S—— has only now found her letter. He is off in a carriage to Granada. The whole house is in an uproar. Most inconvenient for us. We can't stay on here, that's certain. No one dreamt it of her. It's always these quiet women. They'll have dinner as usual, I suppose, but it's most uncomfortable.'

I said that I would not come down to dinner. My headache, bad all day, was now frantic....

A man at dinner the other night said authoritatively:

'Oh, they have no dusk in Spain. Blazing sun one moment, dark the next.'

But I knew better. There is that second of splendour when earth and heaven meet. I had had my second.

Machado has written:

'*Lleva el que deja, y vive que ha vivido*' ('He carries with him who leaves behind, and lives who has lived ').

And so it is.

THE END